CHRISTMAS SPIRITS

Also edited by Peter Haining

Nightcaps and Nightmares
Greasepaint and Ghosts
Dead of Night

CHRISTMAS SPIRITS

Ghost Stories of the Festive Season

Edited by

PETER HAINING

WILLIAM KIMBER · LONDON

This anthology first published in 1983 by
WILLIAM KIMBER & CO. LIMITED
100 Jermyn Street,
London SW1Y 6EE

ISBN 0-7183-0479-9

Photoset in North Wales by
Derek Doyle & Associates, Mold, Clwyd
and printed and bound in Great Britain by
Biddles Ltd., Guildford and Kings Lynn

Contents

Acknowledgements

The Editor and publishers are grateful to the following for permission to include copyright material in this collection: The Executors of the Estate of J.M. Barrie for 'The Ghost of Christmas Eve'; Pearson Longman Ltd for 'The Irtonwood Ghost' by Elinor Glyn; The Estate of Alfred Noyes for 'The *Lusitania* Waits'; A.M. Heath Literary Agency for 'The Festival' by H.P. Lovecraft; The Executors of the Estate of Eden Phillpotts for 'Grimm's Ghost'; The Estate of Stephen Leacock for 'The Christmas Ghost'; Edward Arnold Ltd for 'The Story of a Disappearance and an Appearance' by M.R. James; Denis Dobson Ltd for 'A Christmas Ghost' by A.N.L. Munby; A.P. Watt Literary Agency for 'S.O.S.' by Algernon Blackwood; A.D. Peters Ltd for 'Blind Man's Hood' by John Dickson Carr.

Introduction

There is a famous moment during Shakespeare's play *Hamlet* when Marcellus and the faithful Horatio meet on the battlements of Elsinore Castle. Both are fearful of the imminent arrival of a ghost, yet Marcellus makes a brave attempt to dispel the dark and eerie stillness with the words that:

> At Christmas no spirit dare stir abroad,
> the nights are wholesome ...

Yet should good Horatio really take heart at such a statement? For surely no season of the year is more firmly linked with ghosts than Christmas? No night, indeed, is deemed by tradition as more fitting for the telling of tales of the supernatural than Christmas Eve. Whether, like our grandparents, we huddle before a blazing fire illuminated only by flickering candlelight, or draw tighter the curtains and pull closer to the engulfing magnetism of the television screen, the appeal of the story of ghostly dread has no greater attraction than at this season of festivity.

Of course, in time long past midwinter was regarded by our primitive ancestors with awe, even terror. The sun was at its weakest and lowest, they could clearly observe. Would it ever return from the long, dark night into which it seemed to be sinking? And would its passing release all manner of evil and unnatural beings into the world to plague mankind? Sacrifice was deemed to be necessary to appease the gods of darkness and to ensure that the sun did indeed return the next spring and bring with its warming rays the promise of fertility and growth.

Superstitious nonsense such beliefs may well have been, but time has been quite unable to prevent the shadow of those beguiling spirits remaining as an inseparable part of the festive season. Let that masterful writer of horror stories, Angela Carter, explain a little more evocatively what I mean. 'The winter solstice,' she wrote in the *Radio Times* in 1975, 'is the shortest day, the longest night – the huge, dark, numinous hinge of the year through which all manner of supernatural, half-natural and plainly, straightforwardly unnatural beings creep towards us out of the pagan past, to beguile our Christmas good cheer with a little, delicious shiver of unease.'

And, Miss Carter continues:

> The Christmas ghost-story, the Christmas spine-chiller, horror for Christmas – somehow it's become part and parcel of the whole Dickensy seasonal myth of snow and holly and churchbells and groaning boards. At a time of goodwill to all men, we can contemplate with equanimity the idea that beings might exist that bear us positive malice ... and the titillation of fear adds a special savour to the rich diet, as if a shiver down the spine were an aid to the digestion.

Nowadays, of course, we have come to accept our bill of Christmas horror fare through the medium of the television screen. Yet there are still those who maintain that such tales of supernatural agency are best recounted by the fireside, with flickering shadows on the walls, a wild, night-wind howling around the house, and somewhere out of sight a door creaking like the moan of a lost soul. Should a yule log be crackling on the hearth, all the better!

Yet despite the seeming timelessness of this tradition, it has to be admitted that the idea of creating ghost stories especially for telling at Christmas goes back no further – as Angela Carter has hinted – than the time of Charles Dickens. For he it was who saw the possibility of using the inheritance from our pagan past as the basis of an entertainment ideal for consumption at Christmas.

No reader needs an introduction to Dickens, for his creation of some of the greatest classics in the English language makes his name familiar to one and all. Yet such is his fame that certain elements of his life and work tend to become forgotten in the general story of success – in particular that he was also a highly accomplished journalist and skilful magazine editor. And it was in this later capacity that he began what has since became a universal practice among publishers everywhere of printing a ghost story in the Christmas issues of their newspapers, magazines and periodicals.

Dickens' remarkable achievement was formed in his now immortal story *A Christmas Carol*, published in 1843. Though couched in the form of a ghost story, another important objective of the tale was subtly to make people re-examine their attitudes towards life and one another at a time when it was all too easy to forget such things in the general festivity.

Such was the enormous popularity of the story, and such was its obvious impact on readers, that Dickens determined to write similar tales each ensuing Christmas, as well as encouraging other authors to do the same for the magazine he edited, *Household Words* (which later became known as *All The Year Round*). Not surprisingly, rival editors and publishers quickly realised what Dickens had achieved and began to follow his lead. Within a matter of years the 'Ghost Story for Christmas' had become the kind of tradition that seemed as if it had always existed. And so it has continued to this day.

It was Dickens, also, in this self-same story who perpetrated the enduring idea that Christmas is invariably *white*: a time of snow and ice and frozen landscapes. In fact, a study of weather records shows that the days around Christmas are usually rather mild, even bright, with the bad weather not generally developing until the New Year.

Why Dickens should have painted the dawn of Scrooge's Christmas Day as being snowy is, though, not too difficult to explain. For research has shown that the first eight Christmases of his young life did actually have snow or hard frosts, and though overall these were freakish conditions, they left a strong impression on his mind which he used as a means of emphasising his theme in *A Christmas Carol*.

So it is to Dickens, then, that we especially owe thanks for our Christmas ghost stories, and our delight at being thrilled and chilled around the festive hearth. Naturally, it is only right and proper that he should take pride of place in this assembly of such stories which I offer for your pleasure. And it is also perhaps not surprising that his spirit of Christmas should permeate all the other tales which follow. Each and every one underlines the achievement of his genius.

And, without more ado, as the reformed Scrooge urged Bob Crachit and his family, let us take up a glass of warming cheer, make up the fire, and begin our entertainment ...

PETER HAINING
Christmas, 1982.

I

The Goblins Who Stole a Sexton

Charles Dickens

As I mentioned in my Introduction, Charles Dickens (1812-1870), the journalist-cum-storyteller-turned-editor, was responsible for starting the tradition of writing and publishing ghost stories for Christmas when he gave us A Christmas Carol *in 1843. Interestingly, though, Dickens had* already *written a ghost story set at Christmas prior to this work. The story was called 'The Goblins Who Stole A Sexton' and it formed an episode in the December 1836 instalment of his first novel,* Pickwick Papers. *(Dickens' work was almost all first published in serial form.) What makes this story – which is also about ghostly retribution on Christmas Eve – doubly interesting is that there are strong elements in both the plot and action which Dickens later reworked into* A Christmas Carol *with even more dramatic effect – as the observant reader will soon spot. So settle down by your roaring fire, dim the lights, and prepare to have your flesh creep and your nerve ends tingle as you read this intriguing little tale of the supernatural which can be seen as a forerunner to much that is to follow ...*

In an old abbey town, down in this part of the country, a long, long, while ago – so long, that the story must be a true one, because our great-grandfathers implicitly believed it – there officiated as sexton and grave-digger in the churchyard, one Gabriel Grub. It by no means follows that because a man is a sexton, and constantly surrounded by the emblems of mortality, therefore he should be a morose and melancholy man; your undertakers are the merriest fellows in the world; and I once had the honour of being on intimate terms with a mute, who in private life, and off duty, was as comical and jocose a little fellow as ever chirped out a devil-may-care song, without a hitch in his memory, or drained off the contents of a good stiff glass without stopping for breath. But notwithstanding these precedents to the contrary, Gabriel Grub was an ill-conditioned, cross-grained, surly fellow – a morose and lonely man, who consorted with nobody but himself, and an old wicker bottle which fitted into his large deep waistcoat pocket – and who eyed each merry face, as it passed him by, with such a deep scowl of malice and ill-humour, as it was difficult to meet, without feeling something the worse for.

A little before twilight, one Christmas Eve, Gabriel shouldered his spade, lighted his lantern, and betook himself towards the old churchyard; for he had got a grave to finish by next morning, and, feeling very low, he thought it might raise his spirits, perhaps, if he went on with his work at once. As he went his way, up the ancient street, he saw the cheerful light of the blazing fires gleam through the old casements, and heard the loud laugh and the cheerful shouts of those who were assembled around them; he marked the bustling preparations for next day's cheer, and smelt the numerous savoury odours consequent thereupon, as they steamed up from the kitchen windows in clouds. All this was gall and wormwood to the heart of Gabriel Grub; and when groups of children bounded out of the houses, tripped across the road, and were met, before they could knock at the opposite door, by half a dozen curly-headed little rascals who crowded round them as they flocked upstairs to spend the evening in their Christmas games, Gabriel smiled grimly, and clutched the handle of his spade with a firmer grasp, as he thought of measles, scarlet-fever, thrush, whooping-cough, and a good many other sources of consolation besides.

In this happy frame of mind, Gabriel strode along: returning a short, sullen growl to the good-humoured greetings of such of his neighbours as now and then passed him: until he turned into the dark lane which led to the churchyard. Now, Gabriel had been looking forward to reaching the dark lane, because it was, generally speaking, a nice, gloomy, mournful place, into which the townspeople did not much care to go, except in broad daylight, and when the sun was shining; consequently, he was not a little indignant to hear a young urchin roaring out some jolly song about a merry Christmas, in this very sanctuary, which had been called Coffin Lane ever since the days of the old abbey, and the time of the shaven-headed monks. As Gabriel walked on, and the voice drew nearer, he found it proceeded from a small boy, who was hurrying along, to join one of the little parties in the old street, and who, partly to keep himself company, and partly to prepare himself for the occasion, was shouting out the song at the highest pitch of his lungs. So Gabriel waited until the boy came up, and then dodged him into a corner, and rapped him over the head with his lantern five or six times, to teach him to modulate his voice. And as the boy hurried away with his hand to his head, singing quite a different sort of tune, Gabriel Grub chuckled very heartily to himself, and entered the churchyard, locking the gate behind him.

He took off his coat, put down his lantern, and getting into the unfinished grave, worked at it for an hour or so, with right good will. But the earth was hardened with the frost, and it was no very easy matter to break it up, and shovel it out; and although there was a moon, it was a very young one, and shed little light upon the grave, which was in the shadow of the church. At any other time, these obstacles would have made Gabriel Grub very moody and miserable, but he was so well pleased with having stopped the small boy's singing, that he took little heed of the scanty progress he had made, and looked down into the grave, when he had finished work for the night, with grim satisfaction: murmuring as he gathered up his things:

Brave lodgings for one, brave lodgings for one,
A few feet of cold earth, when life is done;
A stone at the head, a stone at the feet,
A rich, juicy meal for the worms to eat;
Rank grass over head, and damp clay around,
Brave lodgings for one, these, in holy ground!

'Ho! Ho!' laughed Gabriel Grub, as he sat himself down on a flat tombstone which was a favourite resting-place of his; and drew forth his wicker bottle. 'A coffin at Christmas! A Christmas Box. Ho! ho! ho!'

'Ho! ho! ho!' repeated a voice which sounded close behind him.

Gabriel paused, in some alarm, in the act of raising the wicker bottle to his lips: and looked round. The bottom of the oldest grave about him, was not more still and quiet, than the churchyard in the pale moonlight. The cold hoar frost glistened on the tombstones, and sparkled like rows of gems, among the stone carvings of the old church. The snow lay hard and crisp upon the ground; and spread over the thickly-strewn mounds of earth so white and smooth a cover that it seemed as if corpses lay there, hidden only by their winding sheets. Not the faintest rustle broke the profound tranquillity of the solemn scene. Sound itself appeared to be frozen up, all was so cold and still.

'It was the echoes,' said Gabriel Grub, raising the bottle to his lips again.

'It was *not*,' said a deep voice.

Gabriel started up, and stood rooted to the spot with astonishment and terror; for his eyes rested on a form that made his blood run cold.

Seated on an upright tombstone, close to him, was a strange unearthly figure, whom Gabriel felt at once, was no being of this world. His long fantastic legs which might have reached the ground, were cocked up, and crossed after a quaint, fantastic fashion; his sinewy arms were bare; and his hands rested on his knees. On his short round body, he wore a close covering, ornamented with small slashes; a short cloak dangled at his back; the collar was cut into curious peaks, which served the goblin in lieu of ruff or neckerchief; and his shoes curled at his toes into long points. On his head, he wore a broad-rimmed sugar-loaf hat, garnished with a single feather. The hat was covered with the white frost; and the goblin looked as if he had sat on the same tombstone very comfortably, for two or three hundred years. He was sitting perfectly still; his tongue was put out, as if in derision; and he was grinning at Gabriel Grub with such a grin as only a goblin could call up.

'It was *not* the echoes,' said the goblin.

Gabriel Grub was paralysed, and could make no reply.

'What do you do here on Christmas Eve?' said the goblin sternly.

'I came to dig a grave, sir,' stammered Gabriel Grub.

'What man wanders among graves and churchyards on such a night as this?' cried the goblin.

'Gabriel Grub! Gabriel Grub!' screamed a wild chorus of voices that seemed to fill the churchyard. Gabriel looked fearfully round – nothing was to be seen.

'What have you got in that bottle?' said the goblin.

'Hollands, sir,' replied the sexton, trembling more than ever; for he had bought it of the smugglers, and he thought that perhaps his questioner might be in the excise department of the goblins.

'Who drinks Hollands alone, and in a churchyard, on such a night as this?' said the goblin.

'Gabriel Grub! Gabriel Grub!' exclaimed the wild voices again.

The goblin leered maliciously at the terrified sexton, and then raising his voice, exclaimed: 'And who, then, is our fair and lawful prize?'

To this inquiry the invisible chorus replied, in a strain that sounded like the voices of many choristers singing to the mighty swell of the old church organ – a strain that seemed borne to the sexton's ears upon a wild wind, and to die away as it passed onward; but the burden of the reply was still the same, 'Gabriel Grub! Gabriel Grub!'

The goblin grinned a broader grin than before, as he said, 'Well Gabriel, what do you say to this?'

The sexton gasped for breath.

'What do you think of this, Gabriel?' said the goblin, kicking up his feet in the air on either side of the tombstone, and looking at the turned-up points with as much complacency as if he had been contemplating the most fashionable pair of Wellingtons in all Bond Street.

'It's – it's – very curious sir,' replied the sexton, half dead with fright; 'very curious, and very pretty, but I think I'll go back and finish my work, sir, if you please.'

'Work!' said the goblin, 'what work?'

'The grave, sir; making the grave,' stammered the sexton.

'Oh, the grave, eh?' said the goblin. 'Who makes graves at a time when all other men are merry, and takes a pleasure in it?' Again the mysterious voices replied, 'Gabriel Grub! Gabriel Grub!'

'I'm afraid my friends want you, Gabriel,' said the goblin, thrusting his tongue further into his cheek than ever – and a most astonishing tongue it was – 'I'm afraid my friends want you, Gabriel,' said the goblin.

'Under favour, sir,' replied the horror-stricken sexton, 'I don't think they can, sir; they don't know me, sir; I don't think the gentlemen have ever seen me, sir.'

'Oh yes they have,' replied the goblin; 'we know the man with the sulky face and grim scowl, that came down the street tonight, throwing his evil looks at the children, and grasping his burying spade the tighter. We know the man who struck the boy in the envious malice of his heart, because the boy could be merry, and he could not. We know him, we know him.'

Here, the goblin gave a loud shrill laugh, which the echoes returned twenty-fold: and throwing his legs up in the air, stood upon his head, or rather upon the very point of his sugar-loaf hat, on the narrow edge of the tombstone: whence he threw a somerset with extraordinary agility, right to the sexton's feet, at which he planted himself in the attitude in which tailors generally sit upon the shop-board.

'I – I – am afraid I must leave you, sir,' said the sexton, making an effort to move.

'Leave us!' said the goblin, 'Gabriel Grub going to leave us. Ho! ho! ho!'

As the goblin laughed, the sexton observed, for one instant, a brilliant illumination within the windows of the church, as if the whole building were lighted up; it disappeared, the organ pealed forth a lively air, and whole troops of goblins, the very counterpart of the first one, poured into the churchyard, and began playing at leap-frog with the tombstones: never stopping for an instant to take break, but 'overing' the highest among them, one after the other, with the most marvellous dexterity. The first goblin was a most astonishing leaper, and none of the others could come near him; even in the extremity of his terror the sexton could not help observing, that while his friends were content to leap over the common-sized gravestones, the first one took the family vaults, iron railing and all, with as much ease as if they had been so many street-posts.

At last the game reached to a most exciting pitch; the organ played quicker and quicker; and the goblins leaped faster and faster: coiling themselves up, rolling head over heels upon the ground, and bounding over the tombstones like footballs. The sexton's brain whirled round with the rapidity of the motion he beheld, and his legs reeled beneath him, as the spirits flew before his eyes: when the goblin king, suddenly darting towards him, laid his hand upon his collar, and sank with him through the earth.

When Gabriel Grub had had time to fetch his breath, which the rapidity of his descent had for the moment taken away, he found himself in what appeared to be a large cavern, surrounded on all sides by crowds of goblins, ugly and grim; in the centre of the room, on an elevated seat, was stationed his friend of the churchyard; and close beside him stood Gabriel Grub himself, without power of motion.

'Cold tonight,' said the king of the goblins, 'very cold. A glass of something warm, here!'

At this command, half a dozen officious goblins, with a perpetual smile upon their faces, whom Gabriel Grub imagined to be courtiers, on that account, hastily disappeared, and presently returned with a goblet of liquid fire, which they presented to the king.

'Ah!' cried the goblin, whose cheeks and throat were transparent, as he tossed down the flame, 'This warms one, indeed! Bring a bumper of the same, for Mr Grub.'

It was in vain for the unfortunate sexton to protest that he was not in the habit of taking anything warm at night; one of the goblins held him while another poured the blazing liquid down his throat; the whole assembled screeched with laughter as he coughed and choked, and wiped away the tears which gushed plentifully from his eyes, after swallowing the burning draught.

'And now,' said the king, fantastically poking the taper corner of his sugar-loaf hat into the sexton's eye, and thereby occasioning him the most exquisite pain: 'And now, show the man of misery and gloom, a few of the pictures from our own great storehouse!'

As the goblin said this, a thick cloud which obscured the remoter end of the cavern, rolled gradually away, and disclosed, apparently at a great distance, a small and scantily furnished, but neat and clean apartment. A crowd of little children were gathered round a bright fire, clinging to their mother's gown, and gambolling around her chair. The mother occasionally rose, and drew aside the window-curtain, as if to look for some expected object: a frugal meal was placed near the fire. A knock was heard at the door: the mother opened it, and the children crowded round her, and clapped their hands for joy, as their father entered. He was wet and weary, and shook the snow from his garments, as the children crowded round him, and seizing his cloak, hat, stick and gloves, with busy zeal, ran with them from the room. Then, as he sat down to his meal before the fire, the children climbed about his knee, and the mother sat by his side, and all seemed happiness and comfort.

But a change came upon the view, almost imperceptibly. The scene was altered to a small bedroom, where the fairest and youngest child lay dying; the roses had fled from his cheek, and the light from his eye; and even as the sexton looked upon him with an interest he had never felt or known before, he died. His young brothers and sisters crowded round his little bed, and seized his tiny hand, so cold and heavy; but they shrunk back from its touch, and looked with awe on his infant face; for calm and tranquil as it was, and sleeping in rest and peace as the beautiful child seemed to be, they saw that he was dead, and they knew that he was an Angel looking down upon, and blessing them, from a bright and happy Heaven.

Again the light cloud passed across the picture, and again the subject changed. The father and mother were old and helpless now, and the number of those about them was diminished more than half; but content and cheerfulness sat on every face, and beamed in every eye, as they crowded round the fireside, and told and listened to old stories of earlier and bygone days. Slowly and peacefully, the father sank into the grave, and soon after, the sharer of all his cares and troubles followed him to a place of rest. The few, who yet survived them, knelt by their tomb, and watered the green turf which covered it, with their tears; then rose, and turned away; sadly and mournfully, but not with bitter cries, or despairing lamentations, for they knew that they should one day meet again; and once more they mixed with the busy world, and their content and cheerfulness was restored. The cloud settled upon the picture and concealed it from the sexton's view.

'What do you think of *that*?' said the goblin, turning his large face towards Gabriel Grub.

Gabriel murmured out something about its being very pretty, and looked somewhat ashamed, as the goblin bent his fiery eyes upon him.

'*You* a miserable man!' said the goblin, in a tone of excessive contempt. 'You!' He appeared disposed to add more, but indignation choked his utterance, so he lifted up one of his very pliable legs, and flourishing it above his head a little, to insure his aim, administered a good sound kick to Gabriel Grub; immediately after which, all the goblins in waiting, crowded round the wretched sexton, and kicked him without mercy: according to the established and invariable custom of courtiers upon earth, who kick whom royalty kicks, and hug whom royalty hugs.

'Show him some more!' said the king of the goblins.

At these words, the cloud was dispelled, and a rich and beautiful landscape was disclosed to view – there is just such another, to this day, within half a mile of the old abbey town. The sun shone from out the clear blue sky, the water sparkled beneath his rays, and the trees looked greener, and the flowers more gay, beneath his cheering influence. The water rippled on, with a pleasant sound; the trees rustled in the light wind that murmured among their leaves; the birds sang upon the boughs; and the lark carolled on high her welcome to the morning. Yes, it was morning; the bright, balmy morning of summer; the minutest leaf, the smallest blade of grass, was instinct with life. The ant crept forth to her daily toil, the butterfly fluttered and basked in the warm rays of the sun; myriads of insects spread their transparent wings, and revelled in their brief but happy existence. Man walked forth, elated with the scene; and all was brightness and splendour.

'*You* a miserable man!' said the king of the goblins, in a more contemptuous tone than before. And again the king of the goblins gave his leg a flourish; again it descended on the shoulders of the sexton; and again the attendant goblins imitated the example of their chief.

Many a time the cloud went and came, and many a lesson it taught to Gabriel Grub, who, although his shoulders smarted with pain from the frequent applications of the goblins' feet, looked on with an interest that nothing could diminish. He saw that men who worked hard, and earned their scanty bread with lives of labour, were cheerful and happy; and that to the most ignorant, the sweet face of nature was a never-failing source of cheerfulness and joy. He saw those who had been delicately nurtured, and tenderly brought up, cheerful under privations, and superior to suffering that would have crushed many of a rougher grain, because they bore within their own bosoms the materials of happiness, contentment, and peace. He saw that women, the tenderest and most fragile of all God's creatures, were the oftenest superior to sorrow, adversity, and distress; and he saw that it was because they bore, in their own hearts, an inexhaustible well-spring of affection and devotion. Above all, he saw that men like himself, who snarled at the mirth and cheerfulness of others, were the foulest weeds on the fair surface of the earth; and setting all the good of the world against the evil, he came to the conclusion that it was a very decent and respectable sort of world after all. No sooner had he formed it, than the cloud which closed over the last picture, seemed to settle on his senses, and lull him to repose. One by one, the goblins faded from his sight; and as the last one disappeared, he sunk to sleep.

The day had broken when Gabriel Grub awoke, and found himself lying, at full length on the flat gravestone in the churchyard, with the wicker bottle lying empty by his side, and his coat, spade, and lantern, all well whitened by the last night's frost, scattered on the ground. The stone on which he had first seen the goblin seated, stood bolt upright before him, and the grave at which he had worked, the night before, was not far off. At first, he began to doubt the reality of his adventures, but the acute pain in his shoulders when he attempted to rise, assured him that the kicking of the goblins was certainly not ideal. He was staggered again, by observing no traces of footsteps in the snow on which the goblins had played leap-frog with the gravestones, but he speedily accounted for this circumstance when he remembered that, being spirits, they would leave no visible impression behind them. So, Gabriel Grub got on his feet as well as he could, for the pain in his back; and brushing the frost off his coat, put it on, and turned his face towards the town.

But he was an altered man, and he could not bear the thought of returning to a place where his repentance would be scoffed at, and his reformation disbelieved. He hesitated for a few moments; and then turned away to wander where he might, and seek his bread elsewhere.

The lantern, the spade, and the wicker bottle, were found, that day, in the churchyard. There were a great many speculations about the sexton's fate at first, but it was speedily determined that he had been carried away by the goblins; and there were not wanting some very credible witnesses who had distinctly seen him whisked through the air on the back of a chestnut horse blind of one eye, with the hind-quarters of a lion, and the tale of a bear. At length all this was devoutly believed; and the new sexton used to exhibit to the curious, for a trifling emolument, a good-sized piece of the church weathercock which had been accidentally picked up by himself in the churchyard, a year or two afterwards.

Unfortunately, these stories were somewhat disturbed by the unlooked-for re-appearance of Gabriel Grub himself, some ten years afterwards, a ragged, contented, rheumatic old man. He told his story to the clergyman, and also to the mayor; and in course of time it began to be received, as a matter of history, in which form it has continued down to this very day. The believers in the weathercock tale, having misplaced their confidence once, were not easily prevailed upon to part with it again, so they looked as wise as they could, shrugged their shoulders, touched their foreheads, and murmured something about Gabriel Grub having drunk all the Hollands, and then fallen asleep on the flat tombstone; and they affected to explain what he supposed he had witnessed in the goblin's cavern, by saying that he had seen the world, and grown wiser. But this opinion, which was by no means a popular one at any time, gradually died off; and be the matter how it may, as Gabriel Grub was afflicted with rheumatism to the end of his days, this story has at least one moral, if it teach no better one – and that is, that if a man turn sulky and drink by himself at Christmas time, he may make up his mind to be not a bit the better for it; let the spirits be never so good, or let them be even as many degrees beyond proof, as those which Gabriel Grub saw in the goblin's cavern.

II

The Haunted Man
A Christmas Story

Ch-r-s D-c-k-n-s

In the flood of writers and editors who copied Dickens' inspired idea of a ghost story for Christmas, there were those who sought to be inventive and ingenious in their tales, while others blatantly stole his themes and plots: copyright protection being then virtually non-existent. Much of this derivative material was rightly quickly confined to oblivion, and furious though Dickens must have been at much of this piracy he at least saw that his work was earning a durability that has never waned. The success of A Christmas Carol *and his other ghost stories naturally enough also attracted parody, and of the numerous stories I have read which ape Dickens' supernatural tales, none is quite the equal of 'The Haunted Man' which was first published anonymously in America in 1868. Its skilful use of Dickens' style and clever plot construction pointed to it being the work of a talented author. And so it proved when Bret Harte (1836-1902), the American writer who became a US Consul and settled in London, confessed to its authorship in 1870. I make no excuse for including this amusing and neglected little Christmas parody here – nor for the fact that another of Bret Harte's stories appears later in this collection.*

The First Phantom

Don't tell me that it wasn't a knocker. I had seen it often enough, and I ought to know. So ought the three o'clock beer, in dirty highlows, swinging himself over the railing, or executing a demoniacal jig upon the doorstep; so ought the butcher, although butchers as a general thing are scornful of such trifles; so ought the postman, to whom knockers of the most extravagant description were merely human weaknesses, that were to be pitied and used. And so ought, for the matter of that, etc., etc., etc.

But then it was *such* a knocker. A wild, extravagant, and utterly incomprehensible knocker. A knocker so mysterious and suspicious that Policeman X 37, first coming upon it, felt inclined to take it instantly in custody, but compromised with his professional instincts by sharply and sternly noting it with an eye that admitted of no nonsense, but confidently expected to detect its secret yet. An ugly knocker; a knocker with a hard, human face, that was a type of the harder human face within. A human face that held between its teeth a brazen rod. So hereafter in the mysterious future should be held, etc., etc.

But if the knocker had a fierce human aspect in the glare of day, you should have seen it at night, when it peered out of the gathering shadows and suggested an ambushed figure; when the light of the street lamps fell upon it, and wrought a play of sinister expression in its hard outlines; when it seemed to wink meaningly at a shrouded figure who, as the night fell darkly, crept up the steps and passed into the mysterious house; when the swinging door disclosed a black passage into which the figure seemed to lose itself and become a part of the mysterious gloom; when the night grew boisterous and the fierce wind made furious charges at the knocker, as if to wrench it off and carry it away in triumph. Such a night as this.

It was a wild and pitiless wind. A wind that had commenced life as a gentle country zephyr, but wandering through manufacturing towns had become demoralised, and reaching the city had plunged into extravagant dissipation and wild excesses. A roystering wind that indulged in Bacchanalian shouts on the street corners, that knocked off the hats from the heads of helpless passengers, and then fulfilled its duties by speeding away, like all young prodigals – to sea.

He sat alone in a gloomy library listening to the wind that

roared in the chimney. Around him novels and story-books were strewn thickly; in his lap he held one with its pages freshly cut, and turned the leaves wearily until his eyes rested upon a portrait in its frontispiece. And as the wind howled the more fiercely, and the darkness without fell blacker, a strange and fateful likeness to that portrait appeared above his chair and leaned upon his shoulder. The Haunted Man gazed at the portrait and sighed. The figure gazed at the portrait and sighed too.

'Here again?' said the Haunted Man.

'Here again,' it repeated in a low voice.

'Another novel?'

'Another novel.'

'The old story?'

'The old story.'

'I see a child,' said the Haunted Man, gazing from the pages of the book into the fire – 'a most unnatural child, a model infant. It is prematurely old and philosophic. It dies in poverty to slow music. It dies surrounded by luxury to slow music. It dies with an accompaniment of golden water and rattling carts to slow music. Previous to its decease it makes a will; it repeats the Lord's Prayer, it kisses the "boofer lady." That child –'

'Is mine,' said the phantom.

'I see a good woman, undersized. I see several charming women, but they are all undersized. They are more or less imbecile and idiotic, but always fascinating and undersized. They wear coquettish caps and aprons. I observe that feminine virtue is invariably below the medium height, and that it is always babyish and infantine. These women –'

'Are mine.'

'I see a haughty, proud, and wicked lady. She is tall and queenly. I remark that all proud and wicked women are tall and queenly. That woman –'

'Is mine,' said the phantom, wringing his hands.

'I see several things continually impending. I observe that whenever an accident, a murder, or death is about to happen, there is something in the furniture, in the locality, in the atmosphere that foreshadows and suggests it years in advance. I cannot say that in real life I have noticed it – the perception of this surprising fact belongs –'

'To me!' said the phantom. The Haunted Man continued, in a despairing tone:

'I see the influence of this in the magazines and daily papers: I see weak imitators rise up and enfeeble the world with senseless formula. I am getting tired of it. It won't do, Charles! It won't do!' and the Haunted Man buried his head in his hands and groaned. The figure looked down upon him sternly: the portrait in the frontispiece frowned as he gazed.

'Wretched man,' said the phantom, 'and how have these things affected you?'

'Once I laughed and cried, but then I was younger. Now, I would forget them if I could.'

'Have then your wish. And take this with you, man whom I renounce. From this day henceforth you shall live with those whom I displace. Without forgetting me, 'twill be your lot to walk through life as if we had not met. But first you shall survey these scenes that henceforth must be yours. At one to-night, prepare to meet the phantom I have raised. Farewell!'

The sound of its voice seemed to fade away with the dying wind, and the Haunted Man was alone. But the firelight flickered gaily, and the light danced on the walls, making grotesque figures of the furniture.

'Ha, ha!' said the Haunted Man, rubbing his hands gleefully; 'now for a whiskey punch and a cigar.'

The Second Phantom

One! The stroke of the far-off bell had hardly died before the front door closed with a reverberating clang. Steps were heard along the passage; the library door swung open of itself, and the Knocker – yes, the Knocker – slowly strode into the room. The Haunted Man rubbed his eyes – no! there could be no mistake about it – it was the Knocker's face, mounted on a misty, almost imperceptible body. The brazen rod was transferred from its mouth to its right hand, where it was held like a ghostly truncheon.

'It's a cold evening,' said the Haunted Man.

'It is,' said the Goblin, in a hard metallic voice.

'It must be pretty cold out there,' said the Haunted Man, with vague politeness. 'Do you ever – will you – take some hot water and brandy?'

'No,' said the Goblin.

'Perhaps you'd like it cold, by way of change?' continued the Haunted Man, correcting himself, as he remembered the peculiar temperature with which the Goblin was probably familiar.

'Time flies,' said the Goblin coldly. 'We have no leisure for idle talk. Come!' He moved his ghostly truncheon toward the window, and laid his hand upon the other's arm. At his touch the body of the Haunted Man seemed to become as thin and incorporeal as that of the Goblin himself, and together they glided out of the window into the black and blowy night.

In the rapidity of their flight the senses of the Haunted Man seemed to leave him. At length they stopped suddenly.

'What do you see?' asked the Goblin.

'I see a battlemented medieval castle. Gallant men in mail ride over the drawbridge, and kiss their gauntleted fingers to fair ladies, who wave their lily hands in return. I see fight and fray and tournament. I hear roaring heralds bawling the charms of delicate women, and shamelessly proclaiming their lovers. Stay. I see a Jewess about to leap from a battlement. I see knightly deeds, violence, rapine, and a good deal of blood. I've seen pretty much the same at Astley's.'

'Look again.'

'I see purple moors, glens, masculine women, bare-legged men, priggish bookworms, more violence, physical excellence, and blood. Always blood – and the superiority of physical attainments.'

'And how do you feel now?' said the Goblin.

The Haunted Man shrugged his shoulders.

'None the better for being carried back and asked to sympathise with a barbarous age.'

The Goblin smiled and clutched his arm; they again sped rapidly through the black night, and again halted.

'What do you see?' said the Goblin.

'I see a barrack room, with a mess table, and a group of intoxicated Celtic officers telling funny stories, and giving challenges to duel. I see a young Irish gentleman capable of performing prodigies of valour. I learn incidentally that the acme of all heroism is the cornetcy of a dragoon regiment. I hear a good deal of French! No, thank you,' said the Haunted Man hurriedly, as he stayed the waving hand of the Goblin, 'I would rather *not* go to the Peninsula, and don't care to have a private interview with Napoleon.'

Again the Goblin flew away with the unfortunate man, and from a strange roaring below them, he judged they were above the ocean. A ship hove in sight, and the Goblin stayed its flight. 'Look,' he said, squeezing his companion's arm.

The Haunted Man yawned. 'Don't you think, Charles, you're rather running this thing into the ground? Of course, it's very moral and instructive, and all that. But ain't there a little too much pantomime about it? Come now!'

'Look!' repeated the Goblin, pinching his arm malevolently. The Haunted Man groaned.

'Oh, of course, I see Her Majesty's ship *Arethusa*. Of course I am familiar with her stern First Lieutenant, her eccentric Captain, her one fascinating and several mischievous midshipmen. Of course, I know it's a splendid thing to see all this, and not to be sea-sick. Oh, there the young gentlemen are going to play a trick on the purser. For God's sake, let us go,' and the unhappy man absolutely dragged the Goblin away with him.

When they next halted, it was at the edge of a broad and boundless prairie, in the middle of an oak opening.

'I see,' said the Haunted Man, without waiting for his cue, but mechanically, and as if he were repeating a lesson which the Goblin had taught him – 'I see the Noble Savage. He is very fine to look at! But I observe under his war paint, feathers and picturesque blanket – dirt, disease, and an unsymmetrical contour. I observe beneath his inflated rhetoric deceit and hypocrisy. Beneath his physical hardihood, cruelty, malice and revenge. The Noble Savage is a humbug. I remarked the same to Mr Catlin.'

'Come,' said the phantom.

The Haunted Man sighed, and took out his watch. 'Couldn't we do the rest of this another time?'

'My hour is almost spent, irreverent being, but there is yet a chance for your reformation. Come!'

Again they sped through the night, and again they halted. The sound of delicious but melancholy music fell upon their ears.

'I see,' said the Haunted Man, with something of interest in his manner, 'I see an old moss-covered manse beside a sluggish, flowing river. I see weird shapes: witches, Puritans, clergymen, little children, judges, mesmerised maidens, moving to the sound of melody that thrills me with its sweetness and purity.

'But, although carried along its calm and evenly-flowing current, the shapes are strange and frightful: an eating lichen gnaws at the heart of each; not only the clergymen, but witch, maiden, judge, and Puritan, all wear Scarlet Letters of some kind burned upon their hearts. I am fascinated and thrilled, but I feel a morbid sensitiveness creeping over me. I – I beg your pardon.' The Goblin was yawning frightfully. 'Well, perhaps we had better go.'

'One more, and the last,' said the Goblin. They were moving home. Streaks of red were beginning to appear in the eastern sky. Along the banks of the blackly flowing river, by moorland and stagnant fens, by low houses, clustering close to the water's edge, like strange mollusks, crawled upon the beach to dry; by misty black barges, the more misty and indistinct seen through its mysterious veil, the river fog was slowly rising. So rolled away and rose from the heart of the Haunted Man, etc., etc.

They stopped before a quaint mansion of red brick. The Goblin waved his hand without speaking.

'I see,' said the Haunted Man, 'a gay drawing-room. I see my old friends of the club, of the college, of society, even as they lived and moved. I see the gallant and unselfish men whom I have loved, and the snobs whom I have hated. I see strangely mingling with them, and now and then blending with their forms, our old friends Dick Steele, Addison, and Congreve. I observe, though, that these gentlemen have a habit of getting too much in the way. The royal standard of Queen Anne, not in itself a beautiful ornament, is rather too prominent in the picture. The long galleries of black oak, the formal furniture, the old portraits, are picturesque, but depressing. The house is damp. I enjoy myself better here on the lawn, where they are getting up a Vanity Fair. See, the bell rings, the curtain is rising, the puppets are brought out for a new play. Let me see.'

The Haunted Man was pressing forward in his eagerness, but the hand of the Goblin stayed him, and pointing to his feet, he saw between him and the rising curtain, a new-made grave. And bending above the grave in passionate grief, the Haunted Man beheld the phantom of the previous night.

The Haunted Man started, and – woke. The bright sunshine streamed into the room. The air was sparkling with frost. He ran joyously to the window and opened it. A small boy saluted him with 'Merry Christmas'. The Haunted Man instantly gave him a Bank of England note. 'How much like Tiny Tim, Tom and Bobby that boy looked – bless my soul, what a genius this Dickens has!'

A knock at the door, and Boots entered.

'Consider you salary doubled instantly. Have you read *David Copperfield*?'

'Yezzur.'

'Your salary is quadrupled. What do you think of *The Old Curiosity Shop*?'

The man instantly burst into a torrent of tears, and then into a roar of laughter.

'Enough! Here are five thousand pounds. Open a porter-house, and call it, "Our Mutual Friend." Huzza! I feel so happy!' And the Haunted Man danced about the room.

And so, bathed in the light of that blessed sun, and yet glowing with the warmth of a good action, the Haunted Man, haunted no longer, save by those shapes which make the dreams of children beautiful, re-seated himself in his chair, and finished *Our Mutual Friend*.

III

Frights!

George Cruikshank

An important factor in the impact that Charles Dickens' work had on the public was undoubtedly the superb illustrations which appeared with his stories. These striking engravings which evoked all the grimness and poverty that much of his work focused upon, were primarily the work of George Cruikshank (1792-1878). Cruikshank, the son of a prominent caricaturist, followed directly in the footsteps of Rowlandson and Gillray and helped usher in the age of realistic as against stylised engravings. He began his career as a cartoonist for the satirical monthly, The Scourge, *but in 1832 switched to book illustration and not long afterwards began his partnership with Dickens which led to him being described as 'the perfect illustrator for Dickens'. Many editions of Dickens' work still retain Cruikshank's original drawings to this day. What is not generally known about George Cruikshank is that he also enjoyed writing, and shared Dickens' interest in the supernatural. When, in the 1840's and 50's, he edited* George Cruikshank's Omnibus, *he took the opportunity to write a few tales and essays about the macabre, also providing the illustrations. Most of his stories appeared anonymously (as was customary then), and such is the scarcity of these omnibuses that many are now probably lost. However, I have been fortunate enough to unearth the following ghostly yarn which Cruikshank wrote for the Christmas 1841 edition, and I present it here with the observation that the author reveals himself as grimly adept with words as he was with his brush – and every bit as capable of surprising you!*

I remember two of my father's friends who were 'regular story tellers'. Mr O'Brien had a store of Irish legends, and Mr Thomas Smith a variety of ghost stories. Of one of these a haunted house was the scene – a whole family of ghosts the *dramatis personae*. We must premise, that at the time referred to, it was the fashion to wear 'pigtails', and Mr Smith, who had eschewed 'pigtail' and patronised 'short cut' or crop, used to say when asked what he had done with his 'pig-tail' that 'thereby hangs a tail' which joke he retailed at every opportunity. We may also intimate that a good ghost story was in those days a valuable little property. Mr Smith seldom dined at home, and always passed his evenings at other people's firesides. In truth, for more than three parts of the year his ghost story procured him 'bed, board and lodgings' gratis, including coal and candles. Now then, let the reader imagine a small family party seated round the fire on a Christmas Eve, and let Mr Smith tell his own story in his own way.

I was staying (he began) some years back at Squire Calf's, at Danglewitch-Hall, near Nantwich, in Cheshire; my friend, O'Brien here, was also a visitor. ('Sure I was,' says Mr O'B. with a grin – he was a merry fellow that O'B.) One evening the conversation turned upon Clay-hall, an old deserted mansion, that was reported to be haunted. Strange sights, strange sounds, and strange stories, filled the neighbourhood with alarm; and what surprised me at that time was, that all the Danglewitch people seemed firmly to believe in them. Being a little elevated, I bantered the family upon their ridiculous fears – I have since learned to pay more attention to other people's opinions – and so enraged the squire, that he offered to bet fifty guineas to one, that I would not dare to sleep in that house for one night. No sooner said than 'Done,' cried I, and proposed to go immediately. The squire instantly ordered the servant to get the key from the old women at Clay-park lodge, to light a fire in the blue-room, and to provide, besides a pipe and tobacco, a good bottle of brandy. The whole party, in a merry mood, sallied forth to conduct me to my quarters. Soon after I wished them all good night, and fastened the door. I had a brace of pistols and a good sword-stick. I drew my sword and went over the house at once, to see that the fastenings were secure – for though not afraid of ghosts, I objected to being surprised by robbers.

Everything was in a dilapidated state, but I ascertained that the locks and bolts, although rusty, were sufficiently strong to resist an intruder. I was also certain, that no one was concealed. I then proceeded to my apartment, which was on the first floor at the back of the house. I slowly ascended the large staircase. The sound of my footsteps echoed through the empty mansion. As I approached the landing I was startled by a sudden noise, like the slamming of a door, and recollected that one of the upper rooms was without a fastening. All was silent again. I could hear myself breathe. I then held up the light, and looked first up, and then down, the well staircase, and began to feel that I had done a rather foolish thing – there might be after all a secret inlet – I might be robbed, murdered. But it was too late to recede; and the fear of being laughed at overcame every other fear.

I now entered my chamber and secured the door. The bright fire and the candles gave a cheering look to a room otherwise dreary enough; for it was of large dimensions, and its colour was a deep dingy blue. At one end stood a huge four-post bedstead, hung with dark blue tattered damask curtains, edged with black; the head of each post was ornamented with a ragged plume of dark-blue feathers, which gave to it rather a funereal appearance. I examined every part, and beneath the bed perceived a large chest, which I found to be firmly locked. Pushing it aside, I proceeded to explore the two closets that flanked the fire-place. Amongst a quantity of loose lumber, wig boxes, hat boxes, and odd slippers, I discovered an old black letter volume (a good deal nibbled), but as Sir Walter Scott says, 'worth its weight in gold for all that'; it was *God's Revenge against Murther*. I just gave it a bang upon the table to knock out the dust. The blow produced a most tremendous noise that nearly stunned me, and was echoed apparently from every corner of the building, followed by the rattling of falling mortar behind the wainscot, and a scampering as if ten thousand rats were flying in all directions. The cloud of dust almost stifled me; but not quite overcome, I applied myself to my brandy, and filled my pipe, stirred the fire, snuffed the candles, opened my book, and began to read. I read on in silence, broken only by the regular puffing of smoke, the ticking of my watch, and the singing, or rather sighing of the kettle. The book absorbed my whole attention. I was insensibly moved by its revelations. I was so worked upon by it that I felt a kind of lifting of the chair beneath me, and a peeping shadow appeared evermore between the candle and the page. Suddenly, at a most exciting point, I heard a gentle rustling of the bed-curtains. On looking round – horror! never to be forgotten!

I distinctly saw a tall figure enveloped in a long night-dress, which touched the ground. It was standing sideways towards me, so that the face was hidden by a large feminine cap, which, however, it removed and threw upon the bed, discovering a most fearful and ghastly profile. It went through the operation of making its toilet before a small glass, then looked towards the trunk, and then to the bed. After a moment's hesitation, the trunk was opened, and it proceeded to put on an old-fashioned brocade dress. The figure then, after surveying itself in the mirror, slowly turned round, and moved towards me. I felt my blood curdle, my flesh crawl. It passed the foot of the bed, and advanced towards the door. The eyes were cast down; the hand was upon the fastenings. At this instant the village clock struck, or rather tolled out twelve – and as the last stroke of the bell floated on the breeze, the figure gradually raised its head, and fixed upon me a pair of horrible glaring eyes that turned my heart to ice. A sharp sliding noise on the wall opposite made me turn to look, and the two portraits, a lady, and an officer in a blue uniform, appeared to be leaning out of their frames, and watching me intently. The figure then hastily passed out of the room, uttering a screaming note, wilder than the moaning wind. This was answered seemingly from the cellars by a most hideous long drawn howl, followed by the rattling of locks, bolts, and chains, and a confusion of strange unearthly sounds. I sprang up and seized my pistols. There was a dead silence. I could distinctly hear a whispering not only on the stairs, but in the closets, the doors of which were slowly pushed open, and more than one pair of eyes flashed upon me from the dark; in an instant the door of the room creaked slowly, and I beheld two or three parchment faces, with fiery eyes, gazing at me. I made now a desperate effort, and levelling a pistol either way, uttered a fierce menace, threatening to fire, if they advanced. This threat was answered by a queer sort of tittering and shuffling; in desperation I pulled the triggers; the result was a double flash in the pan, which overspread the room like a sheet of blue lightning. Then broke forth – a laugh – ten times more horrible than the laughter of a herd of hyenas – I could endure no longer, and sank into the chair, the pistols dropping from my hands.

There was a dead pause, and I heard something like the mewing of a cat, yet it seemed like the voice of a child in distress; and my attention was attracted by the appearance of a black skeleton of a cat, who was setting up its back, growling and spitting. It then slowly advanced and prowled round the fire-place, and sitting down opposite to the fire with its back towards me, turned its head, and its fearful green eyes met mine. I next heard the whelping of a cur, and the distant, hollow, wolf-like baying of a watch-dog. The sounds approached; the dog-chain rattled up the stairs. I tried to seize my sword, but was paralysed. I could just glance towards the door, whence came a strange, shuffling sound, and the next moment I saw an extraordinary figure enter, with a large carving-knife in his hand. He was dressed in blue livery, with tags – a round paunch – high bony shoulders, and spindle-shanks – he wore a blue Welsh wig – and his nose, which was of enormous size and hooked, was of a deep blue also: it was like burning brimstone. He was followed by a skeleton-like figure; also in livery, and armed like his fellow. These stood and stared at me. They were followed by a figure, marching into the room with an air of consequence. He was not prepossessing: dimly-glaring saucer-eyes, with a decided cast in them; a small, pinched bit of blue nose; a spacious mouth, with a tooth or two exposed; the look of age diffused over all. He was wrapped in a blue dressing-gown, and wore a large curled blue wig. As *he* entered, all appeared blue – the candles, and the fire, whose flames curled themselves into the likeness of some ghastly thing. The whole company, for there were now many intruders, seemed covered with blue mould; they were the children of Mildew and Decay; they looked damp and slippery. The veteran in the dressing-gown advanced to the fireside with dignity, and looked at me with a withering scowl. I guessed at once that he was or *had been* the master of the mansion, and politeness prompted me to rise. He motioned me to be seated, and then took a chair. A little boy was at his side, and the stately figure of a lady also stood near him – other faces peered over his chair. My venerable host then bent forwards, and placing his hands upon his knees, looked sternly in my face and said, in sepulchral tones – '*Pray sir, did you ever hear that this house is haunted*?'

I was thunderstruck! What answer could I make? Not a moment was allowed me for reflection, for I instantly felt a violent tug at my pigtail behind, and the brimstoned-nose butler, leering in my upturned face, exclaimed, 'And you don't believe in ghosts!' My terror was at its height. I heard no more; but I *saw* – I saw the knife flashing, and felt that, though my head was not off, my pigtail was gone! Shouts of exulting malice rent the air –

But here Mr Smith was interrupted by a shout of exulting laughter from one of his listeners. It was Mr O'Brien. 'O, ho!' screamed that gentleman; 'I'll be kilt intirely. A mighty ingenious tale you've made of it, Mr Smith. And sure I must tell the thruth if you hate me for it. Sure and wasn't it the day after we had the stag-hunt, and didn't you get so over head and ears in liquor that you went sleep-walking about the house all night, disturbing the people that were fast asleep; and the night after, sure didn't we tie your pigtail to the bell-rope at the head of the bed, to keep you still, or give us notice of your rambles – and a pretty good notice we got, by the powers! for what wid the bell ringing and your bawling, we thought the house was on fire. I'll never forget seeing you pulling one way and the bell-pull pulling the other – and all we could do, we could not keep you aisy, till we undid your tail; so faith it was Betty, the cook, I remember, who whipt out her scissors, and cut the knot. Oh, oh! och! – and that's the *thrue* way you lost your pigtail, Mr Smith!'

IV

Thurlow's Christmas Story

John Kendrick Bangs

The tradition which Dickens had begun quickly enough spread to America, and over the years which followed one of the most regular, not to say most inventive contributors of ghost stories at Christmas, was the humorist John Kendrick Bangs (1862-1922). Bangs had discovered Dickens' stories as a child, and when his own interest in the supernatural developed along with his natural wit, it came as no surprise that almost half of his output of books – some nineteen works – dealt with ghosts in one way or another. They contributed considerably to the reputation he earned as America's leading humorist at the turn of the century. Bangs initially earned his living as a journalist specialising in satire, then after a time feature writing on the world's first tabloid newspaper, The Daily Continent, *he became editor of the prestigious* Harper's Weekly. *The story here, however, is typical of his supernatural humour, and is a particularly appropriate selection not only because it appeared at Christmas 1895, but because Bangs – as he admits – had to produce it to meet a most punishing deadline. How he utilised these circumstances makes for a superbly ironic tale.*

*

I. – Being the statement of Henry Thurlow, Author, to George Currier, Editor of the Tatler, *a weekly journal of human interest*

I have always maintained, my dear Currier, that if a man wished to be considered sane, and has any particular regard for his reputation as a truth-teller, he would better keep silent as to the singular experiences that enter into his life. I have had many such experiences myself; but I have rarely confided them in detail, or otherwise, to those about me, because I know that even the most trustful of my friends would regard them merely as the outcome of an imagination unrestrained by conscience, or of a gradually weakening mind subject to hallucinations. I know them to be true, but until Mr Edison or some other modern wizard has invented a search-light strong enough to lay bare the secrets of the mind and conscience of man, I cannot prove to others that they are not pure fabrications, or at least the conjurings of a diseased fancy. For instance, no man would believe me if I were to state to him the plain and indisputable fact that one night last month, on my way up to bed shortly after midnight, having been neither smoking nor drinking, I saw confronting me upon the stairs, with the moonlight streaming through the windows behind me, lighting up its face, a figure in which I recognized my very self in every form and feature. I might describe the chill of terror that struck to the very marrow of my bones, and well-nigh forced me to stagger backward down the stairs, as I noticed in the face of this confronting figure every indication of all the bad qualities which I know myself to possess, of every evil instinct which by no easy effort I have repressed heretofore, and realized that that *thing* was, as far as I knew, entirely independent of my true self, in which I hope at least the moral has made an honest fight against the immoral always. I might describe this chill, I say, as vividly as I felt it at that moment, but it would be of no use to do so, because, however realistic it might prove as a bit of description, no man would believe that the incident really happened; and yet it did happen as truly as I write, and it has happened a dozen times since, and I am certain that it will happen many times again, though I would give all that I possess to be assured that never again should that disquieting creation of mind or matter, whichever it may be, cross my path. The experience has made me afraid almost to be alone, and I have found myself unconsciously and uneasily glancing at my face in mirrors, in the plate-glass of show-windows on the shopping streets of the city, fearful lest I should find some of those evil traits which I have struggled to keep under, and have kept under so far, cropping out there where all the world, all *my* world, can see and wonder at, having known me always as a man of right doing and right feeling. Many a time in the night the thought has come to me with prostrating force, what if that thing were to be seen and recognized by others, myself and yet not my whole self, my unworthy self unrestrained and yet recognizable as Henry Thurlow.

I have also kept silent as to that strange condition of affairs which has tortured me in my sleep for the past year and a half; no one but myself has until this writing known that for that period of time I have had a continuous, logical dream-life; a life so vivid and so dreadfully real to me that I have found myself at times wondering which of the two lives I was living and which I was dreaming; a life in which that other wicked self has dominated, and forced me to a career of shame and horror; a life which, being taken up every time I sleep where it ceased with the awakening from a previous sleep, has made me fear to close my eyes in forgetfulness when others are near at hand, lest, sleeping, I shall let fall some speech that, striking on their ears, shall lead them to believe that in secret there is some wicked mystery connected with my life. It would be of no use for me to tell these things. It would merely serve to make my family and my friends uneasy about me if they were told in their awful detail, and so I have kept silent about them. To you alone, and now for the first time have I hinted as to the troubles which have oppressed me for many days, and to you they are confided only because of the demand you have made that I explain to you the extraordinary complication in which the Christmas story sent you last week has involved me. You know that I am a man of dignity; that I am not a school-boy and a lover of childish tricks; and knowing that, your friendship, at least, should have restrained your tongue and pen when, through the former, on Wednesday, you accused me of perpetrating a trifling, and to you excessively embarrassing, practical joke – a charge which, at the moment, I was too overcome to refute; and through the latter, on Thursday, you reiterated the accusation, coupled with a demand for an explanation of my conduct satisfactory to yourself, or my immediate resignation from the staff of the *Tatler*. To explain is difficult, for I am certain that you will find the explanation too improbable for credence, but explain I must. The alternative, that of resigning from your staff, affects not only my own welfare, but that of my children, who must be provided for; and if my post with you is taken from me, then are all resources gone. I have not the courage to face dismissal, for I have not sufficient confidence in my powers to please elsewhere to make me easy in my mind, or, if I could please elsewhere, the certainty of finding the immediate employment of my talents which is necessary to me, in view of the at present overcrowded condition of the literary field.

To explain, then, my seeming jest at your expense, hopeless as it appears to be, is my task; and to do so as completely as I can, let me go back to the very beginning.

In August you informed me that you would expect me to provide, as I have heretofore been in the habit of doing, a story for the Christmas issue of the *Tatler*; that a certain position in the make-up was reserved for me, and that you had already taken steps to advertise the fact that the story would appear. I undertook the commission, and upon seven different occasions set about putting the narrative into shape. I found great difficulty, however, in doing so. For some reason or other I could not concentrate my mind upon the work. No sooner would I start in on one story than a better one, in my estimation, would suggest itself to me; and all the labour expended on the story already begun would be cast aside, and the new story set in motion. Ideas were plenty enough, but to put them properly upon paper seemed beyond my power. One story, however, I did finish; but after it had come back to me from my typewriter I read it, and was filled with consternation to discover that it was nothing more nor less than a mass of jumbled sentences, conveying no idea to the mind – a story which had seemed to me in the writing to be coherent had returned to me as a mere bit of incoherence – formless, without ideas – a bit of raving. It was then that I went to you and told you, as you remember, that I was worn out, and needed a month of absolute rest, which you granted. I left my work wholly, and went into the wilderness, where I could be entirely free from everything suggesting labour, and where no summons back to town could reach me. I fished and hunted. I slept; and although, as I have already said, in my sleep I found myself leading a life that was not only not to my taste, but horrible to me in many particulars, I was able at the end of my vacation to come back to town greatly refreshed, and, as far as my feelings went, ready to undertake any amount of work. For two or three days after my return I was busy with other things. On the fourth day after my arrival you came to me, and said that the story must be finished at the very latest by October 15th, and I assured you that you should have it by that time. That night I set about it. I mapped it out, incident by incident, and before starting up to bed had actually written some twelve or fifteen hundred words of the opening chapter – it was to be told in four chapters. When I had gone thus far I experienced a slight return of one of my nervous chills, and, on consulting my watch, discovered that it was after midnight, which was a sufficient explanation of my nervousness: I was merely tired. I arranged my manuscripts on my table so that I might easily take up the work the following morning. I locked up the windows and doors, turned out the lights, and proceeded upstairs to my room.

It was then that I first came face to face with myself – that other self, in which I recognised, developed to the full, every bit of my capacity for an evil life.

Conceive of the situation if you can. Imagine the horror of it, and then ask yourself if it was likely that when next morning came I could by any possibility bring myself to my work-table in fit condition to prepare for you anything at all worthy of publication in the *Tatler*. I tried. I implore you to believe that I did not hold lightly the responsibilities of the commission you had entrusted to my hands. You must know that if any of your writers has a full appreciation of the difficulties which are strewn along the path of an editor, I, who have myself had an editorial experience, have it, and so would not, in the nature of things, do anything to add to your troubles. You cannot but believe that I have made an honest effort to fulfil my promise to you. But it was useless, and for a week after that visitation was it useless for me to attempt the work. At the end of the week I felt better, and again I started in, and the story developed satisfactorily until – *it* came again. That figure which was my own figure, that face which was the evil counterpart of my own countenance, again rose up before me, and once more was I plunged into hopelessness.

Thus matters went on until the 14th day of October, when I received your peremptory message that the story must be forthcoming the following day. Needless to tell you that it was not forthcoming; but what I must tell you, since you do not know it, is that on the evening of the 15th day of October a strange thing happened to me, and in the narration of that incident, which I almost despair of your believing, lies my explanation of the discovery of October 16th, which has placed my position with you in peril.

At half-past seven o'clock on the evening of October 15th I was sitting in my library trying to write. I was alone. My wife and children had gone away on a visit to Massachusetts for a week. I had just finished my cigar, and had taken my pen in hand, when my front-door bell rang. Our maid, who is usually prompt in answering summonses of this nature, apparently did not hear the bell, for she did not respond to its clanging. Again the bell rang, and still did it remain unanswered, until finally, at the third ringing, I went to the door myself. On opening it I saw standing before me a man of, I should say, fifty odd years of age, tall, slender, pale-faced, and clad in sombre black. He was entirely unknown to me. I had never seen him before, but he had about him such an air of pleasantness and wholesomeness that I instinctively felt glad to see him, without knowing why or whence he had come.

'Does Mr Thurlow live here?' he asked.

You must excuse me for going into what may seem to you to be petty details, but by a perfectly circumstantial account of all that happened that evening alone can I hope to give a semblance of truth to my story, and that it must be truthful I realize as painfully as you do.

'I am Mr Thurlow,' I replied.

'Henry Thurlow, the author?' he said, with a surprised look upon his face.

'Yes,' said I; and then, impelled by the strange appearance of surprise on the man's countenance, I added, 'Don't I look like an author?'

He laughed, and candidly admitted that I was not the kind of looking man he had expected to find from reading my books, and then he entered the house in response to my invitation that he do so. I ushered him into my library, and, after asking him to be seated, inquired as to his business with me.

His answer was gratifying at least. He replied that he had been a reader of my writings for a number of years, and that for some time past he had had a great desire, not to say curiosity, to meet me and tell me how much he had enjoyed certain of my stories.

'I'm a great devourer of books, Mr Thurlow,' he said, 'and I have taken the keenest delight in reading your verses and humorous sketches. I may go further, and say to you that you have helped me over many a hard place in my life by your work. At times when I have felt myself worn out with my business, or face to face with some knotty problem in my career, I have found much relief in picking up and reading your books at random. They have helped me to forget my weariness or my knotty problems for the time being; and to-day, finding myself in this town, I resolved to call upon you this evening and thank you for all that you have done for me.'

Thereupon we became involved in a general discussion of literary men and their works, and I found that my visitor certainly did have a pretty thorough knowledge of what has been produced by the writers of to-day. I was quite won over to him by his simplicity, as well as attracted to him by his kindly opinion of my own efforts, and I did my best to entertain him, showing him a few of my little literary treasures in the way of autograph letters, photographs, and presentation copies of well-known books from the authors themselves. From this we drifted naturally and easily into a talk on the methods of work adapated by literary men. He asked me many questions as to my own methods; and when I had in a measure outlined to him the manner of life which I had adopted, telling him of my days at home, how little detail office-work I had, he seemed much interested with the picture – indeed, I painted the picture of my daily routine in almost too perfect colours, for, when I had finished, he observed quietly that I appeared to him to lead the ideal life, and added that he supposed I knew very little unhappiness.

The remark recalled to me the dreadful reality, that through some perversity of fate I was doomed to visitations of an uncanny order which were practically destroying my usefulness in my profession and my sole financial resource.

'Well,' I replied, as my mind reverted to the unpleasant

predicament in which I found myself, 'I can't say that I know little unhappiness. As a matter of fact, I know a great deal of that undesirable thing. At the present moment I am very much embarrassed through my absolute inability to fulfil a contract into which I have entered, and which should have been filled this morning. I was due to-day with a Christmas story. The presses are waiting for it, and I am utterly unable to write it.'

He appeared deeply concerned at the confession. I had hoped, indeed, that he might be sufficiently concerned to take his departure, that I might make one more effort to write the promised story. His solicitude, however, showed itself in another way. Instead of leaving me, he ventured the hope that he might aid me.

'What kind of a story is it to be?' he asked.

'Oh, the usual ghostly tale,' I said, 'with a dash of the Christmas flavour thrown in here and there to make it suitable to the season.'

'Ah,' he observed. 'And you find your vein worked out?'

It was a direct and perhaps an impertinent question; but I thought it best to answer it, and to answer it as well without giving him any clue as to the real facts. I could not very well take an entire stranger into my confidence, and describe to him the extraordinary encounters I was having with an uncanny other self. He would not have believed the truth, hence I told him an untruth, and assented to his proposition.

'Yes,' I replied, 'the vein is worked out. I have written ghost stories for years now, serious and comic, and I am to-day at the end of my tether – compelled to move forward and yet held back.'

'That accounts for it,' he said, simply. 'When I first saw you to-night at the door I could not believe that the author who had provided me with so much merriment could be so pale and worn and seemingly mirthless. Pardon me, Mr Thurlow, for my lack of consideration when I told you that you did not appear as I had expected to find you.'

I smiled my forgiveness, and he continued:

'It may be,' he said, with a show of hesitation, 'it may be that I have come not altogether inopportunely. Perhaps I can help you.'

I smiled again. 'I should be most grateful if you could,' I said.

'But you doubt my ability to do so?' he put in. 'Oh – well – yes – of course you do; and why shouldn't you? Nevertheless, I have noticed this: At times when I have been baffled in my work a mere hint from another, from one who knew nothing of my work, has carried me on to a solution of my problem. I have read most of your writings, and I have thought over some of them many a time, and I have even had ideas for stories, which, in my own conceit, I have imagined were good enough for you, and I have wished that I possessed your facility with the pen that I might make of them myself what I thought you would make of them had they been ideas of your own.'

The old gentleman's pallid face reddened as he said this, and while I was hopeless as to anything of value resulting from his ideas, I could not resist the temptation to hear what he had to say further, his manner was so deliciously simple, and his desire to aid me so manifest. He rattled on with suggestions for a half-hour. Some of them were good, but none were new. Some were irresistibly funny, and did me good because they made me laugh, and I hadn't laughed naturally for a period so long that it made me shudder to think of it, fearing lest I should forget how to be mirthful. Finally I grew tired of his persistence, and, with a very ill-concealed impatience, told him plainly that I could do nothing with his suggestions, thanking him, however, for the spirit of kindliness which had prompted him to offer them. He appeared somewhat hurt, but immediately desisted, and when nine o'clock came he rose up to go. As he walked to the door he seemed to be undergoing some mental struggle, to which, with a sudden resolve, he finally succumbed, for, after having picked up his hat and stick and donned his overcoat, he turned to me and said –

'Mr Thurlow, I don't want to offend you. On the contrary, it is my dearest wish to assist you. You have helped me, as I have told you. Why may I not help you?'

'I assure you, sir –' I began, when he interrupted me.

'One moment, please,' he said, putting his hand into the inside pocket of his black coat and extracting from it an envelope addressed to me. 'Let me finish: it is the whim of one who has affection for you. For ten years I have secretly been at work myself on a story. It is a short one, but it has seemed good to me. I had a double object in seeking you out to-night. I wanted not only to see you, but to read my story to you. No one knows that I have written it; I had intended it as a surprise to my – to my friends. I had hoped to have it published somewhere, and I had come here to seek your advice in the matter. It is a story which I have written and rewritten and rewritten time and time again in my leisure moments during the ten years past, as I have told you. It is not likely that I shall ever write another. I am proud of having done it, but I should be prouder yet if it – if it could in some way help you. I leave it with you, sir, to print or to destroy; and if you print it, to see it in type will be enough for me; to see your name signed to it will be a matter of pride to me. No one will ever be the wiser, for, as I say, no one knows I have written it, and I promise you that no one shall know of it if you decide to do as I not only suggest but ask you to do. No one would believe me after it has appeared as *yours*, even if I should forget my promise and claim it as my own. Take it. It is yours. You are entitled to it as a slight measure of repayment for the debt of gratitude I owe you.'

He pressed the manuscript into my hands, and before I could reply had opened the door and disappeared into the darkness of the street. I rushed to the sidewalk and shouted out to him to return, but I might as well have saved my breath and spared the neighbourhood, for there was no answer. Holding his story in my hand, I re-entered the house and walked back into my library, where, sitting and reflecting upon the curious interview, I realized for the first time that I was in entire ignorance as to my visitor's name and address.

I opened the envelope hoping to find them, but they were not there. The envelope contained merely a finely written manuscript of thirty odd pages, unsigned.

And then I read the story. When I began it was with a half-smile upon my lips, and with a feeling that I was wasting my time. The smile soon faded, however; after reading the first paragraph there was no question of wasted time. The story was a masterpiece. It is needless to say to you that I am not a man of enthusiasms. It is difficult to arouse that emotion in my breast, but upon this occasion I yielded to a force too great for me to resist. I have read the tales of Hoffmann and of Poe, the wondrous romances of De La Motte Fouqué, the unfortunately little-known tales of the lamented Fitz-James O'Brien, the weird tales of writers of all tongues have been thoroughly sifted by me in the course of my reading, and I say to you now that in the whole of my life I never read one story, one paragraph, one line, that could approach in vivid delineation, in weirdness of conception, in anything, in any quality which goes to make up the truly great story, that story which came into my hands as I have told you. I read it once and was amazed. I read it a second time and was – tempted. It was mine. The writer himself had authorized me to treat it as if it were my own; had voluntarily sacrificed his own claim to its authorship that he might relieve me of my very pressing embarrassment. Not only this; he had almost intimated that in putting my name to his work I should be doing him a favour. Why not do so, then, I asked myself; and immediately my better self rejected the idea as impossible. How could I put out as my own another man's work and retain my self respect? I resolved on another and better course – to send you the story in lieu of my own with a full statement of the circumstances under which it had come into my possession, when that demon rose up out of the floor at my side, this time more evil of aspect than before, more commanding in its manner. With a groan I shrank back into the cushions of my chair, and by passing my hands over my eyes tried to obliterate for ever the offending sight; but it was useless. The uncanny thing approached me, and as truly as I write sat upon the edge of my couch, where for the first time it addressed me.

'Fool!' it said, 'how can you hesitate? Here is your position: you have made a contract which must be filled; you are already behind, and in a hopeless mental state. Even granting that between this and to-morrow morning you could put together the necessary number of words to fill the space allotted to you, what kind of a thing do you think that story would make? It would be a mere raving like that other precious effort of August. The public, if by some odd chance it ever reached them, would think your mind was utterly gone; your reputation would go with that verdict. On the other hand, if you do not have the story ready by to-morrow, your hold on the *Tatler* will be destroyed. They have their announcements printed, and your name and portrait appear among those of the prominent contributors. Do you suppose the editor and publisher will look leniently upon your failure?'

'Considering my past record, yes,' I replied. 'I have never yet broken a promise to them.'

'Which is precisely the reason why they will be severe with you. You, who have been regarded as one of the few men who can do almost any kind of literary work at will – you, of whom it is said that your "brains are on tap" – will they be lenient with *you*? Bah! Can't you see that the very fact of your invariable readiness heretofore is going to make your present unreadiness a thing incomprehensible?'

'Then what shall I do?' I asked. 'If I can't, I can't, that is all.'

'You can. There is the story in your hands. Think what it will do for you. It is one of the immortal stories –'

'You have read it, then?' I asked.

'Haven't you?'

'Yes – but –'

'It is the same,' it said, with a leer and a contemptuous shrug. 'You and I are inseparable. Aren't you glad?' it added, with a laugh that grated in every fibre of my being. I was too overwhelmed to reply, and it resumed: 'It is one of the immortal stories. We agree to that. Published over your name, your name will live. The stuff you write yourself will give you present glory; but when you have been dead ten years people won't remember your name even – unless I get control of you, and in that case there is a very pretty though hardly a literary record in store for you.'

Again it laughed harshly, and I buried my face in the pillows of my couch, hoping to find relief there from this dreadful vision.

'Curious,' it said. 'What you call your decent self doesn't dare look me in the eye! What a mistake people make you say that the man who won't look you in the eye is not to be trusted! As if mere brazenness were a sign of honesty; really, the theory of decency is the most amusing thing in the world. But come, time is growing short. Take that story. The writer gave it to you; begged you to use it as your own. It is yours. It will make your reputation, and save you with your publishers. How can you hesitate?'

'I shall not use it!' I cried, desperately.

'You must – consider your children. Suppose you lose your connection with these publishers of yours?'

'But it would be a crime.'

'Not a bit of it. Whom do you rob? A man who voluntarily came to you, and gave you that of which you rob him. Think of it as it is – and act, only act quickly. It is now midnight.'

The tempter rose up and walked to the other end of the room, whence, while he pretended to be looking over a few of my books and pictures, I was aware he was eying me closely, and gradually compelling me by sheer force of will to do a thing which I abhorred. And I – I struggled weakly against the temptation, but gradually, little by little, I yielded, and finally succumbed altogether. Springing to my feet, I rushed to the table, seized my pen, and signed my name to the story.

'There!' I said. 'It is done. I have saved my position and made my reputation, and am now a thief!'

'As well as a fool,' said the other, calmly. 'You don't mean to say you are going to send that manuscript in as it is?'

'Good Lord!' I cried. 'What under heaven have you been trying to make me do for the last half-hour?'

'Act like a sane thing,' said the demon. 'If you send that manuscript to Currier he'll know in a minute it isn't yours. He knows you haven't an amanuensis, and that handwriting isn't yours. Copy it.'

'True!' I answered. 'I haven't much of a mind for details to-night. I will do as you say.'

I did so. I got out my pad and pen and ink, and for three hours diligently applied myself to the task of copying the story. When it was finished I went over it carefully, made a few minor corrections, signed it, put it in an envelope, addressed it to you, stamped it, and went out to the mailbox on the corner, where I dropped it into the slot, and returned home. When I had returned to my library my visitor was still there.

'Well,' it said, 'I wish you'd hurry and complete this affair. I am tired, and wish to go.'

'You can't go too soon to please me,' said I, gathering up the original manuscripts of the story and preparing to put them away in my desk.

'Probably not,' it sneered. 'I'll be glad to go too, but I can't go until that manuscript is destroyed. As long as it exists there is evidence of your having appropriated the work of another. Why, can't you see that? Burn it!'

'I can't see my way clear in crime!' I retorted. 'It is not in my line.'

Nevertheless, realizing the value of his advice, I thrust the pages one by one into the blazing log fire, and watched them as they flared and flamed and grew to ashes. As the last page disappeared in the embers the demon vanished. I was alone, and throwing myself down for a moment's reflection upon my couch, was soon lost in sleep.

It was noon when I again opened my eyes, and ten minutes after I awakened, your telegraphic summons reached me.

'Come down at once,' was what you said, and I went; and then came the terrible *dénouement*, and yet a *dénouement* which was pleasing to me since it relieved my conscience. You handed me the envelope containing the story.

'Did you send that?' was your question.

'I did – last night, or rather early this morning. I mailed it about three o'clock,' I replied.

'I demand an explanation of your conduct,' said you.

'Of what?' I asked.

'Look at your so-called story and see. If this is a practical joke, Thurlow, it's a d—d poor one.'

I opened the envelope and took from it the sheets I had sent you – twenty-four of them.

They were every one of them as blank as when they left the paper mill!

You know the rest. You know that I tried to speak; that my utterance failed me; and that, finding myself unable at the time to control my emotions, I turned and rushed madly from the office, leaving the mystery unexplained. You know that you wrote demanding a satisfactory explanation of the situation or my resignation from your staff.

This, Currier, is my explanation. It is all I have. It is absolute truth. I beg you to believe it, for if you do not, then is my condition a hopeless one. You will ask me, perhaps, for a *résumé* of the story which I thought I had sent you.

It is my crowning misfortune that upon that point my mind is an absolute blank. I cannot remember it in form or in substance. I have racked my brains for some recollection of some small portion of it to help to make my explanation more credible, but, alas! it will not come back to me. If I were dishonest I might fake up a story to suit the purpose, but I am not dishonest. I came near to doing an unworthy act; I did do an unworthy thing, but by some mysterious provision of fate my conscience is cleared of that.

Be sympathetic Currier, or, if you cannot, be lenient with me this time. *Believe, believe, believe*, I implore you. Pray let me hear from you at once.

(Signed)
HENRY THURLOW

II.– *Being a note from George Currier, Editor of the* Tatler, *to Henry Thurlow, author*

Your explanation has come to hand. As an explanation it isn't worth the paper it is written on, but we are all agreed here that is is probably the best bit of fiction you ever wrote. It is accepted for the Christmas issue. Enclosed please find cheque for one hundred dollars.

Dawson suggests that you take another month up in the Adirondacks. You might put in your time writing up some account of that dream-life you are leading while you are there. It seems to me there are possibilities in the idea. The concern will pay all expenses. What do you say?

Yours ever,
G.C.

V

Our Ghost Party

Jerome K. Jerome

Britain's answer to John Kendrick Bangs was Jerome K. Jerome (1859-1927) whose satirical wit and mastery of the comic story made him a great favourite with readers around the turn of the century. His reputation was made with the classic Three Men In A Boat *(1889), although he was also famous for his work as editor of the humorous magazine,* The Idler. *After years of neglect, his shorter work is enjoying something of a revival of interest now, and I am pleased to be able to continue this trend by returning to print 'Our Ghost Party' which he wrote in 1891. It describes what is almost the archetypal Christmas party at which guests entertain each other with supernatural tales, and I was sorely tempted to use it as the first item in this collection because it so entertainingly sets the mood of seasonal storytelling. However, somewhat fearful of annoying the shade of Dickens, to whom Jerome K. Jerome like everyone else owes his inspiration, I have settled on this position in our line-up and I am sure it loses nothing for the slight delay ...*

It was Christmas Eve.

I begin this way, because it is the proper, orthodox, respectable way to begin, and I have been brought up in a proper, orthodox, respectable way, and taught to always do the proper, orthodox, respectable thing; and the habit clings to me.

Of course, as a mere matter of information it is quite unnecessary to mention the date at all. The experienced reader knows it was Christmas Eve, without my telling him. It always is Christmas Eve, in a ghost story.

Christmas Eve is the ghosts' great gala night. On Christmas

Eve they hold their annual fête. On Christmas Eve everybody in Ghostland who *is* anybody – or rather, speaking of ghosts, one should say, I suppose, every nobody who *is* any nobody – comes out to show himself or herself, to see and to be seen, to promenade about and display their winding-sheets and grave-clothes to each other, to criticise one another's style, and sneer at one another's complexion.

'Christmas Eve parade,' as I expect they themselves term it, is a function, doubtless, eagerly prepared for and looked forward to through Ghostland, especially by the swagger set, such as the murdered Barons, the crime-stained Countesses, and the Earls who came over with the Conqueror, and assassinated their relatives, and died raving mad.

Hollow moans and fiendish grins are, one may be sure, energetically practised up. Blood-curdling shrieks and marrow-freezing gestures are probably rehearsed for weeks beforehand. Rusty chains and gory daggers are overhauled, and put into good working order; and sheets and shrouds, laid carefully by from the previous year's show, are taken down and shaken out, and mended, and aired.

Oh, it is a stirring night in Ghostland, the night of December the twenty-fourth!

Ghosts never come out on Christmas night itself, you may have noticed. Christmas Eve, we suspect, has been too much for them; they are not used to excitement. For about a week after Christmas Eve, the gentlemen ghosts, no doubt, feel as if they were all head, and go about making solemn resolutions to themselves that they will stop in next Christmas Eve; while the lady spectres are contradictory and snappish, and liable to burst into tears and leave the room hurriedly on being spoken to, for no perceptible cause whatever.

Ghosts with no position to maintain – mere middle-class ghosts – occasionally, I believe, do a little haunting on off-nights: on All-hallows Eve, and at Midsummer; and some will even run up for a mere local event – to celebrate, for instance, the anniversary of the hanging of somebody's grandfather, or to prophesy a misfortune.

He does love prophesying a misfortune, does the average British ghost. Send him out to prognosticate trouble to somebody, and he is happy. Let him force his way into a peaceful home, and turn the whole house upside down by foretelling a funeral, or predicting a bankruptcy, or hinting at a coming disgrace, or some other terrible disaster, about which nobody in their senses would want to know sooner than they could possibly help, and the prior knowledge of which can serve no useful purpose whatsoever, and he feels that he is combining duty with pleasure. He would never forgive himself if anybody in his family had a trouble and he had not been there for a couple of months beforehand, doing silly tricks on the lawn, or balancing himself on somebody's bed-rail.

Then there are, besides, the very young, or very conscientious ghosts with a lost will or an undiscovered number weighing heavy on their minds, who will haunt steadily all the year round; and also the fussy ghost, who is indignant at having been buried in the dust-bin or in the village pond, and who never gives the parish a single night's quiet until somebody has paid for a first-class funeral for him.

But these are the exceptions. As I have said, the average orthodox ghost does his one turn a year, on Christmas Eve, and is satisfied.

Why on Christmas Eve, of all nights in the year, I never could myself understand. It is invariably one of the most dismal of nights to be out in – cold, muddy, and wet. And besides, at Christmas time, everybody has quite enough to put up with in the way of a houseful of living relations, without wanting the ghosts of any dead ones mooning about the place, I am sure.

There must be something ghostly in the air of Christmas something about the close, muggy atmosphere that draws up the ghosts, like the dampness of the summer rains brings out the frogs and snails.

And not only do the ghosts themselves always walk on Christmas Eve, but live people always sit and talk about them on Christmas Eve. Whenever five or six English-speaking people meet round a fire on Christmas Even, they start telling each other ghost stories. Nothing satisfies us on Christmas Eve but to hear each other tell authentic anecdotes about spectres. It is a genial, festive season, and we love to muse upon graves, and dead bodies, and murders, and blood.

There is a good deal of similarity about our ghostly

experiences; but this of course is not our fault but the fault of the ghosts, who never will try any new performances, but always will keep steadily to the old, safe business. The consequence is that, when you have been at one Christmas Eve party, and heard six people relate their adventures with spirits, you do not require to hear any more ghost stories. To listen to any further ghost stories after that would be like sitting out two farcical comedies, or taking in two comic journals; the repetition would become wearisome.

There is always the young man who was, one year, spending the Christmas at a country house, and, on Christmas Eve, they put him to sleep in the west wing. Then in the middle of the night, the room door quietly opens and somebody – generally a lady in her night-dress – walks slowly in, and comes and sits on the bed. The young man thinks it must be one of the visitors, or some relative of the family, though he does not remember having previously seen her, who, unable to go to sleep, and feeling lonesome, all by herself, has come into his room for a chat. He has no idea it is a ghost: he is so unsuspicious. She does not speak, however; and, when he looks again, she is gone!

The young man relates the circumstance at the breakfast-table next morning, and asks each of the ladies present if it were she who was his visitor. But they all assure him that it was not, and the host, who has grown deadly pale, begs him to say no more about the matter, which strikes the young man as a singularly strange request.

After breakfast the host takes the young man into a corner, and explains to him that what he saw was the ghost of a lady who had been murdered in that very bed, or who had murdered somebody else there – it does not really matter which: you can be a ghost by murdering somebody else or by being murdered yourself, whichever you prefer. The murdered ghost is, perhaps, the more popular; but, on the other hand, you can frighten people better if you are the murdered one, because then you can show your wounds and do groans.

Then there is the sceptical guest – it is always 'the guest' who gets let in for this sort of thing, by-the-bye. A ghost never thinks much of his own family: it is 'the guest' he likes to haunt who after listening to the host's ghost story, on

Christmas Eve, laughs at it, and says that he does not believe there are such things as ghosts at all; and that he will sleep in the haunted chamber that very night, if they will let him.

Everybody urges him not to be reckless, but he persists in his foolhardiness, and goes up to the, Yellow Chamber (or whatever colour the haunted room may be) with a light heart and a candle, and wishes them all goodnight, and shuts the door.

Next morning he has got snow-white hair.

He does not tell anybody what he has seen: it is too awful.

There is also the plucky guest, who sees a ghost, and knows it is a ghost, and watches it, as it comes into the room and disappears through the wainscot, after which, as the ghost does not seem to be coming back, and there is nothing, consequently, to be gained by stopping awake, he goes to sleep.

He does not mention having seen the ghost to anybody, for fear of frightening them – some people are so nervous about ghosts – but determines to wait for the next night, and see if the apparition appears again.

It does appear again, and, this time, he gets out of bed, dresses himself and does his hair, and follows it; and then discovers a secret passage leading from the bedroom down into the beer-cellar – a passage which, no doubt, was not infrequently made use of in the bad old days of yore.

After him comes the young man who woke up with a strange sensation in the middle of the night, and found his rich bachelor uncle standing by his bedside. The rich uncle smiled a weird sort of smile and vanished. The young man immediately got up and looked at his watch. It had stopped at half-past four, he having forgotten to wind it.

He made inquiries the next day, and found that, strangely enough, his rich uncle, whose only nephew he was, had married a widow with eleven children at exactly a quarter to twelve, only two days ago.

The young man does not attempt to explain the extraordinary circumstance. All he does is to vouch for the truth of his narrative.

And, to mention another case, there is the gentleman who is returning home late at night, from a Freemasons' dinner, and who, noticing a light issuing from a ruined abbey, creeps up, and looks through the keyhole. He sees the ghost of a 'grey sister' kissing the ghost of a brown monk, and is so inexpressibly shocked and frightened that he faints on the spot, and is discovered there the next morning, lying in a heap against the door, still speechless, and with his faithful latch-key clasped tightly in his hand.

All these things happen on Christmas Eve, they are all told of on Christmas Eve. For ghost stories to be told on any other evening than the evening of the twenty-fourth of December would be impossible in English society as at present regulated. Therefore, in introducing the sad but authentic ghost stories that follow hereafter, I feel that it is unnecessary to inform the student of Anglo-Saxon literature that the date on which they were told and on which the incidents took place was – Christmas Eve.

Nevertheless, I do so.

The Ghost of the Blue Chamber
(My Uncle's Story)

'I don't want to make you fellows nervous,' began my uncle in a peculiarly impressive, not to say blood-curdling, tone of voice, 'and if you would rather that I did not mention it, I won't; but, as a matter of fact, this very house, in which we are now sitting, is haunted.'

'You don't say that!' exclaimed Mr Coombes.

'What's the use of your saying I don't say it when I have just said it?' retorted my uncle somewhat pettishly. 'You do talk so foolishly. I tell you the house is haunted. Regularly on Christmas Eve the Blue Chamber [they called the room next to the nursery the 'blue chamber,' at my uncle's, most of the toilet service being of that shade] is haunted by the ghost of a sinful man – a man who once killed a Christmas wait with a lump of coal.'

'How did he do it?' asked Mr Coombes, with eager anxiousness. 'Was it difficult?'

'I do not know how he did it,' replied my uncle; 'he did not explain the process. The wait had taken up a position just inside the front gate, and was singing a ballad. It is presumed that, when he opened his mouth for B flat, the lump of coal was thrown by the sinful man from one of the windows, and that it went down the wait's throat and choked him.'

'You want to be a good shot, but it is certainly worth trying,' murmured Mr Coombes thoughtfully.

'But that was not his only crime, alas!' added my uncle. 'Prior to that he had killed a solo cornet-player.'

'No! Is that really a fact?' exclaimed Mr Coombes.

'Of course it's a fact,' answered my uncle testily; 'at all events, as much a fact as you can expect to get in a case of this sort.

'How very captious you are this evening. The circumstantial evidence was overwhelming. The poor fellow, the cornet-player, had been in the neighbourhood barely a month. Old Mr Bishop, who kept the "Jolly Sand Boys" at a time, and from whom I had the story, said he had never known a more hard-working and energetic solo cornet-player. He, the cornet-player, only knew two tunes, but Mr Bishop said that the man could not have played with more vigour, or for more hours a day, if he had known forty. The two tunes he did play were "Annie Laurie" and "Home, Sweet Home"; and as regarded his performance of the former melody, Mr Bishop said that a mere child could have told what it was meant for.

'This musician – this poor, friendless artist used to come regularly and play in this street just opposite for two hours every evening. One evening he was seen, evidently in response to an invitation, going into this very house, *but was never seen coming out of it*!'

'Did the townsfolk try offering any reward for his recovery?' asked Mr Coombes.

'Not a ha'penny,' replied my uncle.

'Another summer,' continued my uncle, 'a German band visited here, intending – so they announced on their arrival – to stay till the autumn.

'On the second day from their arrival, the whole company, as fine and healthy a body of men as one could wish to see, were invited to dinner by this sinful man, and, after spending the whole of the next twenty-four hours in bed, left the town a broken and dyspeptic crew; the parish doctor, who had attended them, giving it as his opinion that it was doubtful if they would, any of them, be fit to play an air again.

'You – you don't know the recipe, do you?' asked Mr Coombes.

'Unfortunately I do not,' replied my uncle; 'but the chief ingredient was said to have been railway refreshment-room pork pie.

'I forget the man's other crimes,' my uncle went on; 'I used to know them all at one time, but my memory is not what it was. I do not, however, believe I am doing his memory an injustice in believing that he was not entirely unconnected with the death, and subsequent burial, of a gentleman who used to play the harp with his toes; and that neither was he altogether unresponsible for the lonely grave of an unknown stranger who had once visited the neighbourhood, an Italian peasant lad, a performer upon the barrel-organ.

'Every Christmas Eve,' said my uncle, cleaving with low impressive tones the strange awed silence that, like a shadow, seemed to have slowly stolen into and settled down upon the room, 'the ghost of this sinful man haunts the Blue Chamber, in this very house. There, from midnight until cock-crow, amid wild muffled shrieks and groans and mocking laughter and the ghostly sound of horrid blows, it does fierce phantom fight with the spirits of the solo cornet-player and the murdered wait, assisted at intervals by the shades of the German band; while the ghost of the strangled harpist plays mad ghostly melodies with ghostly toes on the ghost of a broken harp.'

Uncle said the Blue Chamber was comparatively useless as a sleeping-apartment on Christmas Eve.

'Hark!' said my uncle, raising a warning hand towards the ceiling, while we held our breath, and listened; 'Hark! I believe they are at it now – in the *Blue Chamber*!'

I rose up and said that *I* would sleep in the Blue Chamber.

Before I tell you my own story, however – the story of what happened in the Blue Chamber – I would wish to preface it with:

A Personal Explanation

I feel a good deal of hesitation about telling you this story of my own. You see, it is not a story like the other kind of stories that I have mentioned, it is a true story. It is not a story told by a person sitting round a fire on Christmas Eve, drinking whisky punch: it is a record of events that actually happened.

Indeed, it is not a 'story' at all, in the commonly accepted meaning of the word: it is a report. It is, I feel, almost out of place in a book of this kind. It is more suitable to a biography, or an English history.

There is another thing that makes it difficult for me to tell you this story, and that is, that it is all about myself. In telling you this story, I shall have to keep on talking about myself; and talking about ourselves is what we modern-day authors have a strong objection to doing. If we literary men of the new school have one praiseworthy yearning more ever present to our minds than another it is the yearning never to appear in the slightest degree egotistical.

I myself, so I am told, carry this coyness – this shrinking reticence concerning anything connected with my own personality, almost too far; and people grumble at me because of it. People come to me and say –

'Well, now, why don't you talk about yourself a bit? That's what we want to read about. Tell us something about yourself.'

But I have always replied, 'No.' It is not that I do not think the subject an interesting one. I cannot myself conceive of any topic more likely to prove fascinating to the world as a whole, or at all events to the cultured portion of it. But I will not do it, on principle. It is inartistic, and it sets a bad example to the younger men. Other writers (a few of them) do it, I know; but I will not – not as a rule.

Under ordinary circumstances, therefore, I should not tell you this story at all. I should say to myself, 'No! It is a good story, it is a moral story, it is a strange, weird, enthralling sort of a story; and the public, I know, would like to hear it; and I should like to tell it to them; but it is all about myself – about what I said, and what I saw, and what I did, and I cannot do it. My retiring, anti-egotistical nature will not permit me to talk in this way about myself.'

But the circumstances surrounding this story are not ordinary, and there are reasons prompting me, in spite of my modesty, to rather welcome the opportunity of relating it.

As I stated at the beginning, there has been unpleasantness in our family over this party of ours, and, as regards myself in particular, and my share in the events I am now about to set forth, gross injustice has been done me.

As a means of replacing my character in its proper light – of dispelling the clouds of calumny and misconception with which it has been darkened, I feel that my best course is to give a simple, dignified narration of the plain facts, and allow the unprejudiced to judge for themselves. My chief object, I candidly confess, is to clear myself from unjust aspersion. Spurred by this motive – and I think it is an honourable and a right motive – I find I am enabled to overcome my usual repugnance to talking about myself, and can thus tell –

My Own Story

As soon as my uncle had finished his story, I, as I have already told you, rose up and said that *I* would sleep in the Blue Chamber that very night.

'Never!' cried my uncle, springing up. 'You shall not put yourself in this deadly peril. Besides, the bed is not made.'

'Never mind the bed,' I replied. 'I have lived in furnished apartments for gentlemen, and have been accustomed to sleep on beds that have never been made from one year's end to the other. Do not thwart me in my resolve. I am young, and have had a clear conscience now for over a month. The spirits will not harm me. I may even do them some little good, and induce them to be quiet and go away. Besides, I should like to see the show.'

Saying which, I sat down again. (How Mr Coombes came to be in my chair, instead of at the other side of the room, where he had been all the evening; and why he never offered to apologise when I sat right down on top of him; and why young Biffles should have tried to palm himself off upon me as my Uncle John, and induced me, under that erroneous impression, to shake him by the hand for nearly three minutes, and tell him that I had always regarded him as father, – are matters that, to this day, I have never been able to fully understand.)

They tried to dissuade me from what they termed my

foolhardy enterprise, but I remained firm, and claimed my privilege. I was 'the guest.' 'The guest' always sleeps in the haunted chamber on Christmas Eve; it is his perquisite.

They said that if I put it on that footing, they had, of course, no answer; and they lighted a candle for me, and accompanied me upstairs in a body.

Whether elevated by the feeling that I was doing a noble action, or animated by a mere general consciousness of rectitude, is not for me to say, but I went upstairs that night with remarkable buoyancy. It was as much as I could do to stop at the landing when I came to it; I felt I wanted to go on up to the roof. But, with the help of the banisters, I restrained my ambition, wished them all good-night, and went in and shut the door.

Things began to go wrong with me from the very first. The candle tumbled out of the candlestick before my hand was off the lock. It kept on tumbling out of the candlestick, and every time I picked it up and put it in, it tumbled out again: I never saw such a slippery candle. I gave up attempting to use the candlestick at last, and carried the candle about in my hand; and, even then, it would not keep upright. So I got wild and threw it out of window, and undressed and went to bed in the dark.

I did not go to sleep – I did not feel sleepy at all – I lay on my back, looking up at the ceiling, and thinking of things. I wish I could remember some of the ideas that came to me as I lay there, because they were so amusing. I laughed at them myself till the bed shook.

I had been lying like this for half an hour or so, and had forgotten all about the ghost, when, on casually casting my eyes round the room, I noticed for the first time a singularly contented-looking phantom, sitting in the easy-chair by the fire, smoking the ghost of a long clay pipe.

I fancied for the moment, as most people would under similar circumstances, that I must be dreaming. I sat up, and rubbed my eyes.

No! It was a ghost, clear enough. I could see the back of the chair through his body. He looked over towards me, took the shadowy pipe from his lips, and nodded.

The most surprising part of the whole thing to me was that I did not feel in the least alarmed. If anything, I was rather pleased to see him. It was company.

I said, 'Good evening. It's been a cold day!'

He said he had not noticed it himself, but dared say I was right.

We remained silent for a few seconds, and then, wishing to put it pleasantly, I said, 'I believe I have the honour of addressing the ghost of the gentleman who had the accident with the wait?'

He smiled, and said it was very good of me to remember it. One wait was not much to boast of, but still, every little helped.

I was somewhat staggered at his answer. I had expected a groan of remorse. The ghost appeared, on the contrary, to be rather conceited over the business. I thought that, as he had taken my reference to the wait so quietly, perhaps he would not be offended if I questioned him about the organ-grinder. I felt curious about that poor boy.

'Is it true,' I asked, 'that you had a hand in the death of that Italian peasant lad who came to the town once with a barrel-organ that played nothing but Scotch airs?'

He quite fired up. 'Had a hand in it!' he exclaimed indignantly. 'Who has dared to pretend that he assisted me? I murdered the youth myself. Nobody helped me. Alone I did it. Show me the man who says I didn't.'

I calmed him. I assured him that I had never, in my own mind, doubted that he was the real and only assassin, and I went on and asked him what he had done with the body of the cornet-player he had killed.

He said, 'To which one may you be alluding?'

'Oh, were there any more then?' I inquired.

He smiled, and gave a little cough. He said he did not like to appear to be boasting, but that, counting trombones, there were seven.

'Dear me!' I replied, 'you must have had quite a busy time of it, one way and another.'

He said that perhaps he ought not to be the one to say so, but that really, speaking of ordinary middle-class society, he thought there were few ghosts who could look back upon a life of more sustained usefulness.

He puffed away in silence for a few seconds, while I sat watching him. I had never seen a ghost smoking a pipe before, that I could remember, and it interested me.

I asked him what tobacco he used, and he replied, 'The ghost of cut cavendish, as a rule.'

He explained that the ghost of all the tobacco that a man smoked in life belonged to him when he became dead. He said he himself had smoked a good deal of cut cavendish when he was alive, so that he was well supplied with the ghost of it now.

I observed that it was a useful thing to know that, and I made up my mind to smoke as much tobacco as ever I could before I died.

I thought I might as well start at once, so I said I would join him in a pipe, and he said, 'Do, old man'; and I reached over and got out the necessary paraphernalia from my coat pocket and lit up.

We grew quite chummy after that, and he told me all his crimes. He said he had lived next door once to a young lady who was learning to play the guitar, while a gentleman who practised on the bass-viol lived opposite. And he, with fiendish cunning, had introduced these two unsuspecting young people to one another, and had persuaded them to elope with each other against their parents' wishes, and take their musical instruments with them; and they had done so, and, before the honeymoon was over, *she* had broken his head with the bass-viol, and *he* had tried to cram the guitar down her throat, and had injured her for life.

My friend said he used to lure muffin-men into the passage and then stuff them with their own wares till they burst and died. He said he had quieted eighteen that way.

Young men and women who recited long and dreary poems at evening parties, and callow youths who walked about the streets late at night, playing concertinas, he used to get together and poison in batches of ten, so as to save expense; and park orators and temperance lecturers he used to shut up six in a small room with a glass of water and a collection-box apiece, and let them talk each other to death.

It did one good to listen to him.

I asked him when he expected the other ghosts – the ghosts

of the wait and the cornet-player, and the German band that Uncle John had mentioned. He smiled, and said they would never come again, any of them.

I said, 'Why; isn't it true, then, that they meet you here every Christmas Eve for a row?'

He replied that it *was* true. Every Christmas Eve, for twenty-five years, had he and they fought in that room; but they would never trouble him nor anybody else again. One by one, had he laid them out, spoilt, and utterly useless for all haunting purposes. He had finished off the last German-band ghost that very evening, just before I came upstairs, and had thrown what was left of it out through the slit between the window-sashes. He said it would never be worth calling a ghost again.

'I suppose you will still come yourself, as usual?' I said. 'They would be sorry to miss you, I know.'

'Oh, I don't know,' he replied; 'there's nothing much to come for now. Unless,' he added kindly, '*you* are going to be here. I'll come if you will sleep here next Christmas Eve.

'I have taken a liking to you,' he continued; 'you don't fly off, screeching, when you see a party, and your hair doesn't stand on end. You've no idea,' he said, 'how sick I am of seeing people's hair standing on end.'

He said it irritated him.

Just then a slight noise reached us from the yard below, and he started and turned deathly black.

'You are ill,' I cried, springing towards him; 'tell me the best thing to do for you. Shall I drink some brandy, and give you the ghost of it?'

He remained silent, listening intently for a moment, and then he gave a sigh of relief, and the shade came back to his cheek.

'It's all right,' he murmured; 'I was afraid it was the cock.'

'Oh, it's too early for that,' I said. 'Why, it's only the middle of the night.'

'Oh, that doesn't make any difference to those cursed chickens,' he replied bitterly. 'They would just as soon crow in the middle of the night as at any other time – sooner, if they thought it would spoil a chap's evening out. I believe they do it on purpose.'

He said a friend of his, the ghost of a man who had killed a water-rate collector, used to haunt a house in Long Acre, where they kept fowls in the cellar, and every time a policeman went by and flashed his bull's-eye down the grating, the old cock there would fancy it was the sun, and start crowing like mad; when, of course, the poor ghost had to dissolve, and it would, in consequence, get back home sometimes as early as one o'clock in the morning, swearing fearfully because it had only been out for an hour.

I agreed, that it seemed very unfair.

'Oh, it's an absurd arrangement altogether,' he continued, quite angrily. 'I can't imagine what our old man could have been thinking of when he made it. As I have said to him, over and over again, "Have a fixed time, and let everybody stick to it – say four o'clock in summer, and six in winter. Then one would know what one was about." '

'How do you manage when there isn't any cock handy?' I inquired.

He was on the point of replying, when again he started and listened. This time I distinctly heard Mr Bowles's cock, next door, crow twice.

'There you are,' he said, rising and reaching for his hat; 'that's the sort of thing we have to put up with. What *is* the time?'

I looked at my watch, and found it was half-past three.

'I thought as much,' he muttered. 'I'll wring that blessed bird's neck if I get hold of it.' And he prepared to go.

'If you can wait half a minute,' I said, getting out of bed, 'I'll go a bit of the way with you.'

'It's very good of you,' he rejoined, pausing, 'but it seems unkind to drag you out.'

'Not at all,' I replied; 'I shall like a walk.' And I partially dressed myself, and took my umbrella; and he put his arm through mine, and we went out together.

Just by the gate we met Jones, one of the local constables.

'Good-night, Jones,' I said (I always feel affable at Christmas-time).

'Good-night, sir,' answered the man a little gruffly, I thought. 'May I ask what you're a-doing of?'

'Oh, it's all right,' I responded, with a wave of my umbrella;

'I'm just seeing my friend part of the way home.'

He said, 'What friend?'

'Oh, ah, of course,' I laughed; 'I forgot. He's invisible to you. He is the ghost of the gentleman that killed the wait. I'm just going to the corner with him.'

'Ah, I don't think I would, if I was you, sir,' said Jones severely. 'If you take my advice, you'll say good-bye to your friend here, and go back indoors. Perhaps you are not aware that you are walking about with nothing on but a night-shirt and a pair of boots and an opera-hat. Where's your trousers?'

I did not like the man's manner at all. I said, 'Jones! I don't wish to have to report you, but it seems to me you've been drinking. My trousers are where a man's trousers ought to be – on his legs. I distinctly remember putting them on.'

'Well, you haven't got them on now,' he retorted.

'I beg your pardon,' I replied. 'I tell you I have; I think I ought to know.'

'I think so, too,' he answered, 'but you evidently don't. Now you come along indoors with me, and don't let's have any more of it.'

Uncle John came to the door at this point, having been awaked, I suppose, by the altercation; and, at the same moment, Aunt Maria appeared at the window in her nightcap.

I explained the constable's mistake to them, treating the matter as lightly as I could, so as not to get the man into trouble, and I turned for confirmation to the ghost.

He was gone! He had left me without a word – without even saying good-bye!

It struck me as so unkind, his having gone off in that way, that I burst into tears; and Uncle John came out, and led me back into the house.

On reaching my room, I discovered that Jones was right. I had not put on my trousers, after all. They were still hanging over the bed-rail. I suppose, in my anxiety not to keep the ghost waiting, I must have forgotten them.

Such are the plain facts of the case, out of which it must, doubtless, to the healthy, charitable mind appear impossible that calumny could spring.

But it has.

Persons – I say 'persons' – have professed themselves unable to understand the simple circumstances herein narrated, except in the light of explanations at once misleading and insulting. Slurs have been cast and aspersions made on me by those of my own flesh and blood.

But I bear no ill-feeling. I merely, as I have said, set forth this statement for the purpose of clearing my character from injurious suspicion.

VI

The Ghost of Christmas Eve

J.M. Barrie

The enduring fame of Sir James Matthew Barrie (1860-1937) rests squarely on his creation of Peter Pan, *one of the most popular of all Christmas pantomimes which has hardly ever been absent from the London stage since it was created almost eighty years ago. Yet Barrie was also an accomplished journalist, a fine theatre critic (under the pseudonym of 'Gavin Ogilvy') and a master of social satire as exemplified in his enormously popular play,* The Admirable Crichton *(1902). Born in the small town of Kirriemuir in Angus, he grew up with an abiding interest in the world of the supernatural, and his stories of local life in Scotland contain frequent references to the belief in the unknown which persists so strongly in rural communities. Yet he was not averse to turning his sardonic wit to bear on such topics as he shows in the following delightful story which appeared in his collection,* My Lady Nicotine *in 1890.*

A few years ago, as some may remember, a startling ghost paper appeared in the monthly organ of the Society for Haunting Houses. The writer guaranteed the truth of his statement, and even gave the name of the Yorkshire manor-house in which the affair took place. The article and the discussion to which it gave rise agitated me a good deal, and I consulted Pettigrew about the advisability of clearing up the mystery. The writer wrote that he 'distinctly saw his arm pass through the apparition and come out at the other side,' and indeed I still remember his saying so next morning. He had a scared face, but I had presence of mind to continue eating my rolls and marmalade as if my briar had nothing to do with the miraculous affair.

Seeing that he made a 'paper' of it, I suppose he is justified in touching up the incidental details. He says, for instance, that we were told the story of the ghost which is said to haunt the house, just before going to bed. As far as I remember, it was only mentioned at luncheon, and then sceptically. Instead of there being snow falling outside and an eerie wind wailing through the skeleton trees, the night was still and muggy. Lastly, I did not know, until the journal reached my hands, that he was put into the room known as the Haunted Chamber, nor that in that room the fire is noted for casting weird shadows upon the walls. This, however, may be so. The legend of the manor-house ghost he tells precisely as it is known to me.

The tragedy dates back to the time of Charles I, and is led up to by a pathetic love-story, which I need not give. Suffice it that for seven days and nights the old steward had been anxiously awaiting the return of his young master and mistress from their honeymoon. On Christmas Eve, after he had gone to bed, there was a great clanging of the door-bell. Flinging on a dressing-gown, he hastened downstairs. According to the story, a number of servants watched him, and saw by the light of his candle that his face was an ashy white. He took off the chains of the door, unbolted it, and pulled it open. What he saw no human being knows; but it must have been something awful, for without a cry the old steward fell dead in the hall. Perhaps the strangest part of the story is this: that the shadow of a burly man, holding a pistol in his hand, entered by the open door, stepped over the steward's body, and, gliding up the stairs, disappeared, no one could say where.

Such is the legend. I shall not tell the many ingenious explanations of it that have been offered. Every Christmas Eve, however, the silent scene is said to be gone through again; and tradition declares that no person lives for twelve months at whom the ghostly intruder points his pistol.

On Christmas Day the gentleman who tells the tale in the scientific journal created some sensation at the breakfast-table by solemnly asserting that he had seen the ghost. Most of the men present scouted his story, which may be condensed into a few words. He had retired to his bedroom at a fairly early hour, and as he opened the door his candle-light was blown out. He tried to get a light from the fire, but it was too low, and eventually he went to bed in the semi-darkness. He was wakened – he did not know at what hour – by the clanging of a bell. He sat up in bed, and the ghost-story came in a rush to his mind. His fire was dead, and the room was consequently dark; yet by and by he knew, though he heard no sound, that his door had opened. He cried out, 'Who is that?' but got no answer. By an effort he jumped up and went to the door, which was ajar. His bedroom was on the first floor, and looking up the stairs he could see nothing. He felt a cold sensation at his heart, however, when he looked the other way.

Going slowly and without a sound down the stairs, was an old man in a dressing-gown. He carried a candle. From the top of the stairs only part of the hall is visible, but as the apparition disappeared the watcher had the courage to go down a few steps after him. At first nothing was to be seen, for the candlelight had vanished. A dim light, however, entered by the long narrow windows which flank the hall-door, and after a moment the onlooker could see that the hall was empty. He was marvelling at this sudden disappearance of the steward, when, to his horror, he saw a body fall upon the hall-floor within a few feet of the door.

The watcher cannot say whether he cried out, nor how long he stood there trembling. He came to himself with a start as he realized that something was coming up the stairs. Fear prevented his taking flight, and in a moment the thing was at his side. Then he saw indistinctly that it was not the figure he had seen descend. He saw a younger man in a heavy overcoat, but with no hat on his head. He wore on his face a look of extravagant triumph. The guest boldly put out his hand towards the figure. To his amazement his arm went through it. The ghost paused for a moment and looked behind it. It was then the watcher realized that it carried a pistol in its right hand. He was by this time in a highly-strung condition, and he stood trembling lest the pistol should be pointed at him. The apparition, however, rapidly glided up the stairs and was soon lost to sight. Such are the main facts of the story; none of which I contradicted at the time.

I cannot say absolutely that I can clear up this mystery; but my suspicions are confirmed by a good deal of circumstantial evidence. This will not be understood unless I explain my strange infirmity. Wherever I went I used to be troubled with a presentiment that I had left my pipe behind. Often even at the dinner-table, I paused in the middle of a sentence as if stricken with sudden pain. Then my hand went down to my pocket. Sometimes, even after I felt my pipe, I had a conviction that it was stopped, and only by a desperate effort did I keep myself from producing it and blowing down it. I distinctly remember once dreaming three nights in succession that I was on the Scotch express without it. More than once, I know, I have wandered in my sleep, looking for it in all sorts of places, and after I went to bed I generally jumped out, just to make sure of it.

My strong belief, then, is that I was the ghost seen by the writer of the paper. I fancy that I rose in my sleep, lighted a candle and wandered down to the hall to feel if my pipe was safe in my coat, which was hanging there. The light had gone out when I was in the hall. Probably the body seen to fall on the hall floor was some other coat which I had flung there to get more easily at my own. I cannot account for the bell; but perhaps the gentleman in the Haunted Chamber dreamt that part of the affair. I had put on the overcoat before redescending; indeed, I may say that next morning I was surprised to find it on a chair in my bedroom, also to notice that there were several long streaks of candle-grease on my dressing-gown. I conclude that the pistol, which gave my face such a look of triumph, was my briar, which I found in the morning beneath my pillow. The strangest thing of all, perhaps, is that when I awoke there was a smell of tobacco-smoke in the bedroom.

VII

The Ghosts of Stukeley Castle

Bret Harte

The American writer Bret Harte (1836-1902) has already made his debut in this collection as the anonymous hand that penned 'The Haunted Man', yet I think he fully deserves a second appearance with this next tale which he published under his own name in 1892. For his interest in the supernatural was long-standing, and the diligent reader will find several outstanding weird and mystery stories in the various collections of his work. Born in Albany, New York, Harte took the advice which has been given to so many young Americans over the years to 'Go West'. He went to California, where he became a compositor on a San Francisco newspaper in 1854. This tempted him to try writing himself, and shortly afterwards he began a series of sketches about the California miners which earned widespread praise. He also began to compose essays and poetry, and in 1868 was appointed editor of the Overland Monthly, *to which he contributed the tales which made up two of his best-known collections,* The Luck of Roaring Camp *and* The Outcasts of Poker Flats. *A surprise change of direction in his career came when he entered the Diplomatic Service, and he was a US Consul in Europe for several years before settling in London where he remained until his death. In the splendid story which follows he gives us what at first might seem like a very traditional ghost story of a haunted castle – but as with any work by Bret Harte it is full of surprises!*

There should have been snow on the ground to make the picture seasonable and complete, but the Western Barbarian had lived long enough in England to know that, except in the pages of a holiday supplement, this was rarely the accompaniment of a Christmas landscape, and he cheerfully accepted, on the 24th of December, the background of a low, brooding sky, on which the delicate tracery of leafless sprays and blacker *chevaux de frise* of pine was faintly etched, as a consistent setting to the turrets and peacefully stacked chimneys of Stukeley Castle. Yet, even in this disastrous eclipse of colour and distance, the harmonious outlines of the long, grey, irregular pile seemed to him as wonderful as ever. It still dominated the whole landscape, and, as he had often fancied, carried this subjection even to the human beings who had created it, lived in it, but which it seemed to have in some dull, senile way dozed over and forgotten. He vividly recalled the previous sunshine of an autumnal house party within its walls, where some descendants of its old castellans, encountered in long galleries or at the very door of their bedrooms, looked as alien to the house as the Barbarian himself.

For the rest it may be found described in the local guide-books, with a view of its 'South Front,' 'West Front,' and 'Great Quadrangle.' It was alleged to be based on an encampment of the Romans – that highly apocryphal race who seemed to have spent their time in getting up picnics on tessellated pavements, where, after hilariously emptying their pockets of their loose coin and throwing round their dishes, they instantly built a road to escape by, leaving no other record of their existence. Stowe and Dugdale had recorded the date when a Norman favourite obtained the Royal licence to 'embattle it;' it had done duty on Christmas cards with the questionable snow already referred to laid on thickly in crystal; it had been lovingly portrayed by a fair countrywoman – the vivacious correspondent of the *East Machias Sentinel* – in a combination of the most delightful feminine disregard of facts with the highest feminine respect for titles. It was rich in a real and spiritual estate of tapestries, paintings, armour, legends, and ghosts. Everything the poet could wish for, and indeed some things that decent prose might have possibly wished out of it, were there.

Yet, from the day that it had been forcibly seized by a Parliamentary General, until more recently, when it had passed by the no less desperate conveyance of marriage into the hands of a Friendly Nobleman known to the Western

Barbarian, it had been supposed to suggest something or other more remarkable than itself.

'Few spectators,' said the guide-book, 'even the most unimpassioned, can stand in the courtyard and gaze upon those historic walls without feeling a thrill of awe,' &c. The Western Barbarian had stood there, gazed, and felt no thrill.

'The privileged guest,' said the grave historian, 'passing in review the lineaments of the illustrious owners of Stukeley, as he slowly paces the sombre gallery, must be conscious of emotions of no ordinary character,' &c, &c. The Barbarian had been conscious of no such emotions. And it was for this reason, and believing he *might* experience them if left there in solitude, with no distracting or extraneous humanity around him, it had been agreed between him and the Friendly Nobleman, who had fine Barbarian instincts, that as he – the Friendly Nobleman – and his family were to spend their holidays abroad, the Barbarian should be allowed, on the eve and day of Christmas, to stay at Stukeley alone.

'But,' added his host, 'you'll find it beastly lonely, and although I've told the housekeeper to look after you – you'd better go over to dine at Audley Friars, where there's a big party, and they know you, and it will be a deuced deal more amusing. And – er – I say – you know – you're really *not* looking out for ghosts, and that sort of thing, are you? You know you fellows don't believe in them – over there.'

And the Barbarian, assuring him that this was a part of his deficient emotions, it was settled then and there that he should come. And that was why, on the 24th of December, the Barbarian found himself gazing hopefully on the landscape with his portmanteau at his feet, as he drove up the avenue.

The ravens did *not* croak ominously from the battlements as he entered. And the housekeeper, although neither 'stately' nor 'tall,' nor full of reminiscences of 'his late lordship, the present Earl's father,' was very sensible and practical. The Barbarian could, of course, have his choice of rooms – but – she had thought – remembering his tastes the last time, that the long blue room? Exactly! The long, low-arched room, with the faded blue tapestry, looking upon the gallery – capital! He had always liked that room. From purely negative evidence he had every reason to believe that it was the one formidable-looking room in England that Queen Elizabeth had *not* slept in.

When the footman had laid out his clothes, and his step grew fainter along the passage, until it was suddenly swallowed up with the closing of a red baize door in the turret staircase, like a trap in an *oubliette*, the whole building seemed to sink back into repose. Quiet it certainly was, but not more so, he remembered, than when the chambers on either side were filled with guests, and floating voices in the corridor were lost in those all-absorbing walls. So far, certainly, this was no new experience. It was past four. He waited for the shadows to gather. Light thickened beyond his windows; gradually the outflanking wall and part of a projecting terrace crumbled away in the darkness, as if Night were slowly reducing the castle. The figures on the tapestry in his room stood out faintly. The gallery seen through his open door, barred with black spaces between the mullioned windows, presently became obliterated, as if invaded by a dull smoke from without. But nothing moved, nothing glimmered. Really this might become in time very stupid.

He was startled, however, while dressing, to see from his windows that the great banqueting hall was illuminated, but on coming down was amused to find his dinner served on a small table in its oaken solitude lit by the large electric chandelier – for Stukeley Castle under its present lord had all the modern improvements – shining on the tattered banners and glancing mail above him. It was evidently the housekeeper's reading of some written suggestion of her noble master. The Barbarian, in a flash of instinct, imagined the passage:

'Humour him as a harmless lunatic; the plate is quite safe.'

Declining the further offer of an illumination of the picture gallery, grand drawing-room, ball-room, and chapel, a few hours later he found himself wandering in the corridor with a single candle and a growing conviction of the hopelessness of his experiment. The castle had as yet yielded to him nothing that he had not seen before in the distraction of company and the garishness of day. It was becoming a trifle monotonous. Yet fine – exceedingly; and now that a change of wind had lifted the fog, and the full moon shone on the lower half of the pictures of the gallery, starting into the most artificial simulation of life a number of Van Dyke legs, farthingales, and fingers that would have deceived nobody, it seemed gracious, gentle, and innocent beyond expression. Wandering down the gallery, conscious of being more like a ghost than any of the painted figures, and that they might reasonably object to him, he wished he could meet the original of one of those pictured gallants and secretly compare his fingers with the copy. He remembered an embroidered pair of gloves in a cabinet and a suit of armour on the wall that, in measurement, did not seem to bear out the delicacy of the one nor the majesty of the other. It occurred to him also to satisfy a yearning he had once felt to try on a certain breastplate and steel cap that hung over an oaken settle. It will be perceived that he was getting a good deal bored. For thus caparisoned he listlessly, and, as will be seen, imprudently, allowed himself to sink back into a very modern chair, and give way to a dreamy cogitation.

What possible interest could the dead have in anything that was here? Admitting that they had any, and that it was not the *living*, whom the Barbarian had always found most inclined to haunt the past, would not a ghost of any decided convictions object to such a collection as his descendant had gathered in this gallery? Yonder idiot in silk and steel had blunderingly and cruelly persecuted his kinsman in leather and steel only a few panels distant. Would they care to meet here? And if their human weaknesses had died with them, what would bring them here at all? And if not *them* – who then?

He stopped short. The door at the lower end of the gallery had opened! Not stealthily, not noiselessly, but in an ordinary fashion, and a number of figures, dressed in the habiliments of a bygone age came trooping in. They did not glide in nor float in, but trampled in awkwardly, clumsily, and unfamiliarly, gaping about them as they walked. At the head was apparently a steward in a kind of livery, who stopped once or twice and seemed to be pointing out and explaining certain objects in the room.

A flash of indignant intelligence filled the brain of the Barbarian! It seemed absurd! – impossible! – but it was true! It was a holiday excursion party of ghosts, being shown over

Stukeley Castle by a ghostly Cicerone! And as his measured, monotonous voice rose on the Christmas morning air, it could be heard that he was actually showing off, not the antiquities of the Castle, but the *modern improvements*!

'This 'ere, gossips' – the Barbarian instantly detected the fallacy of all the so-called mediaeval jargon he had read – 'is the Helectric Bell, which does away with our h'old, h'ordinary 'orn blowin', and the h'attendant waitin' in the 'all for the usual, "Without there, who waits?" which all of us was accustomed to in mortal flesh. You h'observe this button. I press it so, and it instantly rings a bell in the kitchen 'all, and shows in fair letters the name of this 'ere gallery – as we will see later. Will h'any good dame or gaffer press the button? Will *you*, Mistress?' said the Cicerone to a giggling, kerchief-coifed lass.

'Oi soy, Maudlin! – look out – will yer! – It's the soime old gag as them bloomin' knobs you ketched hold of when yer was 'ere las' Whitsuntide,' called out the mediaeval 'Arry of the party.

'It is *not* the Galvanic-Magnetic machine in 'is Lordship's library,' said the Cicerone, severely, 'which is a mere toy for infants, and h'old fashioned. And we have 'ere a much later invention. I open this little door, I turn this 'andle – called a switch – and, h'as you perceive, the gallery is h'instantly h'illuminated.'

There was a hoarse cry of astonishment from the assemblage. The Barbarian felt an awful thrill as this searching insufferable light of the nineteenth century streamed suddenly upon the up-turned, vacant-eyed, and dull faces of those sightseers of the past. But there was no responsive gleam in their eyes.

'It be the sun,' gasped an old woman in a grey cloak.

'Toime to rouse out, Myryan, and make the foire,' said the mediaeval 'Arry. The custodian smiled with superior toleration.

'But what do 'ee want o' my old lanthorne,' asked a yellow-jerkined stable boy, pointing to an old-fashioned horned lantern, *tempus* Edward III, 'with this brave loight?'

'You know,' said the custodian, with condescending familiarity, 'these mortals worship what they call "curios" and the "antique," and 'is Lordship gave a matter of fifty pounds for that same lanthern. That's what the modern folk come 'ere to see – like as ye.'

'Oi've an old three-legged stool in Whitechapel oi'll let his Lordship 'ave cheap – for five quid,' suggested the humorist.

'The 'prentice wight knows not that he speaks truly. For 'ere is a braver jest than 'is. Good folks, wilt please ye to examine yon coffer?' pointing to an oaken chest.

''Tis but poor stuff, marry,' said Maudlin.

''Tis a coffer – the same being made in Wardour Street last year – 'is Lordship gave one hundred pounds for it. Look at these would-be worm-holes – but they were made with an *auger*. Marry, *we* know what worm-holes are!'

A ghastly grin spread over the faces of the spectral assembly as they gathered around the chest with silent laughter.

'Wilt walk 'ere and see the phonograph in the libry, made by Hedison, an Hamerican, which bottles up the voice and preserves it fresh for a hundred years? 'Tis a rare new fancy.'

'Rot,' said 'Arry. Then turning to the giggling Maudlin, he whispered: 'Saw it las' toime. 'Is Lordship got a piece o' moy moind that Oi reeled off into it about this 'ere swindle. Fawncy that old bloke there charging a tanner a piece to us for chaffin' a bit of a barrel.'

'Have you no last new braveries to show us of the gallants and their mistresses, as you were wont?' said Maudlin to the Cicerone. ''Twas a rare show last time – the modish silk gowns and farthingales in the closets.'

'But there be no company this Christmas,' said the custodian, 'and 'is Lordship does not entertain, unless it be the new Fool 'is Lordship sent down 'ere to-day, who has been mopin' and moonin' in the corridors, as is ever the way of these wittol creatures when they are not heeded. He was 'ere in a rare motley of his own choosing, with which he thinks to raise a laugh, a moment ago. Ye see him not – not 'avin' the gift that belongs by right to my dread office. 'Tis a weird privilege I have – and may not be imparted to others – save –'

'Save what, good man steward? Prithee, speak?' said Marian earnestly.

''Tis ever a shillin' extra.'

There was no response. A few of the more bashful ghosts

thrust their hands in their pockets and looked awkwardly another way. The Barbarian felt a momentary relief followed by a slight pang of mortified vanity. He was a little afraid of them. The price was an extortion, certainly, but surely he was worth the extra shilling!

'He has brought but little braveries of attire into the Castle,' continued the Cicerone, 'but I 'ave something 'ere which was found on the top of his portmanteau. I wot ye know not the use of this.' To the Barbarian's intense indignation, the Cicerone produced, from under his, his (the Barbarian's) own opera hat. 'Marry, what should be this? Rede me this riddle! To it – and unyoke!'

A dozen vacant guesses were made as the showman held it aloft. Then with a conjuror's gesture he suddenly placed his thumbs within the rim, released the spring and extended the hat. The assembly laughed again silently as before.

''Tis a hat,' said the Cicerone, with a superior air.

'Nay,' said Maudlin, 'give it here.' She took it curiously, examined it, and then with a sudden coquettish movement lifted it towards her own coifed head, as if to try it on. The Cicerone suddenly sprang forward with a despairing gesture to prevent her. And here the Barbarian was conscious of a more startling revelation. How and why he could not tell, but he *knew* that the putting on of that article of his own dress would affect the young girl as the assumption of the steel cap and corset had evidently affected him, and that he would instantly become as visible to her as she and her companions had been to him. He attempted to rise, but was too late; she had evaded the Cicerone by ducking, and, facing in the direction of the Barbarian, clapped the hat on her head. He saw the swift light of consciousness, of astonishment, of sudden fear spring into her eyes! She shrieked, he started, struggled, and awoke!

But what was this! He was alone in the moonlit gallery, certainly; the ghastly figures and their outlandish garb were gone; he was awake and in his senses, but, in this first flash of real consciousness, he could have sworn that something remained! Something terror-stricken, and retreating even then before him – something of the world, modern – and even as he gazed, vanishing through the gallery door with the material flash and rustle of silk.

He walked quietly to the door. It was open. Ah! No doubt he had forgotten to shut it fast; a current of air or a sudden draught had opened it. That noise had awakened him. More than that, remembering the lightning flash of dream consciousness, it had been the *cause* of his dream. Yet, for a few moments he listened attentively.

What might have been the dull reverberation of a closing door in the direction of the housekeeper's room, on the lower story, was all he heard. He smiled, for even that, natural as it might be, was less distinct and real than his absurd vision.

Nevertheless the next afternoon he concluded to walk over to Audley Friars for his Christmas dinner. Its hospitable master greeted him cordially.

'But do you know, my dear fellow,' he said, when they were alone for a moment, 'if you hadn't come by yourself I'd have sent over there for you. The fact is that A – wrote to us that you were down at Stukeley alone, ghost-hunting or something of that sort, and I'm afraid it leaked out among the young people of our party. Two of our girls – I shan't tell you which – stole over there last night to give you a start of some kind. They didn't see you at all, but, by Jove, it seems they got the biggest kind of a fright *themselves*, for they declare that something dreadful in armour, you know, was sitting in the gallery. Awfully good joke, wasn't it? Of course *you* didn't see anything – did you?'

'No,' said the Barbarian, discreetly.

VIII

The Irtonwood Ghost

Elinor Glyn

The glamorous, larger-than-life figure of Elinor Glyn (1864-1943), whose name is still familiar in literary and cinema circles today, is without doubt the most surprising contributor to this collection. And for a woman who revelled in surprise – 'sensation' might be an even more appropriate word – such a fact would have delighted her. For she was the novelist whose books earned a reputation for 'naughtiness' which kept millions of readers enthralled during much of the first half of this century. Born in Jersey, one of the Channel Islands, she soared to international fame with her book, Three Weeks, *published in 1907, which scandalised certain sections of society but delighted huge numbers of readers. Despite the fact that this book – and many of the others which followed – were nonsensical, high-faluting, even ungrammatical, they sold by the million and Elinor exploited her fame by high-living and outrageous public behaviour which nonetheless endeared her all the more to her admirers. In the 1920's she moved to Hollywood where she helped in the selection of film stars to project on the screen the kind of romantic love she had exemplified in her books. Her fame was further enhanced when she was instrumental in launching Rudolf Valentino and also devised the 'It Girl' (her version of sex appeal) which made Clara Bow world famous. I am delighted to be including Elinor Glyn here with this supernatural story (written in 1911) which is set firmly in the milieu of upper-class Edwardian society which she immortalised in print and on the screen.*

Mrs Charters arrived at Euston in plenty of time for the 2.30 train to Ileton. She was a woman who was well served, and her footman had already got her all that she required, and she retired with a paper to the farther side of the compartment.

'You need not wait, Thomas,' she said. 'There will probably be no one else getting in, and it is a corridor train.'

So Thomas touched his hat and left.

Just before the guard gave the signal to start, a man – evidently a gentleman – opened the door of the carriage and entered.

He had been walking leisurely up and down the platform – and if she had known it, had observed her maid and footman, looked at her luggage, and ascertained her destination. It was the same as his own – Irtonwood Manor, that really charmingly romantic old place Ada Hardress and her obedient husband had just taken from the Walworths for a year.

'It is too exquisitely ghostly, pet!' she had written to Estelle Charters. 'Creaking panelling, underground passages, haunted library, and a big cedarwood bedroom where the White Lady appears. There is no electric light, and a person with your sensibilities can be perfectly certain to receive a thrill! Come and spend Christmas with us!'

And Mrs Charters had accepted – won by this alluring description – and was now, the day before Christmas Eve, on her way thither.

She was a tall, slender woman of twenty-eight or thirty, perhaps. She was not beautiful, but every single thing she put on seemed to enhance her grace. Rather plaintive and distinguished refinement appeared to be the note which first struck strangers about her.

That bore, Algernon Alexander Charters, had joined friends in another world some three years before this Christmas Eve, leaving his widow most comfortably provided for. Only an unpleasant jar had happened, not more than a week ago. The family lawyer had written to inform Estelle that there might be serious trouble ahead, and it might even eventualise in her loss of most of Algernon Alexander's money if a certain marriage certificate could not be found. The whole fortune was being claimed by a descendant of the great-great-grandfather, who contended that Algernon Alexander himself had enjoyed his ten or twelve thousand a year unlawfully.

It appeared that somewhere about 1795 the rich Alderman

Charters' son, delighting to move in circles above him, had contracted a marriage secretly with the daughter of a decayed noble, who would have none of him! – and the lady, regretting her mistake too late, had denied all connection with him, and willingly relinquished her son, whose existence she had concealed, and of whom she was ashamed, she had retired with her father to Italy and there a year or two later had died, the wife of an Italian count!

The abandoned rich City husband had apparently taken the casual behaviour of the noble lady in a philosophical spirit, doting upon her son to whom, although he married again, and had a number of other children, he left the bulk of his great fortune.

These second family seemed to have been complacent people, and had accepted their fate. But now one of their descendants had come forward and claimed that, the will of John Charters expressly stating, 'To my legitimate eldest son and his heirs,' with no name given, the property should come to him as the lineal representative of the eldest son of the second family, there being no proof to be found anywhere of the first marriage with the Lady Marjory Wildacre.

Mrs Charters thought of all these things as she sat in the train. Her attention had scarcely wandered from them even as she glanced up at the intruder in her carriage, but she did casually notice that he was a thin, dark man with something rather attractive-looking about him. And after a while she became conscious that his eyes were fixed upon her, and she felt compelled to look up.

They were too close together, the orbs that met hers, she decided, though their size and shape left nothing to be desired. She had a foolish shiver of foreboding and dislike as she turned away and let her mind revert to the ceaseless question of where on the face of the earth this certificate could be – and how were they to find it.

Presently the stranger leaned forward and said, in a most cultivated voice, which yet had a foreign accent somewhere lurking in the background:

'You are Mrs Charters, I believe? We are both going to the same house. May I introduce myself, I am Ambrose Duval – I am afraid, not quite an Englishman!'

His smile was so pleasant, it made you forget the sinister impression left by his eyes.

Mrs Charters was of the world and not easily disconcerted.

She bowed politely, and a conversation began, in the course of which it became apparent that Mr Ambrose Duval (such a name, it reminds one of 'Claude,' she thought!) had met the Hardresses abroad, and had renewed his acquaintance lately, and was coming down now to this Christmas party.

Nothing could be more polished and smooth than his manner; it had that easy gliding from one subject to another, which makes so agreeable a conversationalist. He skimmed all sorts of interesting topics, and at last arrived at English architecture.

'Irtonwood is a very romantic old place, Mrs Hardress tells me,' he said. 'A fine specimen of Tudor style, with additions of Jacobean. I am longing to study it. Do you know its history?'

'Not in the least,' Estelle replied. 'My friend, Ada Hardress, merely wrote I should be certain to see ghosts! I love the thought of them, although I have never been fortunate enough to encounter one, have you?' and she smiled her fascinating, elusive smile, that was half melancholy and half gay.

Sir George Seafield, who had already arrived at Irtonwood earlier in the day, thought Estelle Charters' smile the most divine thing in the world, but then he was in love – resentfully so at first, then resignedly, and now abjectly!

Ambrose Duval, on the contrary, mused: 'She is no fool for all her gentleness, it is a capable mouth, perhaps her innocence about Irtonwood is all bluff, and she is bent upon the same errand as myself. I must lose no time.'

By four o'clock, when they had reached Ileton, they had each taken stock of the other.

'He makes me creep down my back,' was Mrs Charters' comment, 'although I do feel he is attractive.'

Some more guests got out of another carriage, and there were greetings and chaff, and the whole party entered motors and were whirled to their destination.

Here all was holly and mistletoe and everything to make a real English Christmas. Huge log fires in every grate, and quantities of wax candles tried to make up for the want of electric light.

Nothing could have looked more like a story-book description of things as they were once in the good old days.

Ada Hardress gave her friend a most gushing welcome, and contrived that Sir George Seafield secured a chance for a *tête-à-tête* word in a suitable window-seat, as they drank tea.

'You were cruel to me,' he said, looking devotedly at the lady of his heart with his keen blue eyes – 'promising to be at the junction and never turning up by that train – I came down from Scotland on purpose, and thought I should have been allowed to take care of you from Crewe here.'

'I can take care of myself,' she protested softly, 'and I found I wanted to shop this morning before I left.'

'You think you are capable of looking after yourself always, under any circumstances, I suppose,' he hazarded.

'But, of course – when I feel I cannot, then I shall tell you,' and she smiled.

'I pray fate to let the chance come sooner than you think!' he announced fervently.

But at this pious hope Mrs Charters only looked sweetly disdainful, and changed the conversation to less personal things.

'You won't be a goose, darling, and snub Sir George to death, will you?' Ada Hardress begged, as she took her friend up the stairs. 'You are so provoking with your aloof air, and now wanting to rest until dinner when he is dying to talk to you!'

But Mrs Charters was unimpressed.

'I am really tired, Ada – and it does Englishmen good to be made to wait. I learned that in America,' she said. 'Algernon took me there when I wanted to go to Rome, but I never regretted it – I acquired so many hints from those clever women – Oh! what a heavenly place,' she added, when they got to the Cedar chamber which had been allotted to her, 'fancy it's not having been spoilt in these modern days!'

For it was all panelled and hung with faded orange silk in its three tall windows and capacious four-post bed.

And presently, when Mrs Charters was tucked up upon the rather hard sofa, preparing to have a siesta before dinner, she felt at peace with all the world. It was not long before she was sound asleep and here she had a strange dream.

She felt herself unaccountably moved and perturbed – she had a sensation of breathless, waiting tension, while she stood in some dark place, and suddenly it seemed as though only one spot in the blackness became illuminated, and then she saw an old escritoire. There was nothing else, no furniture, no room – nothing but this old writing bureau standing in space, and there, on it, lay unfolded a yellow parchment, upon which seemed to have fallen some drops of fresh blood!

Estelle woke with a sensation of supernatural excitement and fear. And then she reasoned with herself. Could anything have been more foolish! A dream with no incident, no personages, no action, to cause such a feeling! There was something uncanny about it though – what if the room were really haunted! She was not sure if she liked it after all!

She got up quickly and rang for her maid, glad to have company and lights. But all the while she dressed, she saw nothing but the escritoire, the parchment, and the three drops of blood.

'You look pale and pathetic,' Sir George Seafield told her, with tender anxiety in his voice, as they went in to dinner. 'What has happened? I want to know.'

But it was not until about the first entrée that he could get her to unfold her dream.

Her other hand neighbour was the attractive half-foreigner who had come down in the train with her, and who had no intention of allowing her legitimate partner to monopolise the conversation. He listened attentively as she described minutely the strange incident to Sir George, bending forward so as not to lose a word, much to that gentleman's disgust.

'I hate the brute!' he thought. 'Why cannot he attend to the woman he has taken in?'

'What a very strange dream!' Mr Ambrose Duval said. 'And where was the escritoire – have you any idea?'

'Not in the least,' replied Estelle. 'It was all in space – but why the blood?' And then a thought struck her. 'Of course!' she exclaimed. 'This is some vision sent to tell me where I am to find a most important document – how stupid of me never to have thought of it before!'

'A document?' both men asked; but while Sir George's eyes only expressed deep admiration for the lady herself, Mr

Ambrose Duval's had a concentrated eagerness to hear her words that was arresting.

'Why should this interest him so?' wondered Sir George, and it caused him to feel puzzled and irritated.

Mrs Charters was no chatterer and not in the habit of imparting her private affairs to strangers, so she laughed and changed the conversation now to lighter things, dividing her time equally between the two men until the ladies rose to leave the room.

Sir George Seafield was incensed. Why had his good friend Ada Hardress asked this foreigner to Irtonwood? And why had she put him next to Estelle, the lady of his heart?'

'I believe she is rather drawn towards the jackanapes,' he thought angrily to himself, and with difficulty kept from sparring with him as they sat over the port.

'Ada, where did you meet Mr Duval?' Mrs Charters asked, as a group of women hung over the big drawing-room fire. 'He seems an interesting creature.'

'Doesn't he!' several of them chimed in.

'Mysterious and delightful,' one affirmed.

'So good-looking,' another announced.

'His eyes are too close together,' old Miss Harcourt said in her sententious way. 'I shan't play bridge with him.'

'We met him in Hungary last summer,' the hostess at last got in – 'It seems absurd, but he was an hotel acquaintance, only he knew such a lot of people we did, he seemed like an old friend, and we saw him often, and he was always cheery and nice. He has relations in England that he has come to look up. I am so glad you find him attractive – I do myself! He has been too charming this last fortnight when we were up in town for Christmas shopping, he had just arrived from Paris and I have never had so delightful a companion, so I asked him down for Christmas. He said he would be lonely, and is so absorbed in the study of old houses.'

Then someone began to play the piano and the group broke up, and soon the gentlemen joined them, and a general move to the big oak-panelled hall commenced, when the younger members started a valse, while the 'fiddlers three,' who had come down from London to entertain the Yuletide guests, played merrily.

Sir George Seafield was detained by his host for a second, and had the chagrin to see Mrs Charters whirling in the arms of the foreigner! He shut his firm jaw with an ominous snap.

'I am dashed if I'll put up with it,' he muttered, and went and claimed the next turn the moment the pair paused for breath.

'How cross you look to-night, Sir George!' Mrs Charters said, as they danced, 'My last partner was so agreeable and sympathetic!'

'I want to wring his neck,' was all the answer she got. And then he added, as they stopped and wandered off to a distant sofa in the gallery, 'I am sure he is up to no good, I'd watch the silver if I were Jack Hardress!'

'It is really remarkable to what depths of spite men will descend about one another,' Estelle laughed as they sat down. 'No woman would be so transparent, and all just because Mr Duval is a foreigner and has good manners and does not show – moods!' And she leaned back provokingly among the cushions.

'You like him?' Sir George asked indignantly – and then aggrievedly – 'but anyone can see that!'

'If you are going to be unpleasant,' Mrs Charters said, 'I shall leave you and dance with him again, he waltzes divinely.'

Sir George's eyes blazed.

'If you do, I *will* wring his neck – I could easily,' he blurted out.

'Absurd brute force!' and she smiled plaintively – 'Englishmen are so crude.'

'How you do tease me – Estelle –' Sir George said, and then stopped suddenly.

'Who told you you might call me that?' Mrs Charters frowned. 'A piece of impertinence!' – but here her voice faltered, for she saw that her companion was no longer listening to her, his eyes were fixed with an intense interest upon a picture which hung upon the wall opposite them – the portrait of a lady in late eighteenth-century dress, with the rather high waist, and flowing white draperies, while her hair fell in ruffled, unpowdered curls. It was not by any celebrated artist; but was a pleasing picture, and as Estelle's eyes took it in, she knew why Sir George was so absorbed – for it bore a most wonderful likeness to herself!

'By Jove!' was all he said.

'It certainly might have been painted from me,' she allowed. 'Who can it be?'

But they could not find out. Their host, whom they questioned, did not know – he happened to be passing at that moment and joined them with his foreign guest. They had only taken the place from the Walworths for a year, he said, and the Walworths had bought it just as it stood from someone else. It had changed hands once or twice, and he could not remember now who were the original owners.

'It is supposed to be a portrait of the ghost, I believe,' he told them. 'Some old retainer informed Ada when we came. The White Lady who haunts the library and the Cedar chamber –'

'Where I sleep!' cried Estelle with a note of distress. 'Oh! Jack, I believe I am half afraid!'

'I'll come and watch outside your door if you are,' said Sir George. 'Then you can call me if you feel frightened in the night and I will tackle any ghost for you – I should glory in the act!'

'I do not doubt it!' laughed the host and discreetly walked on.

But Mr Ambrose Duval stayed behind, examining every turn of the brush in the picture with a critical eye.

Estelle had grown very quiet, Sir George noticed – she suddenly felt again that strange sense of excitement, a cold, unpleasant feeling of tension and dread; and she looked up into his face with an appealing pair of soft grey eyes.

'Let us go and dance again,' she said. 'I want to get warm once more – I feel cold.'

And Sir George joyfully encircled her slender waist and held her close as they rejoined the dancers and whirled about.

'Who sleeps next to me?' Mrs Charters asked, as a laughing group of women went up to bed about one in the morning – but she heard with secret dismay that the only other room in this quaint square wing was a sitting-room with a little oratory attached.

'You have always said you adored ghosts and weird things,' Mrs Hardress said, 'or, dearest, I would not have put you in the Cedar room.'

'So I do – of course,' returned Estelle rather half-heartedly. She was a proud woman and ashamed to show her fears.

Everything looked most bright and comfortable when she got to her room, and her devoted maid had waited up for her, and now put her to bed with every care. So, tired out with her dance, Estelle forgot her sense of uneasiness and soon sank to sleep between the slippery, fine sheets, while the dying fire made flickering lights in the vast room.

But in the grey dawn she awoke in mortal fright, for she had dreamed again of the dark space, the escritoire, the parchment, and the drops of fresh blood.

II

Next day was Christmas Eve, and much occupied with all sorts of bygone amusements, in which a Christmas tree for the children figured in the late afternoon. Everyone was particularly gay and cheerful, only Estelle Charters felt heavy as lead. Her dream haunted her, it had certainly some meaning; it was the second time she had experienced it, and the certificate, the loss of which might make such a difference to her, could quite well look like the parchment on the desk. But why there should be any connection with it and this house, of which she had never heard until her friends had taken it, she could not imagine. And if there were some strange thread in it all, why should the picture of the ghost be like herself? The money she could be deprived of had been Algernon's money, and had not come to her through her own family at all, so it would be more sensible and seemingly in sequence if the ghost looked like him or one of her sisters-in-law.

But she could not shake off the unaccountable depression she was filled with, and she tried to divert herself with Mr Ambrose Duval's inspiriting conversation, to the rage of Sir George, who had left Scotland on purpose to be present at this party, and press his suit, feeling full of hope that she would show him some grace. But, for some reason, all had been at sixes and sevens between them, and this hateful foreigner appeared to be the cause.

Towards the end of the day, Sir George's temper had got the better of him, and he had finally gone off and talked to another woman in pique and disgust.

And so once more the night came, and Estelle was left alone in the Cedar room.

Now the conduct of the foreign guest had excited suspicion as well as fury in the breast of Sir George; and he had watched him unconsciously most of the day.

'The brute' had come to Irtonwood with some purpose – he now felt sure of that.

Such extreme interest in all the rooms and the furniture was overdone, if it were really an innocent fancy for old things. The library in particular seemed to have attracted him, and he even contrived to be shown the famous Cedar chamber, while he said most insinuating and admiring things to its present occupant. They had gone there, a company of four or five, after lunch, old Miss Harcourt among them, torn from her bridge.

'I would not sleep here for the world,' she said. 'I wonder how *you* can, Estelle. You must have nerves of iron and a conscience of snow-like purity – it makes me creep even in broad daylight.'

'I am not afraid,' affirmed Mrs Charters, raising her head.

From there the group had returned to the library, and here Mr Duval pointed to an old escritoire which stood in one window, used now as a writing table. Its surface seemed a good deal warped from the sunlight, which had come in upon it, probably for many years.

'This could be as the one you told us about in your dream,' Mr Duval said, furtively watching her face.

And Estelle recognised that it was, indeed, the same, with a sharp thrill. But she laughed a little nervously as she evaded a direct reply.

Mr Duval was examining it closely, passing smooth, finely moving fingers over all its sides and top.

'There is probably some secret spring,' he said. 'It would be amusing if your dream came true, and it disclosed the parchment and the drops of blood.'

But for some reason Estelle did not wish him to find it – if there were any spring. She would examine it herself another time, with Ada alone.

And Sir George, watching now intently, felt all sorts of queer ideas come into his head.

By the time they said good-night, the feeling that there was something going on underneath grew so strong that he determined not to undress or go to bed.

'He is going to have a try at opening that old bureau, I'd make any bet,' he said to himself. 'And I'll baulk him if I can and discover what is up.'

So he pretended to be tired, and go on to his room when the other men moved to the smoking room, which was in a side wing, after the ladies had left, but in reality he waited until he thought the butler would have extinguished the lights in the library and the middle part of the house. Then he lit his candle and softly crept down, and stretched himself upon a sofa rather behind a screen, while the dying embers of the fire shed a mysterious glow all over the rest of the room.

And in the Cedar chamber, Estelle, tired out and rather saddened at the estrangement which she felt had grown up in the day, between herself and her hitherto ardent, would-be lover, got hastily into bed.

It was her own fault she knew; she had been most capricious, and talked far too much to the foreign man, whom she realised now she rather disliked underneath. She had been foolish and nervous and jumpy to-day and she felt quite ashamed of herself.

But in a very short time she grew sleepy, and all became a blank, until, with startling vividness, for the third time the dream returned and to it was added a dim figure, which seemed to beckon to her, and compel her to rise and follow from her warm soft bed.

It seemed that she crept across the room to a panel beside the fireplace, fascinated, but without fear, following the ghostly shape which, when it turned its face, looked so strangely like herself. And the panel glided back, disclosing a dark opening, and still she was impelled to enter its black depths, and all the while, as she felt herself descending a narrow stair, a dim iridescence seemed, like a nimbus, to encircle the head of that faint wraith which was leading her on. Whither?

Meanwhile, in the library, Sir George was almost dozing off to sleep on his sofa in the shadow of the screen. The clock had struck two, and the fire had burnt so very low that hardly a glow now illumined the room; but a broad shaft of moonlight came in from the top part of the window, to which the shutters did not reach. It was composed of small panes, with a coat of arms emblazoned in the centre, and the beams of the moon threw some weird shades upon the floor and upon the old escritoire, which happened to stand in its path of light.

Sir George thought to himself that he had, after all, perhaps been mistaken. The foreigner had probably gone to bed with the rest, and he, too, would turn in.

Then, just as his meditations reached thus far, he heard the faintest noise of the door opening, and someone, with stealthy footsteps, cautiously advanced up the room.

As he sprang to his feet he felt, rather than saw, that it was Ambrose Duval; he, himself, was securely hidden in the black shadow of the screen.

The man went softly to the shutter of the moonlit window, and, with quiet, nervous hands, undid its old-fashioned bolt, letting in a still broader shaft of light, which now allowed every detail of the old bureau to be seen. Then he came eagerly to its side, and Sir George held his breath and leaned forward, not to miss anything of what might be about to happen.

Mr Duval seemed to be feeling the lid, which he opened with care, and then a search began for the secret spring. And once or twice, as he looked up as if for inspiration, his face seemed like a fiend's in the ashen light.

At last he appeared to have discovered something – a drawer flew open with a jerk, and he gave a sharp exclamation of pain. Some part of the steel spring had evidently wounded his hand. But his hesitation was only momentary; with frantic eagerness, he now drew forth a roll from the secret place.

It looked to Sir George like an old yellow parchment, and as Ambrose Duval bent to scrutinise it, with devilish satisfaction upon his face, there dropped from the cut on his hand some drops of blood.

The scene was the exact reproduction of Mrs Charters' dream!

This was the moment, Sir George felt, for him to interfere; but before he could take more than a step, he was arrested by seeing the thief raise his head, and then start and grow livid and shaking with abject terror, as he gazed into a far corner, the parchment dropping from his nerveless fingers back on to the old desk.

And Sir George, following the direction of his eyes, also experienced a thrill which, even to him, was not unmixed with something akin to fear.

For both men could just distinguish, slowly and noiselessly advancing towards them out of the shadows, from a part of the room where there was no door, the tall, slender figure of a woman, in a rather short-waisted white garment, with ruffled curls of unpowdered hair.

She seemed to be ethereal and unreal; but when she got into the moonlight the likeness was unmistakable, the face was the same as the picture in the gallery, which the host had told them represented the Irtonwood Ghost.

The great grey eyes were wide and staring, like the eyes of a corpse, and the whole figure moved slowly with a gliding motion unlike life.

'My God! Is it Estelle?' Sir George gasped to himself, as he waited the turn of events.

If it were his well-beloved, then she must be walking in her sleep. If the denizen of some other world, then something strange and awful might develop when she got to the escritoire.

In either case his best course would be to watch and be ready to spring. For he fully realised the securing of the parchment was to Ambrose Duval, for some reason, a matter of desperate need.

The figure advanced, growing more clear as it reached the goal; Duval was now crouching, an almost inert mass, some paces back, in mortal fright.

The lady – whoever or whatever she was – put out a transparent-looking hand in the moonlight, and, seizing the parchment, was gliding back again from whence she came;

but Ambrose Duval gave the hiss of a snake as he saw the precious paper being taken from his grasp, and, with a half inarticulate cry of rage and terror, bounded forward.

But Sir George was quicker than he, and, ere he could reach the ghost, or woman, he found himself pinioned in the Englishman's strong arms.

Then the two men struggled, Ambrose Duval with mad fear in his breast at this new foe, and Sir George with cool determination to frustrate his opponent's ends.

As they tottered together, they both saw, with an indescribable thrill, the figure disappear, as it were before their eyes, into the darkness of the wall.

And they knew they were alone.

Was she a ghost, or real flesh and blood? That was a question which neither could decide.

But now that there was no more reason to protect Estelle – if it were she – Sir George let Mr Duval go.

He was breathless from rage and fright, and he staggered to a chair.

'How dare you attack me like this!' he exclaimed furiously, drawing a revolver from his pocket and pointing it at his foe.

But Sir George, far more perturbed at the thought of what might have become of his lady love, took no notice of him. He walked over to the fire and poked up the dying embers, which threw up a last small flame, giving enough light for him to find his candlestick, which he had put down beside the sofa in the gloom, beyond the shaft of moonlight. Mr Duval followed him, still livid from fear of the supernatural, and mad with rage at his failure and loss.

'You shall answer to me for this, now, with your life!' he snarled.

'In that case you will be hanged for murder,' Sir George retorted, coolly. 'You had better go quietly in the morning, before I denounce you as a thief.'

'I am no thief!' Mr Duval protested, violently. 'How dare you attack a guest in our friend's house in this murderous fashion! It is I who can denounce you. You must give me satisfaction for this!'

'I shall do nothing of the kind,' said Sir George. 'I should not think of duelling with a thief. Just take my advice and go in the morning without a scandal, and prosecute your scheming tricks elsewhere. I have seen all you did, remember, and can describe it well!'

Then the two men glared at one another there in the old library, the one candle illuminating their angry faces, and the great shaft of moonlight lighting the rifled escritoire. And then Sir George calmed himself.

'You can take what course you please,' he said. 'I have a pistol, too,' and he drew his small Derringer from the pocket where he had been holding it. 'I am rather a good shot sometimes, so we may each hit the other, but there is no use in it, and rats like you are fond of life.'

This reflection seemed to carry weight with Mr Duval, unflattering as it was. For it is quite one thing to shoot at an unarmed man, and quite another to find him possessed of a pistol, too.

With what dignity he could, Mr Duval now drew himself up, and prepared to leave the room.

'You have won this time,' he said, between his teeth, 'but some day I will level things up.'

'I am quite indifferent about that,' Sir George answered, hurriedly. 'Get out now, and get away by the earliest train, I shall give you so much start. Now I have other and more important things to do. Go!'

And he almost drove Duval to the door and up to his room. Then, when he had seen him safely shut in, he paused to think what was the next thing to be done.

To awaken Jack Hardress and his wife, and ascertain if Estelle was safe in her Cedar chamber, seemed to be the best move. So, after some difficulty, he found his host's apartment, and knocked firmly at the door.

'Yes, what is it?' Jack Hardress called out, sleepily.

And Ada's frightened voice piped, 'Oh! who is there?'

Then Sir George explained in as few words as he could, when his host and hostess, clothed in dressing-gowns, appeared in the passage, and they all three, carrying lights, set off for the Cedar room.

But here was deathly silence, no answer came to their knocks, nor could they enter – the door was locked from within.

A sickening icy hand clutched at Sir George's heart. What had happened? Some ill had befallen Estelle.

'If we both rush the door together we can break the lock, Jack,' he said, desperately. 'We must not delay an instant – now!'

And the two men hurled themselves against the stout panels; but, though they shivered, they held. Then, with the strength of despair, Sir George made a rush by himself, and the bolt gave, and he fell headlong into the room.

But, alas! Ada's two candles, which she held high, revealed no occupant. The bed had been slept in and left hastily, the clothes were turned back, but there was no sign of Estelle!

The three people looked at each other with blanched faces – what mystery was here? Sir George began hastily to examine the walls. It followed, his common-sense told him, if the door were locked from within, his beloved lady had left the apartment by some other means. The windows were out of the question; they were too high, and, besides, were closed and the orange curtains drawn. There must be some secret panel, and Estelle must have walked in her sleep – but how weird it all was! And he was filled with dread and foreboding as he felt each part of the wall.

'We *must* discover the entrance, Jack,' he said. 'I saw Mrs Charters – or her ghost – with my own eyes in the library and she disappeared at the end of the room.'

Now, with terrified eagerness, the three set to work, feeling and tapping each cedar panel, while Ada Hardress called continually: 'Estelle! Estelle! Answer if you are there and can here us!'

But only silence greeted them.

And, as the hopelessness of their task made itself felt, a sickening fear grew and grew in each of their hearts.

What if she had fallen down some deep secret place – some oubliette – and were dead? They might pull all the house down, and yet be too late.

At last Ada, almost weeping from grief and fright, subsided upon the sofa, while her husband and Sir George, rigid and grey with anxiety, faced each other, to decide what to do.

'Wake the servants and send for a mason and carpenter,' Sir George said. 'And, meanwhile, can't we get an axe and some tools? I will tear the woodwork down myself, when I have an implement.'

Mrs Hardress went off to wake the household, and send for the required men.

'And get a doctor, too,' Sir George called, and when some tools were found by a frightened footman, and brought, he set to work with such a will that at last a steel bolt was discovered, and the panelling giving way by the fireplace, a very small, narrow door was disclosed in the stonework. The bolts in connection with it were stiff and rusted with age, and how a delicate woman could have moved them was a profound mystery.

The door gave way without much difficulty, and here, by the light of a lamp held high, the very narrowest passage was revealed, which in three paces developed into a stair.

It was so extremely narrow that Sir George was obliged to force his broad shoulders through until he came to the descent. Suddenly, at a sharp turn, he could see the steps rising again on the opposite side, but there, in the space beneath, lay the figure of a woman in white.

With an exclamation of anguish, he saw that it was Estelle – but was she dead?

He handed the lamp to Jack Hardress, who was behind him, and in a second he was beside his love, and had raised her in his arms with difficulty in the confined space; and even in the excitement, he noticed that she still clutched in her hand the paper which seemed to have been the cause of all the tragic events of the night.

He detached it from her fingers, and saw that the blood drops had smeared her hand, as he put the paper in his pocket and lifted her in his arms to carry her back.

A bruise marked where her forehead had struck a projecting stone in the wall; perhaps she was only stunned, and not dead! This hope gave him the strength of a lion, and he clasped her close. But their exit was no easy task; the space had been narrow enough for one person here and there, and was impossible for a man cumbered with a woman in his arms.

Jack Hardress retreated before them, holding the lamp high, and when Sir George came to a turn that he could not pass, he was obliged to lay his precious burden down, and let Jack Hardress pull her through by the arms. Then he lifted her up again. And so, at last, all three were safe in the Cedar room, where a thrilled and excited group awaited them, including the doctor, who had now arrived.

The room was cleared of all but Ada, Sir George, and Estelle's maid, while the doctor bent over the inanimate form. And, at last, he looked up and announced, 'No – she is not dead,' and never were more grateful words sent up to heaven than Sir George's fervent, 'Thank God!'

She was not dead then, his darling, and soon she might open her dear eyes and look into his own.

He could afford to wait in the passage now, as he told the good news to the rest of the alarmed guests.

And presently the doctor and Mrs Hardress came out, and he heard that his beloved was conscious, and rapidly recovering.

'She must have walked in her sleep,' the physician said, 'and her head struck a stone, but it was the stifling air which made her faint, though, no doubt, she was stunned, too, by the blow; if you had been an hour later in finding her, I think she could not have lived.'

So, after all, there were rejoicings on that Christmas morning, which seemed as though it was going to dawn so tragically; and in the excitement of it all no one thought then to remark upon Mr Ambrose Duval's departure by the one and only early train.

His note of farewell to his hostess was a masterpiece, and caused Sir George to smile, as she handed it to him to read.

Late in the afternoon he was allowed to see his sweet lady in Ada's own sitting-room, alone, and in peace. She was lying on the sofa with a bandage round her forehead, and her small face looked ghastly pale against the blue silk cushions, but her eyes shone and she stretched out her hands, as he bent upon his knees to be near her.

'George – you were good to me!' she whispered. 'And I can't take care of myself –' But she could not say any more, because he stooped and kissed her lips. And for some while they were too happy to talk of even a subject so interesting as her dream and the adventure it produced.

But at last they became sane enough to examine the parchment, which proved to be the certificate of marriage between John Charters, bachelor, and Marjorie Wildacre, spinster, celebrated at a little village in Leicestershire, in the year 1795.

So the Irtonwood Ghost had stood Estelle in good stead! For here was her fortune secured beyond any doubt.

But who, then, was Mr Ambrose Duval? and what was his connection with the affair? And why did Estelle, herself, resemble the picture of the Irtonwood Ghost? These were questions which it would take time to answer.

'Though what does anything matter,' exclaimed Sir George, after a while, 'since I have enough for us both? And since you cannot take care of yourself, and are going to let me.'

It was not before the happy pair returned from their honeymoon that all the mystery was unravelled. The lawyers had been busy investigating the while. It appeared that Lady Marjorie Wildacre had lived at Irtonwood, which was her old home, her father having sold it when they went to Italy.

She had had a daughter by her second husband, the Italian Count, who eventually married the great-grandfather of Estelle, thus carrying the likeness into her family

And Estelle often loves to weave a romance round her dream, and imagine how, influenced by this far-back ancestress's unquiet spirit, she must have been drawn to go to the Irtonwood Christmas party and participate in the events which followed.

'You see, George, she probably loved the Italian Count,' Estelle told her husband, 'and wanted their descendant, by him, to benefit, too. That is why she directed me. But I cannot help being sorry for poor Mr Duval.'

'Loathsome foreigner!' was all Sir George said.

His real name was Charters, and he was the claimant to the fortune; but he chose to take his mother's name – she had been a Frenchwoman – the better to pursue his investigations unsuspected.

He had got hold of some letter, among the papers of his branch of the family, which referred to the certificate being at Irtonwood, and Lady Marjorie's residence there; and, hearing that his chance acquaintances, the Hardresses, had taken this place, he cultivated them in order to have access for his search, determining, when he found the certificate, he would destroy it, and then with certainty prosecute his claim.

But Fate takes care of things, and arranges what she thinks best. And even the thoroughly English Sir George Seafield is obliged to own that there are more things in heaven and earth than are dreamed of in our philosophy.

IX

The 'Lusitania' Waits

Alfred Noyes

After the flippancy of 'The Irtonwood Ghost', this next story comes in stark contrast and takes us from the carefree social whirl of the first decade of this century into the grimness of World War I. The author, Alfred Noyes (1880-1958), is perhaps best remembered as a distinguished poet – his lines of 'The Highwayman' are surely one of the most widely selected pieces of verse used to introduce young people to poetry – although he also wrote essays, plays, biographies, novels and short stories: several of which were firmly in the macabre vein. His tale 'The Midnight Express', for instance, has been persistently anthologised for many years. Noyes was also deeply interested in the sea, as many of his verses such as 'Forty Singing Seamen' and the epic 'Drake' (both written in 1908) clearly demonstrate. The wild and mysterious nature of the ocean also appears in some of his short stories, and the terrible disaster of the Cunard liner, Lusitania, *which was sunk by a German submarine on May 7th, 1915 with the loss of 1,200 lives directly inspired Noyes to write the grim little tale which follows. It is one of the most moving supernatural stories of the sea I know.*

On a stormy winter's night three skippers – averaging threescore years and five – were discussing the news, around a roaring fire, in the parlour of the White Horse inn. Five years ago they had retired, each on a snug little pile. They were looking forward to a mellow old age in port and a long succession of evenings at the White Horse, where they gathered to debate the politics of their district. The war had given them new topics; but Captain John Kendrick – who had become a parish councillor and sometimes carried bulky blue documents in his breast-pocket, displaying the edges with careful pride – still kept the local pot a-boiling. He was mainly successful on Saturday nights, when the *Gazette*, their weekly newspaper, appeared. It was edited by a Scot named Macpherson, who had learned his job on the *Arbroath Free Press*.

'Macpherson will never be on the council now,' said Captain Kendrick. 'There's a rumour that he's a freethinker. He says that Christianity has been proved a failure by the war.'

'Well, these chaps of ours now,' said Captain Davidson, 'out at sea on a night like this, trying to kill Germans. It's necessary, I know, because the Germans would kill our own folks if we gave 'em a chance. But don't it prove that there's no use for Christianity? In modern civilisation, I mean.'

'Macpherson's no freethinker,' said Captain Morgan, who was a friend of the editor, and inclined on the strength of it to occupy the intellectual chair at the White Horse. 'Macpherson says we'll have to try again after the war, or it will be blood and iron all round.'

'He's upset by the war,' said Captain Davidson, 'and he's taken to writing poytry in his paper. He'd best be careful, or he'll lose his circulation.'

'Ah!' said Kendrick, 'that's what 'ull finish him for the council. What we want is practical men. Poytry would destroy any man's reputation. There was a great deal of talk caused by his last one, about our trawler chaps. "Fishers of Men," he called it; and I'm not sure that it wouldn't be considered blasphemious by a good many.'

Captain Morgan shook his head. 'Every Sunday evening,' he said, 'my missus asks me to read her Macpherson's pome in the *Gazette*, and I've come to enjoy them myself. Now, what does he say in "Fishers of men"?'

'Read it,' said Kenrick, picking the *Gazette* from the litter of newspapers on the table and handing it to Morgan. 'If you know how to read poytry, read it aloud, the way you do to your missus. I can't make head or tail of poytry myself; but it looks blasphemious to me.'

Captain Morgan wiped his big spectacles, while the other two settled themselves to listen critically. Then he began in his best with his forefinger at a picture in an illustrated paper.

'Here's a wicked thing now,' he said. 'Here's a medal they've struck in Germany to commemorate the sinking of the *Lusitania*. Here's a photograph of both sides of it. On one side, you see the great ship sinking, loaded up with munitions which wasn't there; but not a sign of the women and children that *was* there. On the other side you see the passengers taking their tickets from Death in the New York booking office. Now that's a fearful thing. I can understand 'em making a mistake, but I can't understand 'em wanting to strike a medal for it.'

'Not much mistake about the *Lusitania*,' growled Captain Davidson.

'No, indeed. That was only my argyment,' replied the councillor. 'They're a treacherous lot. It was a fearful thing to do a deed like that. My son's in the Cunard; and, man alive, he tells me it's like sinking a big London hotel. There was ladies in evening dress, and dancing in the big saloons every night; and lifts to take you from one deck to another; and shops with plate-glass windows, and smoking-rooms; and glass around the promenade deck, so that the little children could play there in bad weather, and the ladies lay in their deck-chairs and sun themselves like peaches. There wasn't a soldier aboard, and some of the women was bringing their babies to see their Canadian daddies in England for the first time. Why, man, it was like sinking a nursing home!'

'Do you suppose, Captain Kendrick, that they ever caught that submarine?' asked Captain Morgan. They were old friends, but always punctilious about their titles.

'Ah, now I'll tell you something! Hear that?'

The three old men listened. Through the gusts of wind that battered the White Horse they heard the sound of heavy floundering footsteps, passing down the cobbled street, and a hoarse broken voice bellowing with uncanny abandonment a fragment of a hymn:

While shepherds watched their flocks by night,
All seated on the ground.

'That's poor old Jim Hunt,' said Captain Morgan. He rose and drew the thick red curtains from the window to peer out into the blackness.

'Turn the lamp down,' said the councillor, 'or we'll be arrested under the anti-aircraft laws.'

Davidson turned the lamp down and they all looked out of the window. They saw the figure of a man, black against the glimmering water of the harbour below. He walked with a curious floundering gait that might be mistaken for the effects of drink. He waved his arms over his head like a windmill and bellowed his hymn as he went, though the words were now indistinguishable from the tumult of wind and sea.

Captain Morgan drew the curtains, and the three sat down again by the fire without turning up the lamp. The firelight played on the furrowed and bronzed old faces and revealed them as worthy models for a Rembrandt.

'Poor old Jimmy Hunt!' said Captain Kendrick. 'You never know how craziness is going to take people. Jimmy was a terror for women and the drink, till he was taken off the *Albatross* by that German submarine. They cracked him over the head with an iron bolt, down at the bottom of the sea, because he wouldn't answer questions. He hasn't touched a drop since. All he does is to walk about in bad weather, singing hymns against the wind. But there's more in it than that.'

Captain Kendrick lighted his pipe thoughtfully. The wind rattled the windows. Outside, the sign-board creaked and whined as it swung.

'A man like Jim Hunt doesn't go crazy,' he continued, 'through spending a night in a U-boat, and then floating about for a bit. Jimmy won't talk about it now; won't do nothing but sing that blasted hymn; but this is what he said to me when they first brought him ashore. They said he was raving mad, on account of his experiences. But that don't explain what his experiences *were*. Follow me? And this is what he said. "*I been down,*" he says, half singing like, "*I been down, down, down, in the bloody submarine that sank the 'Lusitania.' And what's more,*" he says, "*I seen 'em!*"

' "Seen what?" I says, humouring him like, and I gave him a cigarette. We were sitting down a little, and speaking right into my ear, as if it was a secret. "It was Christmas Eve the time they took me down. We could hear 'em singing carols on shore; and the captain didn't like it, so he rang a little bell, and the Germans jumped to close the hatchways; and we went down, down, down, to the bottom of the sea.

' "I saw the whole ship," he says; and he described it to me, so that I knew he wasn't raving then. "There was only just room to stand upright," he says, "and overhead there was a track for the torpedo-carrier. The crew slept in hammocks and berths along the wall; but there wasn't room for more than half to sleep at the same time. They took me through a little foot-hole, with an air-tight door, into a cabin.

' "The captain seemed kind of excited, and showed me the medal he got for sinking the *Lusitania*; and I asked him if the Kaiser gave it to him for a Christmas present. That was when he and another officer seemed to go mad; and the officer gave me a blow on the head with a piece of iron.

' "They say I'm crazy," he says, "but it was the men on the U boat that went crazy. I was lying where I fell, with the blood running down my face, but I was watching them," he says, "and I saw them start and listen like trapped weasels. At first I thought the trawlers had got 'em in a net. Then I heard a funny little tapping sound all round the hull of the submarine, like little soft hands it was, tapping, tapping, tapping.

' "The captain went white as a ghost, and shouted out something in German, like as if he was calling '*Who's there?*' and the mate clapped his hands over his mouth, and they both stood staring at one another.

' "Then there was a sound like a thin little voice, outside the ship, mark you, and sixty fathom deep, saying, '*Christmas Eve, the waits, sir!*' The captain tore the mate's hand away and shouted again, like he was asking '*Who's there?*' and wild to get an answer, too. Then, very thin and clear, the little voice came a second time, '*The waits, sir. The 'Lusitania' ladies!*' And at that the captain struck the mate in the face with his clenched fist. He had the medal in it still between his fingers, using it like a knuckle-duster. Then he called to the men like a madman, all in German, but I knew he was telling 'em to rise to the surface, by the way they were trying to obey him.

' "The submarine never budged for all that they could do; and while they were running up and down and squealing out to one another, there was a kind of low sweet sound all round the hull, like a thousand voices all singing together in the sea:

Fear not, said he, for mighty dread
  Had seized their troubled mind,
Glad tidings of great joy I bring
  To you and all mankind.

'"Then the tapping began again, but it was much louder now; and it seemed as if hundreds of drowned hands were feeling over the hull and loosening bolts and pulling at hatchways; and – all at once – a trickle of water came splashing down into the cabin. The captain dropped his medal. It rolled up to my hand and I saw there was blood on it. He screamed at the men, and they pulled out their life-saving apparatus, a kind of air-tank which they strapped on their backs, with tubes to rubber masks for clapping over their mouths and noses. I watched 'em doing it, and managed to do the same. They were too busy to take any notice of me. Then they pulled a lever and tumbled out through a hole, and I followed 'em blindly. Something grabbed me when I got outside and held me for a minute. Then I saw 'em, Captain Kendrick, I saw 'em, hundreds and hundreds of 'em, in a shiny light, and sixty fathom down under the dark sea – they were all waiting there, men and women and poor little babies with hair like sunshine ...

'"And the men were smiling at the Germans in a friendly way, and unstrapping the air-tanks from their backs, and saying, 'Won't you come and join us? It's Christmas Eve, you know.'

'"Then whatever it was that held me let me go, and I shot up and knew nothing till I found myself in Jack Simmonds's drifter, and they told me I was crazy."'

Captain Kendrick filled his pipe. A great gust struck the old inn again and again till all the timbers trembled. The floundering step passed once more, and the hoarse voice bellowed away in the darkness against the bellowing sea:

A Saviour which is Christ the Lord.
  And this shall be the sign.

X

The Festival

H.P. Lovecraft

As is now generally recognised, the sinking of the Lusitania *strengthened anti-German feeling in America, and doubtless Alfred Noyes' story which was first published in the USA where he was then a resident as Professor of Poetry at Princeton (he had also married an American) contributed to this attitude. An American admirer of Noyes' work – his poetry and short stories in particular – was Howard Phillips Lovecraft (1890-1937), creator of the Cthulhu Mythos group of stories, inspirer of generations of macabre story writers, and although virtually ignored during his lifetime except in the pages of the pulp magazine* Weird Tales, *is today hailed as the greatest horror story writer of this century. Although much of Lovecraft's work featured 'nameless horrors' and 'blasphemous entities', he rooted many of his stories in the locality where he was born and spent much of his solitary, unhappy life, Providence, Rhode Island. I have travelled in this bleak and often inhospitable-looking New England locality, and the story which follows superbly evokes the landscape in winter time. As a matter of interest the towns of Kingsport and Arkham which Lovecraft describes, are actually the doubles of Marblehead and Salem respectively. I know I should not like to have shared the Yuletide which the narrator of 'The Festival' is now about to describe …*

I was far from home, and the spell of the eastern sea was upon me. In the twilight I heard it pounding on the rocks, and I knew it lay just over the hill where the twisting willows writhed against the clearing sky and the first stars of evening. And because my fathers had called me to the old town beyond, I pushed on through the shallow, new-fallen snow along the road that soared lonely up to where Aldebaran twinkled among the trees; on toward the very ancient town I had never seen but often dreamed of.

It was the Yuletide, that men call Christmas though they know in their hearts it is older than Bethlehem and Babylon, older than Memphis and mankind. It was the Yuletide, and I had come at last to the ancient sea town where my people had dwelt and kept festival in the elder time when festival was forbidden; where also they had commanded their sons to keep festival once every century, that the memory of primal secrets might not be forgotten. Mine were an old people, and were old even when this land was settled three hundred years before. And they were strange, because they had come as dark furtive folk from opiate southern gardens of orchids, and spoken another tongue before they learnt the tongue of the blue-eyed fishers. And now they were scattered, and shared only the rituals of mysteries that none living could understand. I was the only one who came back that night to the old fishing town as legend bade, for only the poor and the lonely remember.

Then beyond the hill's crest I saw Kingsport outspread frostily in the gloaming; snowy Kingsport with its ancient vanes and steeples, ridge-poles and chimney-pots, wharves and small bridges, willow-trees and graveyards; endless labyrinths of steep, narrow, crooked streets, and dizzy church-crowned central peak that time durst not touch; ceaseless mazes of colonial houses piled and scattered at all angles and levels like a child's disordered blocks; antiquity hovering on grey wings over winter-whitened gables and gambrel roofs; fanlights and small-paned windows one by one gleaming out in the cold dusk to join Orion and the archaic stars. And against the rotting wharves the sea pounded; the secretive, immemorial sea out of which the people had come in the elder time.

Beside the road at its crest a still higher summit rose, bleak and wind-swept, and I saw that it was a burying-ground where black gravestones stuck ghoulishly through the snow like the decayed fingernails of a gigantic corpse. The printless road was very lonely, and sometimes I thought I heard a distant horrible creaking as of a gibbet in the wind. They had hanged four kinsmen of mine for witchcraft in 1692, but I did not know just where.

As the road wound down the seaward slope I listened for the merry sounds of a village at evening, but did not hear them. Then I thought of the season, and felt that these old Puritan folk might well have Christmas customs strange to me, and full of silent hearthside prayer. So after that I did not listen for merriment or look for wayfarers, kept on down past the hushed lighted farmhouses and shadowy stone walls to where the signs of ancient shops and sea taverns creaked in the salt breeze, and the grotesque knockers of pillared doorways glistened along deserted unpaved lanes in the light of little, curtained windows.

I had seen maps of the town, and knew where to find the home of my people. It was told that I should be known and welcomed, for village legend lives long; so I hastened through Back Street to Circle Court, and across the fresh snow on the one full flagstone pavement in the town, to where Green Lane leads off behind the Market House. The old maps still held good, and I had no trouble; though at Arkham they must have lied when they said the trolleys ran to this place, since I saw not a wire overhead. Snow would have hid the rails in any case. I was glad I had chosen to walk, for the white village had seemed very beautiful from the hill; and now I was eager to knock at the door of my people, the seventh house on the left in Green Lane, with an ancient peaked roof and jutting second story, all built before 1650.

There were lights inside the house when I came upon it, and I saw from the diamond window-panes that it must have been kept very close to its antique state. The upper part overhung the narrow grass-grown street and nearly met the over-hanging part of the house opposite, so that I was almost in a tunnel, with the low stone doorstep wholly free from snow. There was no sidewalk, but many houses had high doors reached by double flights of steps with iron railings. It was an odd scene, and because I was strange to New England I had never known its like before. Though it pleased me, I would have relished it better if there had been footprints in the snow, and people in the streets, and a few windows without drawn curtains.

When I sounded the archaic iron knocker I was half afraid. Some fear had been gathering in me, perhaps because of the strangeness of my heritage, and the bleakness of the evening, and the queerness of the silence in that aged town of curious customs. And when my knock was answered I was fully afraid, because I had not heard any footsteps before the door creaked open. But I was not afraid long, for the gowned slippered old man in the doorway had a bland face that reassured me; and though he made signs that he was dumb, he wrote a quaint and ancient welcome with the stylus and wax tablet he carried.

He beckoned me into a low, candle-lit room with massive exposed rafters and dark, stiff, sparse furniture of the seventeenth century. The past was vivid there, for not an attribute was missing. There was a cavernous fireplace and a spinning-wheel at which a bent old woman in loose wrapper and deep poke-bonnet sat back toward me, silently spinning despite the festive season. An indefinite dampness seemed upon the place, and I marvelled that no fire should be blazing. The high-backed settle faced the row of curtained windows at the left, and seemed to be occupied, though I was not sure. I did not like everything about what I saw, and felt again the fear I had had. This fear grew stronger from what had before lessened it, for the more I looked at the old man's bland face the more its very blandness terrified me. The eyes never moved, and the skin was too much like wax. Finally I was sure it was not a face at all, but a fiendishly cunning mask. But the flabby hands, curiously gloved, wrote genially on the tablet and told me I must wait a while before I could be led to the place of the festival.

Pointing to a chair, table, and pile of books, the old man now left the room; and when I sat down to read I saw that the books were hoary and mouldy, and that they included old Morryster's wild *Marvells of Science*, the terrible *Saducismus Triumphatus* of Joseph Glanvil, published in 1681, the shocking *Daemonolatreia* of Remigius, printed in 1595 at Lyons, and worst of all, the unmentionable *Necronomicon* of the mad Arab Abdul Alhazred, in Olaus Wormius' forbidden Latin translation; a book which I had never seen, but of which I had heard monstrous things whispered. No one spoke to me, but I could hear the creaking of signs in the wind outside, and the whir of the wheel as the bonneted old woman continued her silent spinning, spinning. I thought the room and the books and the people very morbid and disquieting, but because an old tradition of my fathers had summoned me to strange feastings, I resolved to expect queer things. So I tried to read, and soon became tremblingly absorbed by something I found in that accursed *Necronomicon*; a thought and a legend too hideous for sanity or consciousness, but I disliked it when I fancied I heard the closing of one of the windows that the settle faced, as if it had been stealthily opened. It had seemed to follow a whirring that was not of the old woman's spinning-wheel. This was not much, though, for the old woman was spinning very hard, and the aged clock had been striking. After that I lost the feeling that there were persons on the settle, and was reading intently and shudderingly when the old man came back booted and dressed in a loose antique costume, and sat down on that very bench, so that I could not see him. It was certainly nervous waiting, and the blasphemous book in my hands made it doubly so. When eleven struck, however, the old man stood up, glided to a massive carved chest in a corner, and got two hooded cloaks; one of which he donned, and the other of which he draped round the old woman, who was ceasing her monotonous spinning. Then they both started for the outer door; the woman lamely creeping, and the old man, after picking up the very book I had been reading, beckoning me as he drew his hood over that unmoving face or mask.

We went out into the moonless and tortuous network of that incredibly ancient town; went out as the lights in the curtained windows disappeared one by one, and the Dog Star leered at the throng of cowled, cloaked figures that poured silently from every doorway and formed monstrous processions up this street and that, past the creaking signs and antediluvian gables, the thatched roofs and diamond-paned windows; threading precipitous lanes where decaying houses overlapped and crumbled together, gliding across open courts and churchyards where the bobbing lanthorns made eldritch drunken constellations.

Amid these hushed throngs I followed my voiceless guides;

jostled by elbows that seemed preternaturally soft, and pressed by chests and stomachs that seemed abnormally pulpy; but seeing never a face and hearing never a word. Up, up, up, the eery columns slithered, and I saw that all the travellers were converging as they flowed near a sort of focus of crazy alleys at the top of a high hill in the centre of the town, where perched a great white church. I had seen it from the road's crest when I looked at Kingsport in the new dusk, and it had made me shiver because Aldebaran had seemed to balance itself a moment on the ghostly spire.

There was an open space around the church; partly a churchyard with spectral shafts, and partly a half-paved square swept nearly bare of snow by the wind, and lined with unwholesomely archaic houses having peaked roofs and overhanging gables. Death-fires danced over the tombs, revealing gruesome vistas, though queerly failing to cast any shadows. Past the churchyard, where there were no houses, I could see over the hill's summit and watch the glimmer of stars on the harbour, though the town was invisible in the dark. Only once in a while a lanthorn bobbed horribly through serpentine alleys on its way to overtake the throng that was now slipping speechlessly into the church. I waited till the crowd had oozed into the black doorway, and till all the stragglers had followed. The old man was pulling at my sleeve, but I was determined to be the last. Crossing the threshold into the swarming temple of unknown darkness, I turned once to look at the outside world as the churchyard phosphorescence cast a sickly glow on the hilltop pavement. And as I did so I shuddered. For though the wind had not left much snow, a few patches did remain on the path near the door; and in that fleeting backward look it seemed to my troubled eyes that they bore no mark of passing feet, not even mine.

The church was scarce lighted by all the lanthorns that had entered it, for most of the throng had already vanished. They had streamed up the aisle between the high pews to the trap-door of the vaults which yawned loathsomely open just before the pulpit, and were now squirming noiselessly in. I followed dumbly down the footworn steps and into the dark, suffocating crypt. The tail of that sinuous line of night-marchers seemed very horrible, and as I saw them wriggling into a venerable tomb they seemed more horrible still. Then I noticed that the tomb's floor had an aperture down which the throng was sliding, and in a moment we were all descending an ominous staircase of rough-hewn stone; a narrow spiral staircase damp and peculiarly odorous, that wound endlessly down into the bowels of the hill past monotonous walls of dripping stone blocks and crumbling mortar. It was a silent, shocking descent, and I observed after a horrible interval that the walls and steps were changing in nature, as if chiselled out of the solid rock. What mainly troubled me was that the myriad footfalls made no sound and set up no echoes. After more aeons of descent I saw some side passages or burrows, leading from unknown recesses of blackness to this shaft of nighted mystery. Soon they became excessively numerous, like impious catacombs of nameless menace; and their pungent odour of decay grew quite unbearable. I knew we must have passed down through the mountain and beneath the earth of Kingsport itself, and I shivered that a town should be so aged and maggoty with subterraneous evil.

Then I saw the lurid shimmering of pale light, and heard the insidious lapping of sunless waters. Again I shivered, for I did not like the things that the night had brought, and wished bitterly that no forefather had summoned me to this primal rite. As the steps and the passage grew broader, I heard another sound, the thin, whining mockery of a feeble flute; and suddenly there spread out before me the boundless vista of an inner world – a vast fungous shore litten by a belching column of sick greenish flame and washed by a wide oily river that flowed from abysses frightful and unsuspected to join the blackest gulfs of immemorial ocean.

Fainting and gasping, I looked at that unhallowed Erebus of titan toadstools, leprous fire and slimy water, and saw the cloaked throngs forming a semicircle around the blazing pillar. It was the Yule-rite, older than man and fated to survive him; the primal rite of the solstice and of spring's promise beyond the snows; the rite of fire and evergreen, light and music. And in the stygian grotto I saw them do the rite, and adore the sick pillar of flame, and throw into the water handfuls gouged out of the viscous vegetation which glittered green in the chlorotic glare. I saw this, and I saw something amorphously squatted far away from the light, piping noisomely on a flute; and as the thing piped I thought I heard noxious muffled flutterings in the foetid darkness where I could not see. But what frightened me most was that flaming column; spouting volcanically from depths profound and inconceivable, casting no shadows as healthy flame should, and coating the nitrous stone with a nasty, venomous verdigris. For in all that seething combustion no warmth lay, but only the clamminess of death and corruption.

The man who had brought me now squirmed to a point directly beside the hideous flame, and made stiff ceremonial motions to the semi-circle he faced. At certain stages of the ritual they did grovelling obeisance, especially when he held above his head that abhorrent *Necronomicon* he had taken with him; and I shared all the obeisances because I had been summoned to this festival by the writings of my forefathers. Then the old man made a signal to the half-seen flute-player in the darkness, which player thereupon changed its feeble drone to a scarce louder drone in another key; precipitating as it did so a horror unthinkable and unexpected. At this horror I sank nearly to the lichened earth, transfixed with a dread not of this or any world, but only of the mad spaces between the stars.

Out of the unimaginable blackness beyond the gangrenous glare of that cold flame, out of the tartarean leagues through which that oily river rolled uncanny, unheard, and unsuspected, there flopped rhythmically a horde of tame, trained, hybrid winged things that no sound eye could ever wholly grasp, or sound brain ever wholly remember. They were not altogether cows, nor moles, nor buzzards, nor ants, nor vampire bats, nor decomposed human beings; but something I cannot and must not recall. They flopped limply along, half with their webbed feet and half with their membranous wings; and as they reached the throng of celebrants the cowled figures seized and mounted them, and rode off one by one along the reaches of that unlighted river, into pits and galleries of panic where poison springs feed frightful and undiscoverable cataracts.

The old spinning woman had gone with the throng, and the

old man remained only because I had refused when he motioned me to seize an animal and ride like the rest. I saw when I staggered to my feet that the amorphous flute-player had rolled out of sight, but that two of the beasts were patiently standing by. As I hung back, the old man produced his stylus and table and wrote that he was the true deputy of my fathers who had founded the Yule worship in this ancient place; that it had been decreed I should come back, and that the most secret mysteries were yet to be performed. He wrote this in a very ancient hand, and when I still hesitated he pulled from his loose robe a seal ring and a watch, both with my family arms, to prove that he was what he said. But it was a hideous proof, because I knew from old papers that that watch had been buried with my great-great-great-great grandfather in 1698.

Presently the old man drew back his hood and pointed to the family resemblance in his face, but I only shuddered, because I was sure that the face was merely a devilish waxen mask. The flopping animals were now scratching restlessly at the lichens, and I saw that the old man was nearly as restless himself. When one of the things began to waddle and edge away, he turned quickly to stop it; so that the suddenness of his motion dislodged the waxen mask from what should have been his head. And then, because that nightmare's position barred me from the stone staircase down which we had come, I flung myself into the oily underground river that bubbled somewhere to the caves of the sea; flung myself into that putrescent juice of earth's inner horrors before the madness of my screams could bring down upon me all the charnel legions these pest-gulfs might conceal.

At the hospital they told me I had been found half-frozen in Kingsport Harbour at dawn, clinging to the drifting spar that accident sent to save me. They told me I had taken the wrong fork of the hill road the night before, and fallen over the cliffs at Orange Point; a thing they deduced from prints found in the snow. There was nothing I could say, because everything was wrong. Everything was wrong, with the broad windows showing a sea of roofs in which only about one in five was ancient, and the sound of trolleys and motors in the street below. They insisted that this was Kingsport, and I could not deny it. When I went delirious at hearing that the hospital stood near the old churchyard on Central Hill, they sent me to St. Mary's Hospital in Arkham, where I could have better care. I liked it there, for the doctors were broad-minded and even lent me their influence in obtaining the carefully sheltered copy of Alhazred's objectionable *Necronomicon* from the library of Miskatonic University. They said something about a 'psychosis', and agreed I had better get any harassing obsessions off my mind.

So I read that hideous chapter, and shuddered doubly because it was indeed not new to me. I had seen it before, let footprints tell what they might; and where it was I had seen it were best forgotten. There was no one – in waking hours – who could remind me of it; but my dreams are filled with terror, because of phrases I dare not quote. I dare quote only one paragraph, put into such English as I can make from the awkward Low Latin.

'The nethermost caverns,' wrote the mad Arab, 'are not for the fathoming eyes that see; for their marvels are strange and terrific. Cursed the ground where dead thoughts live new and oddly bodied, and evil the mind that is held by no head. Wisely did Ibn Schacabao say, that happy is the tomb where no wizard hath lain, and happy the town at night whose wizards are all ashes. For it is old rumour that the soul of the devil-bought hastes not from his charnel clay, but fats and instructs *the very worm that gnaws*; till out of corruption horrid life springs, and the dull scavengers of earth wax crafty to vex it and swell monstrous to plague it. Great holes secretly are digged where earth's pores ought to suffice, and things have learnt to walk that ought to crawl.'

XI

Grimm's Ghost

Eden Phillpotts

Like H.P. Lovecraft, the English writer Eden Phillpotts (1862-1960) wrote stories about ancient mythologies and 'nameless things', although among his prodigious output of over 250 books are works on a whole variety of subjects from detective stories to historical romances, and from fantasy tales to novels of Devon life. Although born in India, Phillpotts came to London as a young man and first tried unsuccessfully to make a career on the stage. An equally fruitless period when he was working for an insurance company finally caused him to try his hand at writing and there followed a remarkable and productive career which stretched for almost sixty years until his death at the ripe old age of 98! Among Phillpotts' best books in the fantasy field must be counted the disaster story, The Owl of Athene *(1936), the werewolf tale,* Lycanthrope *(1937) and a couple of collections,* Loup-Garou *(1899) and* Fancy Free *(1901). My selection of a Christmas ghost tale comes from none of these works, however, but was hidden away in* It Happened Like That *published in 1927. With such a huge output, and with so many of his works now almost impossible to find, I constantly wonder what other fascinating tales of fantasy from the pen of Eden Phillpotts remain to be re-discovered ...*

When Johnny Hartland gave up his work and retired, it was very certain that he would not spend his last years out of sight of Beggar's Manor. Because, man and boy, he'd worked for the Marsdens over sixty years. Beggar's Manor woods and wild places were his home, you might say, and when his only remaining eye began to fail him, and rheumatics gripped hold to the marrow of his bones, and he was bent two-double with it and had to lay down his gun for a pair of stout walking-sticks, then his master broke the news that the old bird had got to stop; and they do say that both Johnny and Sir Frederick dropped a tear when the fatal news was out.

For never were two men nearer in friendship and regard than the master and his head gamekeeper. Johnny had served Sir Fred's father before him, and was what you might call an institution at Beggar's Manor; but his sense had always been equal to his pluck, and he knew very well what was coming six months before the blow fell.

'I ban't going out of sight of the woods, Sir Frederick, whether or no,' said John. 'This be the head keeper's house, and leave it I must; but to go far ways off be out of the question. I'm seventy-four, and but for this here bone-shave in the joints and my blindness and one thing and another, I could have worked a good bit yet, but I shall live, no doubt, so long as my father, who didn't drop afore his eighty-fifth birthday, and I ban't going to be exiled from your face for ten years, and 'tis no use you thinking I am.'

'No, Johnny, that you are not,' answered Sir Fred. 'You and me be far too good friends to part because you'm going to give up work and take your rest. You don't leave Beggar's Manor, and the only question is this – whether I build a new house for you anywhere about where you'd like it and where Mrs Hartland would be content, or if you'll let me repair 'Miser Grimm's.' I'll do whichever you please, but to my own view the house we call 'Miser Grimm's' do stand in such a snug corner of the woods, and also lies so handy for the village and the shops, that I'm all for putting it in good repair. There's only one objection, and that won't worry you, I reckon, though it may decide your missis.'

'And what be that, Sir Fred?' asks Johnny.

'Why, the folk say it's haunted, don't they? Old George Grimm is thought to show up every Christmas Eve, and though a man with your record wouldn't quail before a barrel load of misers' ghosts, I don't know what Mrs Hartland may feel about it.'

Johnny's remaining blue eye twinkled. He weren't a very tall man, but broad as a bear and very near as strong in his prime. His face was brown and his head was bald as a nut;

there was a green shade over his right eye-hole; his shoulders were round and his general build nowadays much like a dor-beetle, but his strength of mind weren't abated, nor yet the amazing courage that had gone to make his fame.

'As for ghosts, your honour,' he said, 'I set no store upon 'em, and if you've tackled the wicked flesh and blood I've been called to tackle, then 'tis little likely you'll be feared of shadows in human shape. A poacher's more to be minded than a wishtness, and as for Miser George, my grandfather knew him in life and told me many a tale about the man. He was close as wax and lived on shell-snails, and would even eat rat to save his pocket. His money was his god without a doubt, through my grandfather had no quarrel with him, and as to fearing the ghostey of the creature – no, and my wife have said a score of times that "Miser Grimm's" was a proper lew house and couldn't be beat. In fact, her heart bled to see the place going down the hill and falling into ruins.'

'Good!' says the master. 'It's yours, Johnny, and by the time you're ready for it the little place shall be ready for you and done up regardless.'

''Tis like your large heart, my dear,' answers Johnny. 'And if anything could temper me to give up, it will to know I'm there, at the edge of the woods and in sight of the Manor House and the work and the game. And I hope you'll get a man a patch on me for first keeper, though 'tis doubtful.'

So things fell out, and by the spring of the following year Grimm's had been made into a proper comely cottage, and a better no deserving man and his wife could have desired.

It stood just north of the big fir woods and new plantations, it had a beautiful cover of laurel and rhododendron behind it, and it faced the eye of the mid-day sun. The front was all made sound and painted with rosy-wash, and the thatch had been laid on fresh, so that the little house looked as if the roof was made of gold. There was a scrap of flower garden afore the porch and a nice half-acre, reclaimed from the woods, behind, and a well in the midst where sweet water might be drawn all the year round. And it wasn't above a mile to the village, neither – a distance that to a spry old gammer like Betty Hartland was nothing at all. A good few neighbours said that Johnny was mad not to have a new house when he might, for Miser Grimm's ghost was well known as a fact; indeed, more than one man, not given to lying, had seen it, owing to chance taking them that way on Christmas Eve; but Johnny chid the folk that thought him wrong. He pointed out that his new house stood in a wonderful sheltered spot, with all the blessings of civilisation but a mile distant, and what was more to him than that, he could see the chimneys of Beggar's Manor over the tree-tops. Also he well knew that not many a week would pass without Sir Fred's pony heaving in sight and his master come along to have a word with him. And Michael Marsden, Sir Frederick's son and heir, he was one of Johnny's heroes also, and though he never shot so straight as his father, he was Marsden all through, as John used to say, and stood to make a very understanding squire when his turn came.

Marsdens were famously rich all times, but their indifference on the subject of money, or their ignorance, it might have been, led to a bit of trouble about six months after Johnny had gone to 'Miser Grimm's,' and, as luck would have it, though nothing happened to make any lasting difference to the squire himself, poor old Hartland was hit terribly hard. Anybody but him would have thrown the blame where it belonged and made no bones about agreeing to Sir Frederick's proposal, which instantly followed the disaster; but Johnny wasn't that sort. He had his own ideas of honesty and they was stark and clean like himself, so when the trouble came he took it in his usual fashion and put Sir Fred in a very awkward fix.

Like this it was, and it comed out in conversation one day, when the Master rode up over to see John and break the bad news.

'John,' he said – of course in his own gentleman's language, not mine – 'do you mind how I put your savings in that new oil company started two year agone?'

'Very well indeed,' says Johnny, 'and I never tire of thinking on your cleverness Sir Frederick, and more don't my wife. One thousand pounds I put in, and for it they send me forty pound twice a year. 'Tis an amazing fine affair, no doubt, and we always buy our drop of oil from 'em. And I hope you get your thousands from it, I'm sure, my dear.'

'When I invested your money, John, I put in ten thousand of my own, and now I'm very sorry to say that the company's in Queer Street. In fact, the matter's gone before the courts – not the Bankruptcy Court, not yet; but I'm told there's not a gleam of hope and we must face the fact that the game's up.'

Hartland chewed and worked his hard old mouth and stared afore him. But it would have took more than the loss of his life's savings to shake his nerve.

'If it's gone, it's gone, master. You done your best and –'

'No, Johnny, I didn't. I ought to have known very well indeed that a new, untried industrial was no investment for a small man. It didn't matter to me – it was a rich man's speculation and all in the day's work – but I made a mistake when I put your thousand pounds into it. And now I'm going to take your shares and invest a thousand for you in something else. You'll get sixty pounds a year instead of eighty, John; but you'll have no more trouble and no more accidents.'

Hartland smiled and shook his head.

'Just like you to offer that, Sir Frederick; but I hope it wouldn't be like me to take it. You meant to do me a good turn, but you couldn't tell there was a screw loose. 'Tis just the fortunes of war, and if you can lose your money, I can make shift to lose mine.'

Squire laughed at that and told John he mustn't talk nonsense; but he very soon found the old boy meant it. Nothing on earth t'other could say or threaten would change him. He reckoned he'd had enough from his master, and he was the faithful, out-of-date sort, who used to go deeper than money in their relations with their employer. He wouldn't budge and said he should stand up to his loss as well as another and live on his pension very clever. Eighty pounds a year meant about a third of his total income, I believe; but he held to it that him and his wife would want not a penny more. And finally he got crusty and swore he wouldn't take another farthing from Sir Frederick, and what Johnny swore to he stuck to.

So the master gave up driving at him for the time being, and went away full of admiration at the old keeper's obstinate sense of justice – and full of annoyance also. He saw it was going to be difficult to get his thousand pounds back to Hartland, and, not being a very clever man, he guessed that he would have to get help in such a delicate matter. And he judged that, so like as not, Johnny's wife might be a tower of strength, because he knew her very well also, and he felt pretty sure she wouldn't take such a high and mighty line about it as her husband. And he was right, for Mrs Hartland opposed John very steadfast from the first, and said he must be a crack-brained loon to suppose they could live the same as they was living now – like a duke and duchess, and not a care, and everything paid for on the nail – if they was going to lose the interest of his lifetime savings. Nor did it trouble Betty over much when he told her that the master stood to lose ten thousand.

'That's his affair,' she said. 'And ten thousand's nought to him. He's a just man, of course, he sees with half an eye that it's up to him to make good what he's lost of yours; and if he couldn't do it without hurting himself, I'd say nothing. But a thousand's a flea-bite to Sir Frederick; and, what's more, it will be a piece of darned impertinence on your part if you refuse to do what he wishes.'

However, Johnny didn't see it so and, for the first time in their lives, that couple had a bit of a jar. Of course Betty meant to get in the last word, but she knew it wouldn't be with her husband. So she left him in peace, after a week of argument, and turned her attention elsewhere. She was very sorry indeed to take sides against Johnny – a thing she'd never thought that life would call upon her to do; but savings be savings, and you couldn't expect her to relinquish the united toil and stint of fifty years just because the ancient man had got it into his head he couldn't in honour receive it back.

The battle began from that hour and it went on for six months, and Johnny won all along the line, for Sir Fred and Betty between 'em weren't clever enough to get round the dogged old blade. They tried all sorts of plans – some cunning, some simple; but John was up to every trick, and even when the squire came again and had a proper famous row with Hartland and pretended to be bursting with rage, 'twas all thrown away, for Johnny saw through it.

With autumn the case seemed lost altogether, and Betty had given up hope and got very snappy and tried to break her husband's will by keeping him short of tobacco.

Then Mr Michael Marsden was down at Beggar's Manor

for the pheasants, and he'd often drop into 'Miser Grimm's' for a chat with Johnny. The old keeper had two great stories: how he'd lost his right eye in a shooting accident, and how his grandfather had known George Grimm and seen his ghost the Christmas after he died; and he told these tales so well that the house-party often dropped in – a few at a time – to hear them.

John delighted to tell how, out shooting, a reckless lad had peppered him.

'Suddenly I felt a bitter pang in my face,' he explained, 'and I clapped my hand to my cheek, and, by gor! there was my poor eye running down my face like a poached egg!'

Johnny could always trust his simile for a sensation and a shiver.

As to his grandfather and Miser Grimm, the tales varied somewhat, but the description of the miser was always the same.

''Twas in the lane, but a stone's throw from this here house, that he saw the man's spirit so large as life,' Johnny declared. 'Christmas Eve was the time and grandfather happed to be going up to Beggar's Manor with a message to squire – Squire Frederick's father as was – from parson. Because my grandfather was vicar's warden at the time, and his reverence wanted to know if squire was wishful to have the stove lit in church o' Christmas morning – it being one of they old-fashioned, snowy seasons, as Nature have lost the trick of nowadays. But there he was – George Grimm – beside a five-barred gate, in a long grey garment like a winding-sheet, with his famous white beard hanging afore him and his white go-to-meeting beaver on his head. And he was looking towards his old house and didn't 'pear to see grandfather. But my old man didn't know fear, and he shouts out to the wishtness, and he says: "God's goodness, George, what be you doing out of your grave on this holy night?" And the miser, he turns and gives grandfather a look out of his ghost's eyes – and just shakes his head and passes on to his old home without a word. And grandfather – a very kindly man – shouts after him: "Well, God be with you, George Grimm, and a Merry Christmas wherever you be called to spend it!" '

Johnny told this story on an occasion when Mr Michael

came with others, and a few half-crowns appeared at the finish.

'Was it ever seen again, John?' asked Michael Marsden.

''Twas rumoured to be seen again three years later on Christmas Eve,' answered the old keeper; 'but the man who saw it that time was a drinker, and I have my doubts. Charles Scobhull saw it, however, but two years agone, and his word's good.'

'Perhaps you'll see it, Johnny.'

'So my wife says.'

'You wouldn't be frightened?'

'Frightened, Mr Michael? Why for? I'd be very glad to have a tell with the creature, if he's still a wanderer and have got the use of his tongue. For I've seen and spoke with most living things as go on two feet, or four for that matter, but a spectrum, no. 'Twould be a great adventure.'

'You must keep your weather eye lifting on Christmas Eve, Johnny,' said young Marsden, and Johnny promised to do so.

'If the poor soul had parts to take a drink, or blow a cloud, I'd be very pleased to befriend him with glass and pipe,' he said. 'But I ban't hopeful that he'll show up to a man like me, and I'd much sooner think of him safe in Abraham's bosom than messing about round here. Grandfather always said he weren't a bad man, and perfectly honest in his dealings, only cruel close-fisted and a lot too fond of his beastly money.'

'What became of it, Mr Hartland?' asked a listener.

'It went to a nephew, master, and he married on the strength of it, but didn't have no luck with his wife.'

Then Betty spoke. She had produced some famous sloe gin of her own making.

''Tis said that a good few thought as all his savings never saw light. The people poked about this place a lot after he was took, and dug over the garden also, but they never found a halfpenny.'

Thus talked Johnny when any would listen, and often he hobbled out to watch sport also. The autumn passed; he continued obdurate concerning his savings, and his old master had abandoned the subject when Christmas came again, and with it the usual cheerful company at Beggar's Manor.

A week before Christmas half a dozen men dropped into

Miser Grimm's for a cup of tea after shooting, and Johnny told his two stories once more and reaped a harvest of half-crowns.

And then came Christmas Eve, and Betty sat with John on a dark and moonless night, while the west wind shouted over the woods, and from far away, fitfully borne home, there fell a cry of singing men and women.

Mrs Hartland was nervous and had been so since darkness fell.

'What's that?' she cried, clutching her husband's arm, as the eight-day clock struck eleven.

'The Christmas waits up over at the House,' he answered. 'The wind fetches their carols across the woods. There's a good rally of neighbours gone up, and there'll be some pretty drinking afterwards, no doubt.'

'Let's be off to bed then. 'Tis long past the time and you've had your nightcap.'

But for answer Johnny pulled up the blind and showed a glimpse of the black and blusterous night through his latticed window.

'Not till twelve have struck,' he answered. ''Tis the appointed hour for ghosteys, and I'm very wishful, for my own sake, that George Grimm's shadow will blow along out of the churchyard, because I dearly like to get a fine new tale to tell the people. I'll give him till half after midnight; but if you'd rather not be a party to it and don't want to see him, you'd best to go.'

'Sitting up for a ghost!' yowled Betty, with her eyes glazing out of her head. 'You'm mad! The creature will do 'e a mischief so like as not.'

'Fear nothing. I've sat up for a lot worse than him, and come out with nought worse than a broken nose and a few bruises,' he answered. 'These here spectrums, you must know, be little more than shadows at best; and if you face 'em with a clean conscience in the Lord's name, they can't hurt a hair of your whiskers!'

Well, Betty prayed the man for half an hour, if only for her sake, to turn it up and pull down the blind and come to bed; but he rebuked her fear and axed the old woman where was her faith. Then she wept and, dreading every moment what might look in the window, lighted her chamber cannel and went off. He heard her up over, stumping about and hurrying into bed, and he laughed; but he didn't laugh long, for not ten minutes later – just when his old clock was creaking and clearing its throat afore it sounded the midnight hour – if he didn't hear a hand tapping at the casement. And he jumped up from his peat fire and looked round, and there was the phantom miser peering in the window!

John, he just gave a gasp and went to the lattice and threw it open. Then, as he never tired of telling after, the vision stared hollow-eyed upon him, and the old keeper spoke.

'I'm proper proud to see you, Mr Grimm,' he said, 'and I do hope you'll walk in your old house and have a tell.'

The ghost was grey all over, as if he'd been wrapped in cobweb, and his white beard flowed out upon his chest and his white beaver was perched upon his head. He looked at John and answered in a very slow, rumbly sort of a voice. He weren't vexed about nothing in particular, but he appeared dreadful tired.

'I would speak with you, John Hartland,' he said, and Johnny told him he'd like nothing better.

'I'll ope the door for 'e, Grimm,' he answered, and the wishtness came round and very soon stole within the house.

'Put out your lamp,' was his first command. 'Light does not suit me, John. The fire will be enough.'

'Have 'e got a sit-down, my dear?' asked John doubtfully, 'because, if so, there's my dog-eared chair as you'm welcome to; but I suppose it ain't no manner of use axing you to join me in a drop of Hollands and a yard of clay?'

Well, the spectrum evidently had the power of sitting, for he took John's chair and even spread out his long white hands to the fire. The red light played fitfully over him and 'peared to streak his cobwebs with blood; but Hartland always said after that he weren't particular awful, but only rather depressing and low-spirited.

'He was a melancholy object, with hollow eyes and a face so white as curds,' Johnny admitted, 'and a mouse wouldn't have feared him, but you couldn't help being a bit sorry for the poor toad.'

However, 'twas beyond Miser Grimm's power to take

refreshment, it seemed.

'Such good things are not for me,' he said in his tired voice when Johnny offered to pour out a drop of liquor. 'My drinking days are done, John Hartland; and as for a pipe of Virginny and a "church-warden," they be delights I can never expect where I am now.'

'And where might that be, George Grimm, if it ain't a rude question?' axed Johnny.

'In the Middle Place,' answered the grey creature.

'Can you catch heat from the fire, my dear?'

'No,' answered Grimm's ghost. 'Heat and cold are all alike to me. I only stretch out my hands from force of habit.'

'If I can serve 'e in any way, or buck you up, I shall be exceeding pleased so to do,' declared Hartland.

'On the contrary,' answered the ghost, 'I be come to serve *you.* On Christmas Eve, for a brief hour or two, I am permitted to revisit these scenes of my earthly pilgrimage and given an opportunity to do the living a good turn. Alas, John, I did my neighbours not many a good turn in life. But it is even now not too late, and once I have been able to benefit a human being, then I shall be translated from the Middle Place to something better. You understand? For many years now I have sought this opportunity on Christmas Eve, but my range and hours of operations were alike limited, and until the present anniversary I have never had a real chance. Now it has come, and I wish nothing better than to advance your welfare, because your grandfather, Gregory Hartland, was an old friend of mine. Not only did he treat me well in life, but also wished me a 'Merry Christmas' after death. And I have not forgotten it.'

'He always owned you was too fond of the dibs, my dear, but he never had no other quarrel with you,' answered Johnny.

'Yes,' replied the spectrum. 'I was too fond of the dibs, as you say; but let us forget that. There's no dibs where I am now. But it happens that a precious part of my treasure was never recovered. When my time came I popped off sudden, *and nobody ever heard where I put my Sheffield plate!* For that matter, nobody knew I'd got any. But at last the chance offers to tell a living man, and I'm going to make over the famous stuff to you and your wife, John Hartland – lock, stock and barrel!'

Well, Johnny was almost too astonished to say anything. He just stared, and the ghost, who seemed pretty near tired of talking, shut his eyes and heaved a sigh.

'Such things as Sheffield plate be less than the dust under your feet where I am now,' he went on, 'but my collection was worth a tidy figure even in my own life, and I dare say to-day, owing to the passion the rich have got for everything old, it may be worth a long sight more than ever I paid for it. But 'tis yours, John, and I'm very glad indeed that it should be yours.'

'Like your gracious goodness, I'm sure, and a properly kind thing to do, and I hope you'll be rewarded by Higher Hands,' answered Johnny. 'And if I can ever return such handsome treatment, both me and my wife would be properly pleased to do so.'

'Gratitude is welcome, even to a spirit,' answered the wishtness. 'And it only remains for me to tell you where you shall find the treasure. There stands a great spruce at the corner of the Northern Plantation, where the river Glazebrook runs. 'Tis a solitary tree in a clearing surrounded by silver birches and fern. Measure ten clear yards due north from the base of the trunk, Mr Hartland, then dig four feet into the earth and reap your reward.'

'I know the tree so well as I know my own hand,' answered Johnny, 'and I take your ghostly word that this be all right and honest and above-board; and if you'd like for me to spend a five-pound note in having your tombstone freshed up and your name cut a bit deeper in the slate, it shall be done, my dear.'

The spectrum considered, then he shook his head.

'No, better leave it alone,' he said. 'I'm not wishful for any advertisement to my bones. The churchyard's a scandal anyhow, though we unremembered people don't sleep none the worse for the docks and darnel 'pon top of us.'

'Shall you be coming around this way again next Christmas, George?' asked Johnny, and the shadow shook his head once more.

'No,' he answered. 'My work's done in Devonshire now, and I'm hopeful as it won't be needful for me to walk again. One thing you may do, however. You can pray for me sometimes when you be at your prayers.'

Johnny weren't sure, however.

'It have always been against my principles to pray prayers for dead folk,' he said, 'because they are in the Hands of their Maker and beyond our reach. But I'll stretch a point and beg the Lord in His good time to let you win your eternal crown. Then you'll be able to leave off thickly old beaver, no doubt.'

After that the ghost rose up and prepared to depart.

'I don't mind the owls hooting,' he said, 'but I mustn't hear no cock crow, for 'tis a sound as do always make a spirit feel queer. You mind what I've told you. Ten yards to the north of that great spruce beside Glazebrook, where it runs out under the hanger.'

Johnny offered for to shake hands, but the grey thing couldn't or wouldn't. It just heaved a sigh and walked quietly out of the room; and Hartland wished him a grateful good-night and watched the poor soul slink away into the darkness, and then put home the door. After that he lighted his lamp again, drank an extra drop of spirits, to the eternal salvation of Grimm's ghost, and went up to tell Betty the gay news. She was sound asleep, or so he thought, but he waked her up and told his amazing tale; and she refused to believe a single word of it and told him he was smelling of Hollands something shocking, and would bring her white hair with sorrow to the grave yet.

But day brought the wondrous news that Miser Grimm's ghost was a plain dealer. Every word he'd said came out true, and before he'd ate his Christmas dinner, Johnny proved it. He went with his spade and barrow, and Betty went with him, and they found the exact spot and took turns digging through the fine leaf mould of the forest. Presently Betty struck on a lot of mouldering wood, and then Johnny took the spade and got to the treasure. A proper dollop of teapots and sugar-basins and cannel-sticks and trinkrums was down under, and though a bit shabby to the eye, Mrs Hartland, who understood 'em, said 'twas true Sheffield plate without a doubt!

But John gave her the shock of her life and said he weren't by no means certain whether he'd got any right to the stuff after all.

'God's goodness!' cried Betty, 'what will you say next? Here's a ghostey comes clean out of his grave to give you a gift and you talk this rummage and nonsense. The stuff was Miser

Grimm's and never belonged to nobody else but him, and he's given it to you, and if you part with a snuff-box to squire, or anybody else, so like as not the phantom will get wicked and haunt you in season and out to your dying day.'

'Master shall decide,' her husband answered. 'He's famed for his Sheffield plate, as we all know, and he may feel that we have no right to say what was dug out of his ground belongs to any man but him.'

Then Betty breathed again, because she knew a darned sight more about Grimm's ghost than half-blind old John, for all she'd never seen it. In truth, she'd heard and helped in the plot three months afore, when Sir Frederick had at last discovered how to get back on Johnny. And though he'd had to buy more than a thousand pounds' worth of Sheffield plate to do it, that was of no account to him and only meant adding more to his collection.

'Let Sir Fred decide, I ax nothing fairer,' agreed Betty with her husband. And his master declared there weren't no question whatever about the ownership of the treasure.

''Tis all yours, beyond any shadow of doubt,' spoke he. 'But this I will beg, Johnny. I'll ask you to let me have first refusal of the lot, because I set store by such things. They must be valued in open market. They are very fine pieces indeed I may tell you, and I shall be properly delighted to take 'em off your hands, if you and your missis have got no use for them.'

Everybody at Beggar's Manor came to see the plate next day – everybody but one guest, a friend of Mr Michael's, a play-actor. But he gived Johnny a wide berth and there was a very good reason why he should.

Twelve hundred pounds the old man made by that silver plate, and he loved telling the tale far better than getting the money; and though it fretted his wife something cruel that she should have lived to keep a secret from him, she managed to do so, and he died full of years, but never learned the trick.

'I'm feared of my life he'll make it hot for me when us meet again where no secrets be hid,' Betty would often say to her friends; and when her turn came to go under the daisies she was a lot more put about as to what Johnny had got brewing for her than what her Maker had.

XII

The Christmas Ghost

Stephen Leacock

As we (figuratively speaking) sit around our Christmas fireplace enjoying these seasonal ghost stories, I think it is time for another change of style. After three such grim tales, it is surely the moment for a little light relief – and who better to serve it up than the splendid Canadian humorist, Stephen Leacock (1869-1944). My admiration for this University lecturer on Economics who in his spare time wrote some of the funniest essays and parodies you can find anywhere, is well known – and here once again is a contribution which bears the unique hallmark of his work: taking a long-established tradition and turning it uproariously on its head. Leacock was, of course, a great admirer of Charles Dickens (he wrote a biography of the great Englishman in 1933) and was naturally also interested in the ghost story tradition that Dickens founded. He tackled the theme in 'The Christmas Ghost' which he sub-titled, 'Unemployment in one of our Oldest Industries'. It appeared in one of his lesser-known collections, Winnowed Wisdom, *published in 1926, and I am glad to be returning it to print here. I am sure the reader will be equally glad, too, when he has read it!*

The other night I was sitting up late – away after nine o'clock – thinking about Christmas because it was getting near at hand. And, like everybody else who muses on that subject, I was thinking of the great changes that have taken place in regard to Christmas. I was contrasting Christmas in the old country house of a century ago, with the fires roaring up the chimneys, and Christmas in the modern apartment on the ninth floor with the gasolene generator turned on for the maid's bath.

I was thinking of the old stage coach on the snowy road with its roof piled high with Christmas turkeys and a rosy-faced 'guard' blowing on a key-bugle and the passengers getting down every mile or so at a crooked inn to drink hot spiced ale – and I was comparing all that with the upper berth No. 6, car 220, train No. 53.

I was thinking of the Christmas landscape of long ago when night settled down upon it with the twinkle of light from the houses miles apart among the spruce trees, and contrasting the scene with the glare of motor lights upon the highway of to-day. I was thinking of the lonely highwayman shivering round with his clumsy pistols, and comparing the poor fellow's efforts with the high-class bandits of to-day blowing up a steel express car with nitro-glycerine and disappearing in a roar of gasolene explosions.

In other words, I was contrasting yesterday and to-day. And on the whole yesterday seemed all to the good.

Nor was it only the warmth and romance and snugness of the old Christmas that seemed superior to our days, but Christmas carried with it then a special kind of thrill with its queer terrors, its empty heaths, its lonely graveyards, and its house that stood alone in a wood, haunted.

And thinking of that it occurred to me how completely the ghost business seems to be dying out of our Christmas literature. Not so very long ago there couldn't be a decent Christmas story or Christmas adventure without a ghost in it, whereas nowadays –

And just at that moment I looked and saw that there was a ghost in the room.

I can't imagine how he got in, but there he was, sitting in the other easy chair in the dark corner away from the firelight. He had on my own dressing-gown and one saw but little of his face.

'Are you a ghost?' I asked.

'Yes,' he said, 'worse luck, I am.'

I noticed as he spoke that he seemed to wave and shiver as if he were made of smoke. I couldn't help but pity the poor fellow, he seemed so immaterial.

'Do you mind,' he went on in the same dejected tone, 'if I sit here and haunt you for a while?'

'By all means,' I said, 'please do.'

'Thanks,' he answered, 'I haven't had anything decent to work on for years and years. This is Christmas Eve, isn't it?'

'Yes,' I said, 'Christmas Eve.'

'Used to be my busiest night,' the ghost complained, 'best night of the whole year – and now – say,' he said, 'would you believe it! I went down this evening to that dinner-dance they have at the Ritz-Carlton and I thought I'd haunt it – thought I'd stand behind one of the tables as a silent spectre, the way I used to in King George III's time –'

'Well?' I said.

'They put me out!' groaned the ghost. 'The head waiter came up to me and said they didn't allow silent spectres in the dining-room. I was put out.'

He groaned again.

'You seem,' I said, 'rather down on your luck?'

'Can you wonder?' said the ghost, and another shiver rippled up and down him. 'I can't get anything to do. Talk of the unemployed – listen!' he went on, speaking with something like animation, 'let me tell you the story of my life –'

'Can you make it short?' I said.

'I'll try. A hundred years ago –'

'Oh, I say!' I protested.

'I committed a terrible crime, a murder on the highway –'

'You'd get six months for that nowadays,' I said.

'I was never detected. An innocent man was hanged. I died, but I couldn't rest. I haunted the house beside the highway where the murder had been done. It had happened on Christmas Eve and so, every year on that night –'

'I know,' I interrupted, 'you were heard dragging round a chain and moaning and that sort of thing; I've often read about it.'

'Precisely,' said the ghost, 'and for about eighty years it worked out admirably. People became afraid, the house was deserted, trees and shrubs grew thick around it, the wind whistled through its empty chimneys and its broken windows, and at night the lonely wayfarer went shuddering past and heard with terror the sound of a cry scarce human, while a cold sweat –'

'Quite so,' I said, 'a cold sweat. And what next?'

'The days of the motor-car came and they paved the highway and knocked down the house and built a big garage there, with electricity as bright as day. You can't haunt a garage, can you? I tried to stick on and do a little groaning, but nobody seemed to pay any attention; and anyway, I got nervous about the gasolene. I'm too immaterial to be round where there's gasolene. A fellow would blow up, wouldn't he?'

'He might,' I said, 'so what happened?'

'Well, one day somebody in the garage actually *saw* me and he threw a monkey wrench at me and told me to get to hell out of that garage. So I went.'

'And after that?'

'I haunted round; I've kept on haunting round, but it's no good, there's nothing in it. Houses, hotels, I've tried it all. Once I thought that if I couldn't make a hit any other way, at least I could haunt children. You remember how little children used to live in terror of ghosts and see them in the dark corners of their bedrooms? Well, I admit it was a low-down thing to do, but I tried that.'

'And it didn't work?'

'Work! I should say not. I went one night to a bedroom where a couple of little boys were sleeping and I started in with a few groans and then half materialized myself, so that I could just be seen. One of the kids sat up in bed and nudged the other and said, "Say! I do believe there's a ghost in the room!" And the other said, "Hold on; don't scare him. Let's get the radio set and see if it'll go right through him."

'They both hopped out of bed as brisk as bees and one called downstairs, "Dad, we've got a ghost up here! We don't know whether he's just an emanation or partially material. We're going to stick radio into him –" Believe me,' continued the ghost, 'that was all I waited to hear. Electricity just knocks me edgeways.'

He shuddered. Then he went on.

'Well, it's been like that ever since – nowhere to go and nothing to haunt. I've tried all the big hotels, railways stations, everywhere. Once I tried to haunt a Pullman car, but I had hardly started before I observed a notice, "*Quiet is requested for those already retired*," and I had to quit.'

'Well, then,' I said, 'why don't you just get immaterial or dematerial or whatever you call it, and keep so? Why not go away wherever you belong and stay there?'

'That's the worst of it,' answered the ghost, 'they won't let us. They haul us back. These spiritualists have learned the trick of it and they just summon us up any time they like. They get half-a-crown apiece for each materialization, but what do *we* get?'

The ghost paused, and a sort of spasm went all through him. 'Gol darn it!' he exclaimed, 'they're at me now. There's a group of fools somewhere sitting round a table at a Christmas Eve party and they're calling up a ghost just for fun – a darned poor notion of fun, I call it – I'd like to – like to –'

But his voice trailed off. He seemed to collapse as he sat and my dressing-gown fell to the floor. And at that moment I heard the ringing of the bells that meant it was Christmas Eve midnight, and I knew that the poor fellow had been dragged off to work.

XIII

The Story of a Disappearance and an Appearance

M.R. James

It is a satisfying feeling in a collection such as this to follow one of my favourite writers with another, Montague Rhodes James (1862-1936), who is justifiably regarded as the finest ghost story writer of the twentieth century. M.R. James was, of course, a man of scholarly inclinations (being Provost of King's College, Cambridge and later Provost of Eton), and devoted much of his spare time to antiquarian studies. Yet the supernatural likewise fascinated him, and although he wrote just three dozen ghost stories, they are each and every one superior examples of their kind and remain very popular to this day. It is interesting to note that James – in the tradition of Dickens – first began writing these stories when he was at King's College with the express purpose of reading them to friends at Christmas. The first such was 'Canon Alberic's Scrapbook' (1894) which demonstrated both his knowledge of the supernatural and of old books and manuscripts. Such was its reception among his friends, as well as their demand for more, that James found himself repeating the task each Christmas. Eventually, all the tales found their way into the various collections such as Ghost Stories of an Antiquary *(1904) and* A Thin Ghost And Others *(1919) from which my selection is made. Another interesting fact to note about James is that his stories have, in turn, become something of a tradition of their own at Christmas – for each Christmas Eve for the past decade one or other of them has been adapted for radio or television as a suitably chilling prelude to the festive season. Producers of such programmes might like to note that the following story has not yet been so treated …*

The letters which I now publish were sent to me recently by a person who knows me to be interested in ghost stories. There is no doubt about their authenticity. The paper on which they are written, the ink, and the whole external aspect put their date beyond the reach of question.

The only point which they do not make clear is the identity of the writer. He signs with initials only, and as none of the envelopes of the letters are preserved, the surname of his correspondent – obviously a married brother – is as obscure as his own. No further preliminary explanation is needed, I think. Luckily the first letter supplies all that could be expected.

Letter I

Great Chrishall, *Dec*. 22, 1837.

My Dear Robert, – It is with great regret for the enjoyment I am losing, and for a reason which you will deplore equally with myself, that I write to inform you that I am unable to join your circle for this Christmas: but you will agree with me that it is unavoidable when I say that I have within these few hours received a letter from Mrs Hunt at B—, to the effect that our Uncle Henry has suddenly and mysteriously disappeared, and begging me to go down there immediately and join the search that is being made for him. Little as I, or you either, I think, have ever seen of Uncle, I naturally feel that this is not a request that can be regarded lightly, and accordingly I propose to go to B— by this afternoon's mail, reaching it late in the evening. I shall not go to the Rectory, but put up at the King's Head, and to which you may address letters. I enclose a small draft, which you will please make use of for the benefit of the young people. I shall write you daily (supposing me to be detained more than a single day) what goes on, and you may be sure, should the business be cleared up in time to permit of my coming to the Manor after all, I shall present myself. I have but a few minutes at disposal. With cordial greetings to you all, and many regrets, believe me, your affectionate Bro.,

W.R.

Letter II

King's Head, *Dec.* 23, '37.

My Dear Robert, – In the first place, there is as yet no news of Uncle H., and I think you may finally dismiss any idea – I won't say hope – that I might after all 'turn up' for Xmas. However, my thoughts will be with you, and you have my best wishes for a really festive day. Mind that none of my nephews or nieces expend any fraction of their guineas on presents for me.

Since I got here I have been blaming myself for taking this affair of Uncle H. too easily. From what people here say, I gather that there is very little hope that he can still be alive; but whether it is accident or design that carried him off I cannot judge. The facts are these. On Friday the 19th, he went as usual shortly before five o'clock to read evening prayers at the Church; and when they were over the clerk brought him a message, in response to which he set off to pay a visit to a sick person at an outlying cottage the better part of two miles away. He paid the visit, and started on his return journey at about half-past six. This is the last that is known of him. The people here are very much grieved at his loss; he had been here many years, as you know, and though, as you also know, he was not the most genial of men, and had more than a little of the *martinet* in his composition, he seems to have been active in good works, and unsparing of trouble to himself.

Poor Mrs Hunt, who has been his housekeeper ever since she left Woodley, is quite overcome: it seems like the end of the world to her. I am glad that I did not entertain the idea of taking quarters at the Rectory; and I have declined several kindly offers of hospitality from people in the place, preferring as I do to be independent, and finding myself very comfortable here.

You will, of course, wish to know what has been done in the way of inquiry and search. First, nothing was to be expected from investigation at the Rectory; and to be brief, nothing has transpired. I asked Mrs Hunt – as others had done before – whether there was either any unfavourable symptom in her master such as might portend a sudden stroke, or attack of illness, or whether he had ever had reason to apprehend any such thing: but both she, and also his medical man, were clear that this was not the case. He was quite in his usual health. In the second place, naturally, ponds and streams have been dragged, and fields in the neighbourhood which he is known to have visited last, have been searched – without result. I have myself talked to the parish clerk and – more important – have been to the house where he paid his visit.

There can be no question of any foul play on these people's part. The one man in the house is ill in bed and very weak: the wife and the children of course could do nothing themselves, nor is there the shadow of a probability that they or any of them should have agreed to decoy poor Uncle H. out in order that he might be attacked on the way back. They had told what they knew to several other inquirers already, but the woman repeated it to me. The Rector was looking just as usual: he wasn't very long with the sick man – 'He ain't,' she said, 'like some what has a gift in prayer; but there, if we was all that way, 'owever would the chapel people get their living?' He left some money when he went away, and one of the children saw him cross the stile into the next field. He was dressed as he always was: wore his bands – I gather he is nearly the last man remaining who does so – at any rate in this district.

You see I am putting down everything. The fact is that I have nothing else to do, having brought no business papers with me; and, moreover, it serves to clear my own mind, and may suggest points which have been overlooked. So I shall continue to write all that passes, even to conversation if need be – you may read or not as you please, but pray keep the letters. I have another reason for writing so fully, but it is not a very tangible one.

You may ask if I have myself made any search in the fields near the cottage. Something – a good deal – has been done by others, as I mentioned; but I hope to go over the ground to-morrow. Bow Street has now been informed, and will send down by to-night's coach, but I do not think they will make much of the job. There is no snow, which might have helped us. The fields are all grass. Of course I was on the *qui vive* for any indication to-day both going and returning; but there was a thick mist on the way back, and I was not in trim for wandering about unknown pastures, especially on an evening when bushes looked like men, and a cow lowing in the distance might have been the last trump. I assure you, if Uncle Henry had stepped out from among the trees in a little copse which borders the path at one place, carrying his head under his arm, I should have been very little more uncomfortable than I was. To tell you the truth, I was rather expecting something of the kind. But I must drop my pen for the moment: Mr Lucas, the curate, is announced.

Later. Mr Lucas has been, and gone, and there is not much beyond the decencies of ordinary sentiment to be got from him. I can see that he has given up any idea that the Rector can be alive, and that, so far as he can be, he is truly sorry. I can also discern that even in a more emotional person than Mr Lucas, Uncle Henry was not likely to inspire strong attachment.

Besides Mr Lucas, I have had another visitor in the shape of my Boniface – mine host of the 'King's Head' – who came to see whether I had everything I wished, and who really requires the pen of a Boz to do him justice. He was very solemn and weighty at first. 'Well, sir,' he said, 'I suppose we must bow our 'ead beneath the blow, as my poor wife had used to say. So far as I can gather there been neither hide nor yet hair of our late respected incumbent scented out as yet; not that he was what the Scripture terms a hairy man in any sense of the word.'

I said – as well as I could – that I supposed not, but could not help adding that I had heard he was sometimes a little difficult to deal with. Mr Bowman looked at me sharply for a moment, and then passed in a flash from solemn sympathy to impassioned declamation. 'When I think,' he said, 'of the language that man see fit to employ to me in this here parlour over no more a matter than a cask of beer – such a thing as I told him might happen any day of the week to a man with a family – though as it turned out he was quite under a mistake, and that I knew at the time, only I was that shocked to hear him I couldn't lay my tongue to the right expression.'

He stopped abruptly and eyed me with some embarrassment. I only said, 'Dear me, I'm sorry to hear you had any little differences: I suppose my uncle will be a good deal missed in the parish?' Mr. Bowman drew a long breath. 'Ah, yes!' he said; 'your uncle! You'll understand me when I say that for the moment it had slipped my remembrance that he was a relative; and natural enough, I must say, as it should, for as to you bearing any resemblance to – to him, the notion of any such a thing is clean ridiculous. All the same, 'ad I 'ave bore it in my mind, you'll be among the first to feel, I'm sure, as I should have abstained my lips, or rather I should *not* have abstained my lips with no such reflections.'

I assured him that I quite understood, and was going to have asked him some further questions, but he was called away to see after some business. By the way, you need not take it into your head that he has anything to fear from the inquiry into poor Uncle Henry's disappearance – though, no doubt, in the watches of the night it will occur to him that *I* think he has, and I may expect explanations tomorrow.

I must close this letter: it has to go by the late coach.

Letter III

Dec. 25, '37.

My Dear Robert, – This is a curious letter to be writing on Christmas Day, and yet after all there is nothing much in it. Or there may be – you shall be the judge. At least, nothing decisive. The Bow Street men practically say that they have no clue. The length of time and the weather conditions have made all tracks so faint as to be quite useless: nothing that belonged to the dead man – I'm afraid no other word will do – has been picked up.

As I expected, Mr Bowman was uneasy in his mind this morning; quite early I heard him holding forth in a very distinct voice – purposely so, I thought – to the Bow Street officers in the bar, as to the loss that the town had sustained in their Rector, and as to the necessity of leaving no stone unturned (he was very great on this phrase) in order to come at the truth. I suspect him of being an orator of repute at convivial meetings.

When I was at breakfast he came to wait on me, and took an opportunity when handing a muffin to say in a low tone, 'I 'ope, sir, you reconize as my feelings towards your relative is not actuated by any taint of what you may call melignity – you can leave the room, Eliza, I will see the gentleman 'as all he requires with my own hands – I ask your pardon, sir, but you must be well aware a man is not always master of himself: and when that man has been 'urt in his mind by the application of expressions which I will go so far as to say 'ad not ought to have been made use of (his voice was rising all this time and his face growing redder); no, sir; and 'ere, if you will permit of it, I should like to explain to you in a very few words the exact state of the bone of contention. This cask – I might more truly call it a firkin – of beer –'

I felt it was time to interpose, and said that I did not see that it would help us very much to go into that matter in detail. Mr Bowman acquiesced, and resumed more calmly:

'Well, sir, I bow to your ruling, and as you say, be that here or be it there, it don't contribute a great deal, perhaps, to the present question. All I wish you to understand is that I am prepared as you are yourself to lend every hand to the business we have afore us, and – as I took the opportunity to say as much to the Orficers not three-quarters of an hour ago – to leave no stone unturned as may throw even a spark of light on this painful matter.'

In fact, Mr Bowman did accompany us on our exploration, but though I am sure his genuine wish was to be helpful, I am afraid he did not contribute to the serious side of it. He appeared to be under the impression that we were likely to meet either Uncle Henry or the person responsible for his disappearance, walking about the fields – and did a great deal of shading his eyes with his hands and calling our attention, by pointing with his stick, to distant cattle and labourers. He held several long conversations with old women whom we met, and was very strict and severe in his manner – but on each occasion returned to our party saying, 'Well, I find she don't seem to 'ave no connexion with this sad affair. I think you may take it from me, sir, as there's little or no light to be looked for from that quarter; not without she's keeping somethink back intentional.'

We gained no appreciable result, as I told you at starting; the Bow Street men have left the town, whether for London or not, I am not sure.

This evening I had company in the shape of a bagman, a smartish fellow. He knew what was going forward, but though he has been on the roads for some days about here, he had nothing to tell of suspicious characters – tramps, wandering sailors or gipsies. He was very full of a capital Punch and Judy Show he had seen this same day at W—, and asked if it had been here yet, and advised me by no means to miss it if it does come. The best Punch and the best Toby dog, he said, he had ever come across. Toby dogs, you know, are the last new thing in the shows. I have only seen one myself, but before long all the men will have them.

Now why, you will want to know, do I trouble to write all this to you? I am obliged to do it, because it has something to do with another absurd trifle (as you will inevitably say), which in my present state of rather unquiet fancy – nothing more, perhaps – I have to put down. It is a dream, sir, which I am going to record, and I must say it one of the oddest I have had. Is there anything in it beyond what the bagman's talk and Uncle Henry's disappearance could have suggested? You, I repeat, shall judge: I am not in a sufficiently cool and judicial frame to do so.

It began with what I can only describe as a pulling aside of curtains: and I found myself seated in a place – I don't know whether in doors or out. There were people – only a few – on either side of me, but I did not recognize them, or indeed think much about them. They never spoke, but, so far as I remember, were all grave and pale-faced and looked fixedly before them. Facing me there was a Punch and Judy Show, perhaps rather larger than the ordinary ones, painted with black figures on a reddish-yellow ground. Behind it and on each side was only darkness, but in front there was a sufficiency of light. I was 'strung up' to a high degree of expectation and listened every moment to hear the panpipes and the Roo-too-too-it. Instead of that there came suddenly an enormous – I can use no other word – and enormous single toll of a bell, I don't know from how far off – somewhere behind. The little curtain flew up and the drama began.

I believe someone once tried to re-write Punch as a serious tragedy; but whoever he may have been, this performance would have suited him exactly. There was something Satanic about the hero. He varied his methods of attack: for some of his victims he lay in wait, and to see his horrible face – it was yellowish white, I may remark – peering round the wings made me think of the Vampyre in Fuseli's foul sketch. To others he was polite and carneying – particularly to the unfortunate alien who can only say *Shallabalah* – though what Punch said I never could catch. But with all of them I came to dread the moment of death. The crack of the stick on their skulls, which in the ordinary way delights me, had here a crushing sound as if the bone was giving away, and the victims quivered and kicked as they lay. The baby – it sounds more ridiculous as I go on – the baby, I am sure, was alive. Punch wrung its neck, and if the choke or squeak which it gave were not real, I know nothing of reality.

The stage got perceptibly darker as each crime was consummated, and at last there was one murder which was done quite in the dark, so that I could see nothing of the victim, and took some time to effect. It was accompanied by hard breathing and horrid muffled sounds, and after it Punch came and sat on the foot-board and fanned himself and looked at his shoes, which were bloody, and hung his head on one side, and sniggered in so deadly a fashion that I saw some of those beside me cover their faces, and I would gladly have done the same. But in the meantime the scene behind Punch was clearing, and showed, not the usual house front, but something more ambitious – a grove of trees and the gentle slope of a hill, with a very natural – in fact, I should say a real – moon shining on it. Over this there rose slowly an object which I soon perceived to be a human figure with something peculiar about the head – what, I was unable at first to see. It did not stand on its feet, but began creeping or dragging itself across the middle distance towards Punch, who still sat back to it; and by this time, I may remark (though it did not occur to me at the moment) that all pretence of this being a puppet show had vanished. Punch was still Punch, it is true, but, like the others, was in some sense a live creature, and both moved themselves at their own will.

When I next glanced at him he was sitting in malignant reflection; but in another instant something seemed to attract his attention, and he first sat up sharply and then turned round, and evidently caught sight of the person that was approaching him and was in fact now very near. Then, indeed, did he show unmistakable signs of terror: catching up his stick, he rushed towards the wood, only just eluding the arm of his pursuer, which was suddenly flung out to intercept him. It was with a revulsion which I cannot easily express that I now saw more or less clearly what this pursuer was like. He was a sturdy figure clad in black, and, as I thought, wearing bands: his head was covered with a whitish bag.

The chase which now began lasted I do not know how long, now among the trees, now along the slope of the field, sometimes both figures disappearing wholly for a few seconds, and only some uncertain sounds letting one know that they were still afoot. At length there came a moment when Punch, evidently exhausted, staggered in from the left and threw himself down among the trees. His pursuer was not long after him, and came looking uncertainly from side to side. Then, catching sight of the figure on the ground, he too threw himself down – his back was turned to the audience – with a swift motion twitched the covering from his head, and thrust his face into that of Punch. Everything on the instant grew dark.

There was one long, loud, shuddering scream, and I awoke to find myself looking straight into the face of – what in all the world do you think? – but a large owl, which was seated on my window-sill immediately opposite my bed-foot, holding up its wings like two shrouded arms. I caught the fierce glance of its yellow eyes, and then it was gone. I heard the single enormous bell again – very likely, as you are saying to yourself, the church clock; but I do not think so – and then I was broad awake.

All this, I may say, happened within the last half-hour. There was no probability of my getting to sleep again, so I got up, put on clothes enough to keep me warm, and am writing this rigmarole in the first hours of Christmas Day. Have I left out anything? Yes, there was no Toby dog, and the names over the front of the Punch and Judy booth were Kidman and Gallop, which were certainly not what the bagman told me to look out for.

By this time, I feel a little more as if I could sleep, so this shall be sealed and wafered.

Letter IV

Dec. 26, '37.

My Dear Robert, – All is over. The body has been found. I do not make excuses for not having sent off my news by last night's mail, for the simple reason that I was incapable of putting pen to paper. The events that attended the discovery bewildered me so completely that I needed what I could get of a night's rest to enable me to face the situation at all. Now I can give you my journal of the day, certainly the strangest Christmas Day that ever I spent or am likely to spend.

The first incident was not very serious. Mr Bowman had, I think, been keeping Christmas Eve, and was a little inclined to be captious: at least, he was not on foot very early, and to judge from what I could hear, neither men or maids could do anything to please him. The latter were certainly reduced to tears; nor am I sure that Mr Bowman succeeded in preserving a manly composure. At any rate, when I came downstairs, it was in a broken voice that he wished me the compliments of the season, and a little later on, when he paid his visit of ceremony at breakfast, he was far from cheerful: even Byronic, I might almost say, in his outlook on life.

'I don't know,' he said, 'if you think with me, sir; but every Christmas as comes round the world seems a hollerer thing to me. Why, take an example now from what lays under my own eye. There's my servant Eliza – been with me now for going on fifteen years. I thought I could have placed my confidence in Eliza, and yet this very morning – Christmas morning too, of all the blessed days in the year – with the bells a ringing and – and – all like that – I say, this very morning, had it not have been for Providence watching over us all, that girl would have put – indeed I may go so far to say, 'ad put the cheese on your breakfast table –' He saw I was about to speak, and waved his hand at me. 'It's all very well for you to say, "Yes, Mr Bowman, but you took away the cheese and locked it up in the cupboard," which I did, and have the key here, or if not the actual key one very much about the same size. That's true enough, sir, but what do you think is the effect of that action on me? Why it's no exaggeration for me to say that the ground is cut from under my feet. And yet when I said as much to Eliza, not nasty, mind you, but just firm like, what was my return? "Oh," she said: 'Well," she says, "there wasn't no bones broke, I suppose." Well, sir, it 'urt me, that's all I can say: it 'urt me, and I don't like to think of it now.'

There was an ominous pause here, in which I ventured to say something like, 'Yes, very trying,' and then asked at what hour the church service was to be. 'Eleven o'clock,' Mr Bowman said with a heavy sigh. 'Ah, you won't have no such discourse from poor Mr Lucas as what you would have done from our late Rector. Him and me may have had our little differences, and did do, more's the pity.'

I could see that a powerful effort was needed to keep him off the vexed question of the cask of beer, but he made it. 'But I will say this, that a better preacher, nor yet one to stand faster by his rights, or what he considered to be his rights – however, that's not the question now – I for one, never set under. Some might say, "Was he an eloquent man?" and to that my answer would be: "Well, there you've a better right per'aps to speak of your own uncle than what I have." Others might ask, "Did he keep a hold of his congregation?" and there again I should reply, "That depends." But as I say – Yes, Eliza, my girl, I'm coming – eleven o'clock, sir, and you inquire for the King's Head pew.' I believe Eliza had been very near the door, and shall consider it in my vail.

The next episode was church: I felt Mr Lucas had a difficult task in doing justice to Christmas sentiments, and also to the feeling of disquiet and regret which, whatever Mr Bowman might say, was clearly prevalent. I do not think he rose to the occasion. I was uncomfortable. The organ wolved – you know what I mean: the wind died – twice in the Christmas Hymn, and the tenor bell, I suppose owing to some negligence on the part of the ringers, kept sounding faintly about once in a minute during the sermon. The clerk sent up a man to see to it, but he seemed unable to do much. I was glad when it was over. There was an odd incident, too, before the service. I went in rather early, and came upon two men carrying the parish bier back to its place under the tower. From what I overheard them saying, it appeared that it had been put out by mistake, by some one who was not there. I also saw the clerk busy folding up a moth-eaten velvet pall – not a sight for Christmas Day.

I dined soon after this, and then, feeling disinclined to go out, took my seat by the fire in the parlour, with the last number of *Pickwick*, which I had been saving up for some days. I thought I could be sure of keeping awake over this, but I turned out as bad as our friend Smith. I suppose it was half-past two when I was roused by a piercing whistle and laughing and talking voices outside in the market-place. It was a Punch and Judy – I had no doubt the one that my bagman had seen at W—. I was half delighted, half not – the latter because my unpleasant dream came back to me so vividly; but, anyhow, I determined to see it through, and I sent Eliza out with a crownpiece to the performers and a request that they would face my window if they could manage it.

The show was a very smart new one; the names of the proprietors, I need hardly tell you, were Italian, Foresta and Calpigi. The Toby dog was there, as I had been led to expect. All B— turned out, but did not obstruct my view, for I was at the large first-floor window and not ten yards away.

The play began on the stroke of a quarter to three by the church clock. Certainly it was very good; and I was soon relieved to find that the disgust my dream had given me for Punch's onslaughts on his ill-starred visitors was only transient. I laughed at the demise of the Turncock, the Foreigner, the Beadle, and even the baby. The only drawback was the Toby dog's developing a tendency to howl in the wrong place. Something had occurred, I suppose to upset him, and something considerable: for, I forget exactly at what point, he gave a most lamentable cry, leapt off the foot-board, and shot away across the market-place and down a side street.

There was a stage-wait, but only a brief one. I suppose the men decided that it was no good going after him, and that he was likely to turn up again at night.

We went on. Punch dealt faithfully with Judy, and in fact with all comers; and then came the moment when the gallows was erected, and the great scene with Mr Ketch was to be enacted. It was now that something happened of which I can certainly not yet see the import fully. You have witnessed an execution, and know what the criminal's head looks like with the cap on. If you are like me, you never wish to think of it again, and I do not willingly remind you of it. It was just such a head as that, that I, from my somewhat higher post, saw in the inside of the show-box; but at first the audience did not see it. I expected it to emerge into their view, but instead of that there slowly rose for a few seconds an uncovered face, with an expression of terror upon it, of which I have never imagined the like. It seemed as if the man, whoever he was, was being forcibly lifted, with his arms somehow pinioned or held back, towards the little gibbet on the stage. I could just see the nightcapped head behind him. Then there was a cry and a crash. The whole show-box fell over backwards; kicking legs were seen among the ruins, and then two figures – as some said; I can only answer for one – were visible running at top speed across the square and disappearing in a lane which leads to the fields.

Of course everybody gave chase. I followed; but the pace was killing, and very few were in, literally, at the death. It happened in a chalk pit: the man went over the edge quite blindly and broke his neck. They searched everywhere for the other, until it occurred to me to ask whether he had ever left the market-place. At first everyone was sure that he had; but when we came to look, he was there, under the show-box, dead too.

But in the chalk pit it was that poor Uncle Henry's body was found, with a sack over the head, the throat horribly mangled. It was a peaked corner of the sack sticking out of the soil that attracted attention. I cannot bring myself to write in greater detail.

I forgot to say the men's real names were Kidman and Gallop. I feel sure I have heard them, but no one here seems to know anything about them.

I am coming to you as soon as I can after the funeral. I must tell you when we meet what I think of it all.

XIV

A Christmas Ghost

A.N.L. Munby

Just as Charles Dickens attracted followers, so M.R. James has inspired a school of writers in the supernatural genre. Among most critics the man to have inherited James' mantle was Alan Noel Latimer Munby (1913-1974), himself a fellow scholar and antiquarian. Munby was likewise educated at King's College, Cambridge, became fascinated with antiquarian subjects and later returned to the College to become its librarian with access to the books and manuscripts he so cherished. Munby wrote a number of volumes of essays and biographies, but actually created the group of ghost stories which made his reputation under the most unusual circumstances. While serving as a soldier in the Second World War, he was taken prisoner by the Germans and thrown into captivity. To pass the time he began writing ghost stories which he delighted in reading to fellow POW's. After the war he published these tales in book form as The Alabaster Hand *(1950) and prefaced the collection with the information that 'all these stories were written between 1943 and 1945 in a prison-camp just outside the ancient walled town on Eichstätt in Upper Franconia.' I can think of no more bizarre surroundings for the creation of ghost stories – and certainly not one like the ingenious 'A Christmas Ghost' which actually takes us far away from the horrors of war, yet nevertheless right into the arms of terror ...*

The old country doctor who told me these strange events has died during the late war at the age of about eighty-five. He was a medical student at the time of the incidents which he related, so they can be assigned to the late 'seventies of the last century. I made profuse notes of his narrative, and I gave it, as far as possible, in his own words.

I was spending Christmas with my family in Dorset – my father was a solicitor in Dorchester, and we lived in a comfortable Victorian house about three miles south of the town. The party in the house was a large one. It included my mother and her two unmarried sisters – my Aunts Emily and Gertrude – my younger brother Edward, who was then a schoolboy at Blundell's, and my two small sisters, Bella and Felicity, aged sixteen and ten respectively. In addition, we had staying with us our young cousin Giles; and a number of young people in the neighbourhood were constantly coming to see us, so everything indicated that we should have a festive Christmas holiday. I myself, the eldest son, was a medical student in London, and I arrived home on the afternoon of December the 22nd. Rather to my surprise my father was away when I got there, for he led a fairly leisurely existence, and normally took a clear week off for Christmas. I was told, however, that he had had to go to Exeter on business and would be returning that night.

It was about nine o'clock when I heard the wheels of our dogcart on the drive and I ran out to greet my father. I was astonished to see that he was not alone; for nothing had been said about his returning with a guest. However, a tall, elderly man dismounted with him, very much muffled up, who was introduced to me as Mr Fenton. My father asked me to take the dogcart round to the yard and to see to the horse, and he passed into the house with the stranger. When I returned, I met my mother in the hall. She seemed to have lost some of her normal placidity.

'Really,' she said, 'your dear father is the most impulsive man. He met Mr Fenton in Exeter, and apparently he knew him years and years ago. On hearing that he had nowhere to go for Christmas, he asked him to come and stay with us. He *is* so hospitable, and says that he couldn't bear the thought of anyone spending Christmas alone at an inn. I know that I ought to feel the same, but I *had* been looking forward so much to having just the family round me, and however nice Mr Fenton may be, he will still be a stranger. However, we must just make the best of it. Giles will have to move into Edward's room ...' and she digressed into domestic affairs.

In the drawing-room I was first able to get a proper view of our guest. He was old, I should think sixty-five, but he carried himself well. His face was bronzed and he had a high colour; his nose was aquiline and he had a patrician air about him. His expression was not a kindly one – it was hard, even forbidding in repose, and I could picture him as being given to fits of imperious anger. Altogether I fully shared my mother's regrets that such a stranger should have been introduced into our family circle at the Christmas season. Nevertheless, he greeted me politely and expressed his gratitude that my father had taken pity on his solitary condition, and he said that he hoped his presence would not in any way interfere with our plans. As a matter of fact, he proved a singularly unobtrusive guest, and seemed quite content to withdraw to my father's study with his book and his cigar, or to take long, solitary walks. At meals he took his share in the family small talk and made himself quite a favourite with my aunts.

It was a meal – dinner on Christmas Eve – that I committed inadvertently what seemed to be a *faux pas*. Something in our guest's conversation had given me the idea that he had travelled extensively. In some way or other discussion at table had turned itself to the topic of New Zealand, and in order to bring Mr Fenton into the conversation, I asked him if he had ever been there. He replied with the curt monosyllable 'Yes' and at once changed the subject. I caught a warning glance from my father's eye at the top of the table, and he gave an almost imperceptible shake of the head. After dinner he drew me to one side.

'I shouldn't raise the topic of New Zealand with Mr Fenton,' he said. 'I have done so myself on one occasion and he obviously found it distasteful. I know that he spent some years as a young man in the Colonial service, and I believe now that I remember hearing that some sort of scandal was circulating at the time of his retirement. I never knew the details – it was the merest rumour and nearly thirty years ago now.'

'When did you know him before?' I asked.

'As a boy,' he replied. 'His father owned considerable property in these parts, but he made a number of unwise speculations in railway stocks and died a comparatively poor man. That was no doubt the reason why his son went into the

Colonial service. He has really changed very little since I first knew him. I recognised him at once.'

Christmas Day passed pleasantly enough. No doubt modern children would have found it intolerably dull, but we were content with simpler pleasures. The whole household went to church in the morning, and after luncheon the young people went for a walk with the dogs. It was not until we'd had our tea that the serious business of the day began. We all went into the drawing-room, where the Christmas-tree had been set up; the servants filed in under the watchful eye of Watkins, our old butler, and we all received our presents. I was gratified to get a sovereign, neatly wrapped in tissue paper, from Mr Fenton, and my younger brother and two sisters received half a sovereign apiece from the same source. He seemed to be entering into the spirit of the occasion, and was quite genial at dinner, which followed at six. After the meal my smallest sister, Felicity, was sent up to bed, which occasioned a few tears, and the rest of us proceeded to play various games, such as Dumb Crambo and Forfeits, and the evening passed merrily.

At half-past eleven we started to play a game which had become almost a family institution. It was simple in the extreme. The lights were extinguished and a screen was drawn in front of the fire; then my father began to tell us a horrid tale, which gave rise to many delicious shudders. We children knew it almost by heart, but it never lost its appeal. It was my rôle to assist him in this, by passing round in the darkness certain objects which illustrated the story. I expect our modern psycho-analysts would say that it was harmful to the young, but in those days, thank God, we weren't burdened with that sort of moonshine. I still recall the plot of my father's tale. It described how a lonely traveller in North America had to pass through a dark, almost impenetrable forest. Night overtook him before he had reached his destination, and he became aware that stealthy footsteps were following him. Suddenly he heard the dreaded sound of the Indian's war-whoop, and he was surrounded by a band of yelling savages who despatched him with their tomahawks. The abandoned wretches proceeded to dismember the corpse – first the scalp was removed. This was my cue to pass round the circle an old strip of a fur rug, which was greeted with much giggling and with exclamations of disgust from my aunts. Then my father described how the tongue of the victim was cut out, and I sent passing from hand to hand a small padded wash-leather bag, which I had carefully damped with glycerine. Finally the unfortunate man's eyes were gouged out, and this was the signal for my *pièce de résistance*. Two large muscatelle grapes had been peeled and I picked them up to hand them to my neighbour. This was Mr Fenton. He seemed unwilling to receive them, but I found his left hand in the darkness and thrust into it the slimy horrors. To my astonishment he gave an inarticulate half-cry of disgust, and rising from his seat he snatched aside the firescreen and hurled the grapes into the flames. Then he took a step back and slumped into his chair, breathing heavily. An embarrassed silence fell upon the room, broken by my father's anxious query of 'Are you all right, Fenton?' There was no reply. In the flickering firelight I could see my father fumbling with a lamp. As the light came up we could see that our guest was lolling back in his chair with his head drooping at an unnatural angle. He was very pale and his eyes were closed. I expect you can imagine the confusion that broke out. My sister burst into tears, and one of my aunts started to scream hysterically, until my mother led her from the room. My father sent my cousin Giles post-haste for the doctor, and in the meantime he tried to revive Fenton with brandy. In the midst of all this, I was the only one present who looked into the fire. I suppose I wondered subconsciously why our guest had reacted so strangely to the grapes I had passed him. Anyhow I bent down to look into the grate for them. You won't believe me when I say what I saw. I swear that instead of grapes there was a pair of eyes, sizzling and sputtering in the flames. I know I wasn't mistaken, and I know they were human eyes. I'd seen enough in the dissecting-room to make no error about that. I was dreadfully shocked, but in some curious way I didn't question the evidence of my senses. I realised that I had come face to face with something outside the scope of my comprehension – something in which all my scientific training would be of no avail. I resolved to keep my discovery to myself – for I could visualise the effect that any disclosure on my part would have upon that overwrought room. So I seized the poker and brought the flaming logs tumbling down, and those dreadful relics were buried from sight.

All this took only a few seconds, and I was quickly helping my father to revive the prostrate man. A cursory examination showed that he was the victim of some sort of stroke – a condition beyond the range of my elementary medical knowledge. I was therefore relieved when Giles returned in a few minutes with the doctor, who was a near neighbour. He seemed to take a grave view of our guest's appearance. Under his direction we carried the unconscious figure up to his bedroom and undressed him, leaving him alone in the doctor's care.

By this time it was very late. The other members of the household had gone quickly off to their beds, and I went to my room, where I sat down for a few minutes to try to collect my thoughts. The house was now almost silent, and I was oppressed by my extraordinary experience. I tried to persuade myself that I'd been the victim of some sort of optical illusion – that the eyes had existed only in my imagination; but I had seen them so distinctly – the pupil, the iris, every detail. They had been dark brown, almost black. The more I thought about it, the more I was appalled and dismayed. The transition from the cheerful atmosphere of the Christmas party had been terrifyingly abrupt. It was as though a curtain had been lifted for a moment, and beyond it I had glimpsed another world, exempted from the laws of Nature. I recalled an old piece of ecclesiastical dogma that I'd heard quoted, 'God may work above Nature, but never contrary to Nature.' If I had observed a miracle, it had certainly no Divine origin.

My meditations were interrupted by a noise from downstairs, the intermittent scratching and whining of a dog, and I recollected that in our excitement of the evening, no one had put our spaniel, Danny, outside before locking up. I went down and let him out through the door in the drawing-room, which led on to the terrace. Then, as I had a few moments to wait I lit the lamp and seated myself on the sofa. The idea of waiting in that room without a light did not appeal to me. The fire had died to a few glowing embers, and whatever had been put there had been utterly consumed.

The minutes passed and I became impatient. I went to the door and whistled, but Danny did not come. He was normally a most obedient dog, and his behaviour seemed quite unaccountable. Suddenly he began to howl, low at first but increasing in mournful intensity, making an eerie sound that sent shivers down my spine. I realised that he had gone down the drive into the shrubbery, and I called him again sharply, but again with no result. Seriously irritated, I went out to find him and after some difficulty I located him in the laurels. He was still whining and whimpering when I came upon him, and as he paid no attention to my command to follow me back to the house, I stopped and picked him up. I was surprised to find that he was trembling violently, and as soon as he was in my arms he pushed his head inside my jacket and kept it there, while his body twitched and quaked. I turned towards the house and took a few steps up the drive. Then I stopped as though transfixed.

I had left the garden door of the drawing-room open, and through it the light was streaming out on to the terrace. Into this ray of light a figure was moving, approaching the open door with faltering steps. It became silhouetted in the doorway, and I was able to see its outlines clearly. It was a fantastic, incredible form to see in the familiar setting of my Dorset home. It was not a white man. I could see the gleam of a golden-brown body and a head covered with glossy black hair. One side of the face was visible and it was heavily tattooed. A short skirt of rush or flax was its sole covering, and its feet were bare. In one hand it held a stick, and I realised that it was blind, for it tapped gently upon the paving-stones and felt its way towards the door. In another moment it had passed into the room and was lost to my view.

I silently changed my position in order to see more, and in doing so I came nearer to the house. The figure came once more into my range of vision, and I saw that it was on its knees before the chair in which our guest had been sitting, and that it was searching feverishly upon the floor, groping blindly round the chairlegs with clawlike hands. I was near enough to hear it give a deep sigh of vexation as it found nothing. Then it turned to the remains of the fire and with fascinated horror I watched it plunge its hands into the still glowing embers and pull them out on to the hearth. It scrabbled in the red-hot ashes for a moment or two, then it gave a low cry, almost heart-rending in its bitterness and despair. No soul in limbo could have given vent to a sound more fraught with desolation. As I stood watching, it rose silently to its feet and moved across the room, out of my sight once more.

For some reason I was no longer afraid, just amazed and curious. I take no particular credit for this; I divined in some obscure way that the apparition, or whatever it may have been, was not malevolent to myself. So you need not think that I was exceptionally brave when I tell you that I strode quickly across the terrace and in through the door. The room was deserted; a second's glance told me this, and as I stood there the inner door of the room opened and my father came in. If the strange visitant had left, it could only have done so by the door at which he entered, and he must surely have passed it in the passage.

'Did you see anyone as you came in here?' I asked.

My father frowned and replied sharply. 'What are you talking about? Why on earth don't you go to bed? Shut the door and go upstairs at once. It's nearly two o'clock.'

I glanced at the fireplace before replying. There were the embers, scattered about the hearth – unshatterable testimony that my eyes had not deceived me. But I didn't say anything to my father about it. I went somewhat in awe of him, as did many sons at that date, and there was no very complete and frank understanding between us. I feared his anger and I feared his ridicule: I knew that any revelation on my part must bring both upon my head. So I stammered out something about having let the dog out, holding out the now quiescent Danny as evidence for my words. Then I quickly locked up. My father waited until I'd finished.

'Fenton's pretty bad, I'm afraid,' he said; 'but the doctor says that there's a chance of recovery. I'm glad I asked him here. I wouldn't like to think of any friend of mine being taken ill staying alone at some inn. I'm sorry that it has spoilt our Christmas, though.'

We went up the stairs together, and on the landing my

father wished me good night. As he did so, we heard a confused noise from Fenton's room. The old man must have recovered consciousness, for we could perceive quite distinctly his rather high, querulous tones intermingled with the quieter phrases of the doctor. As we listened the patient's voice became louder and we caught his words.

'Keep him off – keep him away,' he was shouting, 'for God's sake, don't let him come near me.'

Some reassuring remarks of the doctor's followed, but Fenton didn't seem to be pacified.

'Can't you see him?' he cried. 'Over there by the window!' His voice became shriller and he lapsed into some foreign language that I did not understand. The doctor's tones became louder and more authoritative as he said:

'Lie down, sir, lie down. I tell you there's nothing there. I assure you that there's no one in the room but you and myself.'

I looked questioningly at my father for direction, but he shook his head and said:

'I don't think we'd better go in. There's nothing we can do. Leave it to the doctor.'

He was interrupted by another series of cries, culminating in the sound of a struggle, as though Fenton were being forcibly held down upon his bed. Then, quite suddenly, there was utter silence for a period of perhaps two minutes. We waited, straining our ears. Our vigil was broken by the door being opened; the doctor stood upon the threshold, looking pale and tired.

'I'm afraid he's gone,' he said simply. Then, as my father stepped forward, he held up his hand and added:

'I should not go inside. The poor devil was in the grip of some terrifying hallucination at the end, and he didn't have a very peaceful passage. His appearance would only upset you. You go off to bed. I'll make all the necessary arrangements.'

We obeyed and tiptoed quietly away. When I got to my room I found that I still had Danny in my arms, and very glad I was of his company for the remainder of that night.

It must have been quite ten years later, when I was qualified and in practice at Cheltenham, that I met a man who knew Fenton's name. He was a retired sheep farmer who had spent twenty-five years in New Zealand, and though he was too young to have known Fenton personally, he knew him by repute. It was from him that I learned some details of the scandal that surrounded Fenton's retirement from the Colonial service. Dark stories of his ruthlessness and brutality as an administrator had for a time been circulating, but finally there had been an incident which the authorities could not ignore. Under Fenton's direction an alleged malefactor had been subjected to torture, in order to wring a confession from him. When other methods had failed, he had been threatened with blinding, and upon his still remaining obdurate, this dire threat had been carried out. A subsequent enquiry had established the native's innocence, but for the sake of British prestige there had been no public denunciation of the public servant, who had so grossly exceeded his powers. Fenton's only punishment was to be sent home. But though his retribution was light at the hands of men, it would seem that finally he was called to account before a different and a higher court.

XV

S.O.S.

Algernon Blackwood

It was in the years immediately after the Second World War that I first became aware of the tradition of ghost story-telling at Christmas time. It was not through the medium of television, as would be the case today – but by courtesy of the radio: and one broadcaster in particular. In the view of quite a substantial number of people, the radio can have a much greater impact on its audience than television: the voices and sound effects building up a picture in the listener's mind that can be more thrilling and frightening than anything created by make-up and special-effects on the television screen. Anyone who has listened to a master storyteller at work on the radio will, I am sure, know what I mean – and all those fortunate enough to have heard Algernon Blackwood (1869-1951) reading his ghost and horror stories during the late forties will be in no doubt whatsoever! 'The Ghost Man', as Blackwood was known to his audience (myself among them) used to evoke the most terrifying scenes with that slow, sonorous voice of his, and remembering some of the tales he related still brings a shiver to my spine today! He gave to his stories all the rich experience of a lifetime of travel: as a young man in Canada (where he first encountered the supernatural on a haunted island), as a reporter in America (living for a time in a house in New York which had a most active ghost) and latterly in Europe (brushing with the terrible powers of black magic). Back in Britain he utilised these encounters as the basis for numerous stories which appeared in a dozen collections and were later adapted for the radio. In time, some even made their way onto television. The story here, 'S.O.S' was, I recall, first read on Christmas Eve, 1949, and it strikingly evokes the mountain landscape of that part of Europe where Christmas is always celebrated in the snowy conditions Dickens would have us believe were universal. It is a tale to chill the blood and make one glad to be reading it far from the winter climes it describes …

It is a question how many witnesses shall be required to establish the veracity of an occurrence so singular, especially when one of such witnesses is a dog.

Three of us, two men and a girl, had skimmed the snow-covered Jura slopes on our ski since noon, arriving towards four o'clock at the deserted chalet where the fourth was to meet us. Upon the arrival of that fourth hung all the future happiness of the girl, and he was to come from a village far away on the other side. The Christmas rendezvous had been carefully arranged.

We had brought provisions for making a hot supper in the empty building, a lonely farm-house used only in summer, and our plan was to ski back all together by moonlight.

'Put on your extra sweaters before you begin to cool,' said the older man, coming round the corner with an armful of logs from the frozen woodpile. 'I'll get the fire going. Here, Dot,' – turning to his niece – 'stack your ski, and get the food out. He'll be hungry as a bear.'

The three of us bustled about over the crisp snow, and the older man had a wood fire blazing upon the great open hearth in less than ten minutes. The interior of the big room lit up, shadows flew overhead among the rafters, and shafts of cheery yellow light flashed even into the recesses of the vaulted barn that opened out into the cow-sheds in the rear. Outside, the dusk visibly deepened from one minute to the next.

The cold was bitter; but our heated bodies fairly steamed. The big St Bernard ran, sniffing and prancing, after each of us in turn, and from time to time flew up the mounds of snow outside, where he stood, with head flung back and muzzle up, staring against the sunset. He knew perfectly well that someone else was expected and the direction from which he would come. The effect of the firelight streaming through door and cracks of muffled window into the last hour of daylight was peculiar; night and day met together on the threshold of the chalet, under the shadows of that enormous snow-laden roof. For the sun was now below the rim of the Suchet ridges, flaming with a wonderful sheet of red and yellow light over the huge white plateau, and the isolated trees threw vague shadows that easily ran into a length of half a kilometre. Rapidly they spread, assuming monstrous shapes, half animal, half human; then, deceiving the sight, merged into the strange uniform glow that lies upon a snow-field in the twilight. The forest turned purple; the crests of the pines cut into the sky like things of steel and silver. Everything shone, crackled, sparkled; the cold increased.

'Dorothy, where are you going?' sounded the older man's voice from the door, for the girl was out on her ski again. Her slim young figure, topped by the pointed, white snow-cap, was sprite-like.

'Just a little way over the slopes – to meet him,' came her reply. She seemed to float above the snow, not on it.

With decision he called her in, and it was the warning in his tone that perhaps made her obey.

'Better rest,' he said briefly; 'we've got a long run home in the moonlight.' On her ski she came 'sishing' back down the gleaming slope to his side, neat and graceful, her shadow shooting ahead like black lightning, enormously elongated. 'The Creux du Van precipices, besides, lie over that way,' he continued. 'They begin without warning – a sheer drop, and nothing to show the edge.'

'I know them,' she said, pouting a little.

'He knows them, too,' her uncle answered, putting a hand on her shoulder. 'He'll take the higher slopes. He'll get around all right.' He had noticed the look in her soft, brown eyes that betrayed – it was the merest passing flash – an eagerness lying too close upon the verge of anxiety. 'Harry knows these ridges even better than I do.'

He helped her stack the ski, then turned to whistle in the dog, which had stayed behind on the summit of the slope she had just left, and it was at this instant, I think, that I first suddenly became aware of an unusual significance lying behind the little scene. Such moments are beyond explanation or analysis; one can only report them. They pertain, some hold, to a kind of vision. I can merely affirm that the flash came to me in this wise: I saw the big dog, his outline sharply silhouetted against the sky-line and his head turned westward, refusing for the first time that day to obey instantly a whistle that for him was a summons always to be obeyed. His master, noticing nothing, had already gone inside; but the girl saw what I saw, caught a flash similar to my own, and recognised in the animal's insignificant disobedience a corroboration of something in herself that touched uneasiness. I cannot prove it – she has never spoken of it – only, as she stood there a moment, with the sunset in her face and her tumbled hair half over her eyes, I intercepted the swift glance that ran upward to the St Bernard, travelled beyond him to the huge, distant snow-slopes, and then fell upon me. It was love, perhaps, that carried and interpreted thus the instantaneous wireless message – the love that lay undelivered in my heart, as in her own, and, since she was foresworn already, lay unrecognised. In view of what followed, I cannot wholly say. My sight held clearer and steadier than her own, and it came to me that my strange perception, sharpened to bitter sweetness as if by sacrifice, approached possibly to some kind of inferior divination of the wounded soul. The next minute the great dog came bounding down, and we entered the chalet together, busying ourselves with fire, benches, table, and supper. The portable little kettle of aluminum already steamed upon the hearth.

With us – with myself, at any rate – came into the cosy fire-lit interior a sensation that was new. I felt the terror and desolation of these vast, snow-covered mountains, immense, trackless, silent, lying away from the world of men below the coming stars. Winter, like a winter of the polar regions, held them fast. In the brilliant sunshine of the day they had been friendly, enticing, sympathetic. Now, with the icy dusk creeping over their bare, white faces, the freezing wind sifting with long sighs through the forests below, and the silent Terror of the Frost stalking from cliff to ridge with his head among the stars, they turned terrible. With the coming of the night they awoke to their true power. They showed their teeth. Our own insignificance became curiously emphasised. I thought of the Creux du Van precipices, sweeping, crater-like with their semicircle of dark grandeur, a gulf of snow-drifts about their dreadful lips, six hundred feet of shadows yawning within, and shuddered.

'You're cold,' said Dot softly, pulling me to the fire, where.

she warmed her steaming boots. 'I'm cold, too.' We piled the wood on; the flames leaped and crackled; shadows flew among the rafters.

'Harry's due any minute,' said her uncle. 'We'll drop the eggs in as soon as we hear his whistle.' He stooped down to pat the St Bernard, which lay now with head stretched on his forepaws before the fire, staring, listening. 'You'll hear him first,' he laughed cheerily, giving the beast a resounding pat. 'Long before we do.'

The dog growled low, making no other response to a caress that usually brought him leaping to his master's breast. We heard the wind keening round the wooden walls, rushing with a long faint whistle over the roof, and we drew closer to the fire. For a long time no one spoke. The minutes passed and passed.

It was then, quite suddenly, that we heard a step in the snow; but not before the dog had heard it first and bounded to his feet with a growl that was more like a human roar than any animal sound I have ever heard. He fairly leaped toward the door, and the same second Dot and I were also upon our feet.

'What's the matter?' exclaimed her uncle, startled and surprised. 'That's only wind, or snow falling from the roof.'

Behind us the wooden walls gave out sharp, cracking reports as the heated air made them expand; but in my heart something turned into ice with a cold that lay beyond all cold of winter. The terror I at first experienced, however, was not for myself, but for this soft, brown-eyed little maid who shot so swiftly by me and opened the heavy door. I was ready there to catch her, ready to protect and shield, yet knowing by some strange authority within me that she stood already safe, held by a power that lay beyond all little efforts of my own.

For into that great, fire-lit interior stepped at once the figure of a peasant, large, uncouth, lumbering, his face curiously concealed either by the play of the shadows or by the fall of his hair and beard – to this day I know not which – filling the threshold with his bulk, the freezing wind rushing in past his great, sheathed legs, and an eddy of dry snow veiling him like a flying cloak beyond. He stood there a second with an atmosphere of power about him that seemed to dwarf everything, and of such commanding stature that into my mind, bewildered and confused a little with the sudden entrance, ran the thought of a bleak and towering peak of mountain. It came to me that the chalet must crumble, the huge beams split, and fall upon our heads. There was a rush of freezing wind, a touch of ice, and at the same time I was aware of some strange, intolerable beauty, as of wild nature, that made me hide my eyes. It was only long afterward that I remembered there was no snow upon his feet, that his eyes remained hidden, and also that he spoke not a word.

'The door's blown open!' cried the uncle. 'For God's sake –'

All this, moreover, in the tenth of the first second, for immediately I saw that the St Bernard was bounding round the figure with an unfeigned delight that knew no fear; and next, that he had stretched his arms out toward the girl with a gesture of tenderness and invitation possibly only in this whole world to the arms of a woman. Terrible, yet inconceivably winning, was that gesture, as of a child. And the same moment, to my amazement, she had leaped forward and was gone. With her, barking and leaping, went the St Bernard dog.

'Dot, you silly child, where in the world are you going? Do shut the door! It's not Harry yet. It was a false alarm.' It was the matter-of-fact tone of her uncle's voice that let me into the secret – that only she, I, and the dog had witnessed anything at all.

'I'll go with her and see her safe,' I shouted back, and it was only then, as I turned toward the door again after saying it, that I understood there was no one standing there, and that her leap had been really a springing run toward the corner where her ski lay. Already, I saw, they were on her feet. She was away. I saw the dog bounding over the frozen slope beside her. He was a little in front. He held her skirt in his teeth, guidingly. In that pale wintry light of the rising moon, I saw their two outlines against the snow. They were alone.

'Bring brandy and a blanket!' I had the sense to call back into the room, and was after her in my turn. But the frozen fastenings of my ski had never seemed so obstinate. It was a whole minute before I was whizzing down the mile-long slope. The speed was tremendous and the ski skidded on the crust. She left only faint indications of her trail. It was the barking of the dog that guided me best, and far away below me in the yellow moonlight the little speeding spot of black that showed me where she flew, heading straight for the Creux du Van.

At any other time such a descent as we two then made would have been sheer lunacy, even in daylight. The tearing speed, the angle of the huge slope, the iciness of that gleaming crust, all were invitation to disaster; and with the gaping chasm of the Creux du Van lying waiting at the bottom, it was simply a splendid race into suicide. The water poured from my eyes, the frozen mounds whipped by like giant white waves, and no sooner was the black line of some isolated pine-tree sighted than it was past, like the telegraph-poles to an express train. Only the yellow face of the big rising moon held steady.

She had soon outstripped the dog, and as I shot past him, wildly cantering, with his tongue out and steaming, open jaws, he caught vainly at my puttees. The next moment he was a hundred yards behind me.

But Dot, guided by some power that the mountains put into her little feet, knew her direction well, and went as straight as a die to the edge of the awful gulf; then stopped dead, buried to her neck in a drift that climbed wave-like upon the very lips of the chasm. It stopped her, as ten minutes before it had also stopped another, coming down from the slopes that lay to the westward. I saw the hole of the valley gaping at our very feet as a successful 'telemark' flung me backward beside her just in the nick of time.

'Quick!' I heard her cry. 'He's still sliding!' It was then that I realised that the third body, lying there unconscious where the drift had likewise stopped it, was slowly moving with the weight of snow toward the edge. One ski already projected horribly over the actual brink. I heard a mass of snow detach itself and drop even as she said it.

It took less than a second to detach my belt and fasten it to his leg; but even then I firmly believe the strain of our slow pulling must have landed us all three into the gulf below had not the arrival of the St Bernard put a different complexion upon the scene. It was the grandest thing I have ever witnessed. A second he stood there, the supreme instinct of his noble race judging the problem. He knew the softness of the drift that must engulf him if he advanced; he also saw it sliding. Very slowly, like a courageous human being, on all fours, calculating distance, angle, and tensions, as it were, by his superb animal divination, he crawled round to another side. He crept gingerly along the very edge. His teeth fastened upon the boot and ski-straps. We pulled together. God! I cannot understand to this day how it was that the four of us were not gone! He knew, that splendid dumb creature. We merely followed his magnificent lead.

A moment later we were safe on hard, solid snow. As we lay back exhausted, the snow immediately at our feet slid with a hiss, and disappeared into the valley hundreds of feet below. But the St Bernard, still pulling carefully and gently by himself, was next busily licking the boy's white face and breathing his heat upon him, when help arrived with the brandy and the blankets. I believe it was the tireless and incessant attentions of that great dog that really saved the life, for he lay upon the form with his whole body, keeping him warm, and letting go only when he understood that the blankets and our arms, carrying him to the chalet, might replace his own self-sacrificing love.

'I heard a voice crying outside the door, in the wind,' she told me afterward. 'It was his voice, you see, and it called me by name. I don't know what guided me to the place, for I think I shut my eyes the whole way till I fell at his side.'

XVI

Blind Man's Hood

John Dickson Carr

Among all those modern stories which have been deliberately created to follow in the style of Dickens and James, this next item is arguably the best example and as such makes a most fitting finale to the collection. This opinion is shared by that doyen of fantasy editors, Anthony Boucher, who wrote of 'Blind Man's Hood' in Fantasy and Science Fiction, *1955: 'The ghost-story-for-Christmas is one of the most ancient and honourable of English-speaking customs, pre-eminently observed by Dickens (both as writer and editor) and by M.R. James – in this instance Mr Carr adds his own typical impossible-murder problem to a ghost story in the richest Jamesian tradition producing a perfect Christmas tale complete with 'a bright fire … cold fowl on the sideboard, a great bowl of chestnuts …' and a spectre at once pitiful and subtly terrifying.'*

John Dickson Carr (1906-1977), the author, was born in America, the son of a lawyer who specialised in sensational criminal cases, and not surprisingly he grew up with a fascination in detection. His first novel, It Walks By Night *was published when he was only 24, and he went on to issue a steady stream of books which established him as one of the most versatile masters of the 'impossible crime' story. Because of a profound admiration for G.K. Chesterton's Father Brown detective stories, and the fact he married an English girl, Carr settled in Britain and during World War II he scripted a very popular radio series called* Appointment With Fear. *These gave expression to his interest in the supernatural, and elements of the weird and the uncanny can also be found in his short stories like the example here. Although Carr later returned to live in America, his work has remained very popular on this side of the Atlantic. 'Blind Man's Hood' brings to a conclusion this gathering of festive spirits. Whether malevolent or humorous, terrifying or amusing, I hope they have all entertained you in the manner which one expects of surely the most popular season of the year. And I am sure that Charles Dickens himself would be delighted if he could see the extent to which the tradition he began has now spread. Or, possibly, his shade is watching now,* very well aware *of what has happened ...*

Although one snowflake had already sifted past the lights, the great doors of the house stood open. It seemed less a snowflake than a shadow; for a bitter wind whipped after it, and the doors creaked. Inside, Rodney and Muriel Hunter could see a dingy, narrow hall paved in dull red tiles, with a Jacobean staircase at the rear. (At that time, of course, there was no dead woman lying inside.)

To find such a place in the loneliest part of the Weald of Kent – a seventeenth-century country house whose floors had grown humped and its beams scrubbed by the years – was what they had expected. Even to find electricity was not surprising. But Rodney Hunter thought he had seldom seen so many lights in one house, and Muriel had been equally startled by the display. 'Clearlawns' lived up to its name. It stood in the midst of a slope of flat grass, now wiry white with frost, and there was no tree or shrub within twenty yards of it. Those lights contrasted with a certain inhospitable and damp air about the house, as though the owner were compelled to keep them burning all the time.

'But why is the front door *open*?' insisted Muriel.

In the drive-way, the engine of their car coughed and died. The house was now a secret blackness of gables, emitting light at every chink, and silhouetting the stalks of the wisteria vines which climbed it. On either side of the front door were little-paned windows whose curtains had not been drawn. Towards their left they could see into a low dining-room, with table and sideboard set for a cold supper; towards their right was a darkish library moving with the reflections of a bright fire.

The sight of the fire warmed Rodney Hunter, but it made him feel guilty. They were very late. At 5 o'clock, without fail, he had promised Jack Bannister, they would be at 'Clearlawns' to inaugurate the Christmas party.

Engine-trouble in leaving London was one thing; idling at a

country pub along the way, drinking hot ale and listening to the wireless sing carols until a sort of Dickensian jollity stole into you, was something else. But both he and Muriel were young; they were very fond of each other and of things in general; and they had worked themselves into a glow of Christmas, which – as they stood before the creaking doors of 'Clearlawns' – grew oddly cool.

There was no real reason, Rodney thought, to feel disquiet. He hoisted their luggage, including a big box of presents for Jack and Molly's children, out of the rear of the car. That his footsteps should sound loud on the gravel was only natural. He put his head into the doorway and whistled. Then he began to bang the knocker. Its sound seemed to seek out every corner of the house and then come back like a questing dog; but there was no response.

'I'll tell you something else,' he said. 'There's nobody in the house.'

Muriel ran up the three steps to stand beside him. She had drawn her fur coat close around her, and her face was bright with cold.

'But that's impossible!' she said 'I mean, even if they're out, the servants –! Molly told me she keeps a cook and two maids. Are you sure we've got the right place?'

'Yes. The name's on the gate, and there's no other house within a mile.

With the same impulse they craned their necks to look through the windows of the dining-room on the left. Cold fowl on the sideboard, a great bowl of chestnuts; and, now they could see it, another good fire, before which stood a chair with a piece of knitting put aside on it. Rodney tried the knocker again, vigorously, but the sound was all wrong. It was as though they were even more lonely in that core of light, with the east wind rushing across the Weald, and the door creaking again.

'I suppose we'd better go in,' said Rodney. He added, with a lack of Christmas spirit: 'Here, this is a devil of a trick! What do you think has happened? I'll swear that fire has been made up in the last fifteen minutes.'

He stepped into the hall and set down the bags. As he was turning to close the door, Muriel put her hand on his arm.

'I say, Rod. Do you think you'd better close it?'

'Why not?'

'I – I don't know.'

'The place is getting chilly enough as it is,' he pointed out, unwilling to admit that the same thought had occurred to him. He closed both doors and shot their bar into place; and, at the same moment, a girl came out of the door to the library on the right.

She was such a pleasant-faced girl that they both felt a sense of relief. Why she had not answered the knocking had ceased to be a question, she filled a void. She was pretty, not more than twenty-one or two, and had an air of primness which made Rodney Hunter vaguely associate her with a governess or a secretary, though Jack Bannister had never mentioned any such person. She was plump, but with a curiously narrow waist; and she wore brown. Her brown hair was neatly parted, and her brown eyes – long eyes, which might have given a hint of secrecy or curious smiles if they had not been so placid – looked concerned. In one hand she carried what looked like a small white bag of linen or cotton. And she spoke with a dignity which did not match her years.

'I am most terribly sorry,' she told them. 'I *thought* I heard someone, but I was so busy that I could not be sure. Will you forgive me?'

She smiled. Hunter's private view was that his knocking had been loud enough to wake the dead; but he murmured conventional things. As though conscious of some faint incongruity about the white bag in her hand, she held it up.

'For Blind Man's Bluff,' she explained. 'They do cheat so, I'm afraid, and not only the children. If one uses an ordinary handkerchief tied round the eyes, they always manage to get a corner loose. But if you take this, and you put it fully over a person's head, and you tie it round the neck' – a sudden gruesome image occurred to Rodney Hunter – 'then it works so much better, don't you think?' Her eyes seemed to turn inward, and to grow absent. 'But I must not keep you talking here. You are –?'

'My name is Hunter. This is my wife. I'm afraid we've arrived late, but I understood Mr Bannister was expecting –'

'He did not tell you?' asked the girl in brown.

'Tell me what?'

'Everyone here, including the servants, is always out of the house at this hour on this particular date. It is the custom; I believe it has been the custom for more than sixty years. There is some sort of special church service.'

Rodney Hunter's imagination had been devising all sorts of fantastic explanations: the first of them being that this demure lady had murdered the members of the household, and was engaged in disposing of the bodies. What put this nonsensical notion into his head he could not tell, unless it was his own profession of detective-story writing. But he felt relieved to hear a commonplace explanation. Then the woman spoke again.

'Of course, it's a pretext really. The rector, that dear man, invented it all those years ago to save embarrassment. What happened here had nothing to do with the murder, since the dates were so different; and I suppose most people have forgotten now why the tenants *do* prefer to stay away during 7 and 8 o'clock on Christmas Eve. I doubt if Mrs Bannister even knows the real reason, though I should imagine Mr Bannister must know it. But what happens here cannot be very pleasant, and it wouldn't do to have the children see it – would it?'

Muriel spoke with such sudden directness that her husband knew she was afraid. 'Who are you?' Muriel said. 'And what on earth are you talking about?'

'I am quite sane, really,' their hostess assured them, with a smile that was half-cheery and half-coy. 'I dare say it must be all very confusing to you, poor dear. But I am forgetting my duties. Please come in and sit down before the fire, and let me offer you something to drink.'

She took them into the library on the right, going ahead with a walk that was like a bounce, and looking over her shoulder out of those long eyes. The library was a long, low room with beams. The windows towards the road were uncurtained; but those in the side-wall, where a faded red-brick fireplace stood, were bay windows with draperies closed across them. As their hostess put them before the fire, Hunter could have sworn he saw one of the draperies move.

'You need not worry about it,' she assured him, following his glance towards the bay. 'Even if you looked in there, you might not see anything now. I believe some gentleman did try it once, a long time ago. He stayed in the house for a wager. But when he pulled the curtain back, he did not see anything in the bay – at least, anything quite. He felt some hair, and it moved. That is why they have so many lights nowadays.'

Muriel had sat down on a sofa, and was lighting a cigarette: to the rather prim disapproval of their hostess, Hunter thought.

'May we have a hot drink?' Muriel asked crisply. 'And then, if you don't mind, we might walk over and meet the Bannisters coming from church.'

'Oh, please don't do that!' cried the other. She had been standing by the fireplace, her hands folded and turned outwards. Now she ran across to sit down beside Muriel; and the swiftness of her movement, no less than the touch of her hand on Muriel's arm, made the latter draw back.

Hunter was now completely convinced that their hostess was out of her head. Why she held such fascination for him, though, he could not understand. In her eagerness to keep them there, the girl had come upon a new idea. On a table behind the sofa, book-ends held a row of modern novels. Conspicuously displayed – probably due to Molly Bannister's tact – were two of Rodney Hunter's detective stories. The girl put a finger on them.

'May I ask if you wrote these?'

He admitted it.

'Then,' she said with sudden composure, 'it would probably interest you to hear about the murder. It was a most perplexing business, you know; the police could make nothing of it, and no one ever has been able to solve it.' An arresting eye fixed on his. 'It happened out in the hall there. A poor woman was killed where there was no one to kill her, and no one could have done it. But she was murdered.'

Hunter started to get up from his chair; then he changed his mind, and sat down again. 'Go on,' he said.

'You must forgive me if I am a little uncertain about dates,' she urged. 'I think it was in the early eighteen-seventies, and I am sure it was in early February – because of the snow. It was a bad winter then; the farmers' livestock all died. My people have been bred up in the district for years, and I know that. The house here was much as it is now, except that there was none of this lighting (only paraffin lamps, poor girl!); and you were obliged to pump up what water you wanted; and people read the newspaper quite through, and discussed it for days.

'The people were a little different to look at, too. I am sure I do not understand why we think beards are so strange nowadays; they seem to think that men who had beards never had any emotions. But even young men wore them then, and looked handsome enough. There was a newly married couple living in this house at the time: at least, they had been married only the summer before. They were named Edward and Jane Waycross, and it was considered a good match everywhere.

'Edward Waycross did not have a beard, but he had bushy side-whiskers which he kept curled. He was not a handsome man, either, being somewhat dry and hard-favoured; but he was a religious man, and a good man, and an excellent man of business, they say: a manufacturer of agricultural implements at Hawkhurst. He had determined that Jane Anders (as she was) would make him a good wife, and I dare say she did. The girl had several suitors. Although Mr Waycross was the best match, I know it surprised people a little when she accepted him, because she was thought to have been fond of another man – a more striking man, whom many of the young girls were after. This was Jeremy Wilkes: who came of a very good family, but was considered wicked. He was no younger than Mr Waycross, but he had a great black beard, and wore white waistcoats with gold chains, and drove a gig. Of course, there had been gossip, but that was because Jane Anders was considered pretty.'

Their hostess had been sitting back against the sofa, quietly folding the little white bag with one hand, and speaking in a prim voice. Now she did something which turned her hearers cold.

You have probably seen the same thing done many times. She had been touching her cheek lightly with the fingers of the other hand. In doing so, she touched the flesh at the corner under her lower eyelid, and accidentally drew down the corner of that eyelid – which should have exposed the red part of the inner lid at the corner of the eye. It was not red. It was of a sickly pale colour.

'In the course of his business dealing,' she went on, 'Mr Waycross had often to go to London, and usually he was obliged to remain overnight. But Jane Waycross was not afraid to remain alone in the house. She had a good servant, a staunch old woman, and a good dog. Even so, Mr Waycross commended her for her courage.'

The girl smiled. 'On the night I wish to tell you of, in February, Mr Waycross was absent. Unfortunately, too, the old servant was absent; she had been called away as a midwife to attend her cousin, and Jane Waycross had allowed her to go. This was known in the village, since all such affairs are well known, and some uneasiness was felt – this house being isolated, as you know. But she was not afraid.

'It was a very cold night, with a heavy fall of snow which had stopped about 9 o'clock. You must know, beyond doubt, that poor Jane Waycross was alive after it had stopped snowing. It must have been nearly half-past 9 when a Mr Moody – a very good and sober man who lived in Hawkhurst – was driving home along the road past this house. As you know, it stands in the middle of a great bare stretch of lawn; and you can see the house clearly from the road. Mr Moody saw poor Jane at the window of one of the upstairs bedrooms, with a candle in her hand, closing the shutters. But he was not the only witness who saw her alive.

'On that same evening, Mr Wilkes (the handsome gentleman I spoke to you of a moment ago) had been at a tavern in the village of Five Ashes with Dr Sutton, the local doctor, and a racing gentleman named Pawley. At about half-past 11 they started to drive home in Mr Wilkes's gig to Cross-in-Hand. I am afraid they had been drinking, but they were all in their sober senses. The landlord of the tavern remembered the time because he had stood in the doorway to watch the gig, which had fine yellow wheels, go spanking away as though there were no snow; and Mr Wilkes in one of the new round hats with a curly brim.

'There was a bright moon. "And no danger," Dr Sutton always said aftewards; "shadows of trees and fences as clear as though a silhouette-cutter had made 'em for sixpence." But when they were passing this house Mr Wilkes pulled up sharp. There was a bright light in the window of one of the downstairs rooms – this room, in fact. They sat out there looking round the hood of the gig, and wondering.

'Mr Wilkes spoke: "I don't like this," he said. "You know, gentlemen, that Waycross is still in London; and the lady in question is in the habit of retiring early. I am going up there to find out if anything is wrong."

'With that he jumped out of the gig, his black beard jutting out and his breath smoking. He said: "And if it is a burglar, then, by Something, gentlemen" – I will not repeat the word he used – "by Something, gentlemen, I'll settle him." He walked through the gate and up to the house – they could follow every step he made – and looked into the windows of this room here. Presently he returned looking relieved (they could see him by the light of the gig lamps), but wiping the moisture off his forehead.

' "It is all right," he said to them; "Waycross has come home. But, by Something, gentlemen, he is growing thinner these days, or it is shadows."

'Then he told them what he had seen. If you look through the front windows – there – you can look sideways and see out through the doorway into the main hall. He said he had seen Mrs Waycross standing in the hall with her back to the staircase, wearing a blue dressing-wrap over her nightgown, and her hair down round her shoulders. Standing in front of her, with his back to Mr Wilkes, was a tallish, thin man like Mr Waycross, with a long greatcoat and a tall hat like Mr Waycross's. *She* was carrying either a candle or a lamp; and he remembered how the tall hat seemed to wag back and forth, as though the man were talking to her or putting out his hands towards her. For he said he could not see the woman's face.

'Of course, it was not Mr Waycross; but how were they to know that?

'At about 7 o'clock next morning, Mrs Randall, the old servant, returned. (A fine boy had been born to her cousin the night before.) Mrs Randall came home through the white dawn and the white snow, and found the house all locked up. She could get no answer to her knocking. Being a woman of great resolution, she eventually broke a window and got in. But, when she saw what was in the front hall, she went out screaming for help.

'Poor Jane was past help. I know I should not speak of these things; but I must. She was lying on her face in the hall. From the waist down her body was much charred and – unclothed, you know, because fire had burnt away most of the nightgown and the dressing-wrap. The tiles of the hall were soaked with blood and paraffin oil having come from a broken lamp with a thick blue-silk shade which was lying a little distance away. Near it was a china candlestick with a candle. This fire had also charred a part of the panelling of the wall, and a part of the staircase. Fortunately, the floor is of brick tiles, and there had not been much paraffin left in the lamp, or the house would have been set afire.

'But she had not died from burns alone. Her throat had been cut with a deep slash from some very sharp blade. But she had been alive for a while to feel both things, for she had crawled forward on her hands while she was burning. It was a cruel death, a horrible death for a soft person like that.'

There was a pause. The expression on the face of the narrator, the plump girl in the brown dress, altered slightly. So did the expression of her eyes. She was sitting beside Muriel; and moved a little closer.

'Of course, the police came. I do not understand such things, I am afraid, but they found that the house had not been robbed. They also noticed the odd thing I have mentioned, that there was both a lamp *and* a candle in a candlestick near her. The lamp came from Mr and Mrs Waycross's bedroom upstairs, and so did the candlestick: there were no other lamps or candles downstairs except the lamps waiting to be filled next morning in the back kitchen. But the police thought she would not have come downstairs carrying both the lamp *and* the candle as well.

'She must have brought the lamp, because that was broken. When the murderer took hold of her, they thought, she had dropped the lamp, and it went out; the paraffin spilled, but did not catch fire. Then this man in the tall hat, to finish his work after he had cut her throat, went upstairs, and got a candle, and set fire to the spilled oil. I am stupid at these things; but even I should have guessed that this must mean someone familiar with the house. Also, if she came downstairs, it must have been to let someone in at the front door; and that could not have been a burglar.

'You may be sure all the gossips were like police from the start, even when the police hemm'd and haw'd, because they knew Mrs Waycross must have opened the door to a man who was not her husband. And immediately they found an indication of this, in the mess that the fire and blood had made in the hall. Some distance away from poor Jane's body there was a medicine-bottle, such as chemists use. I think it had been broken in two pieces; and on one intact piece they found sticking some fragments of a letter that had not been quite burned. It was in a man's handwriting, not her husband's, and they made out enough of it to understand. It was full of – expressions of love, you know, and it made an appointment to meet her there on that night.'

Rodney Hunter, as the girl paused, felt impelled to ask a question.

'Did they know whose handwriting it was?'

'It was Jeremy Wilkes's,' replied the other simply. 'Though they never proved that, never more than slightly suspected it, and the circumstances did not bear it out. In fact, a knife stained with blood was actually found in Mr Wilkes's possession. But the police never brought it to anything, poor souls. For, you see, not Mr Wilkes – or anyone else in the world – could possibly have done the murder.'

'I don't understand that,' said Hunter, rather sharply.

'Forgive me if I am stupid about telling things,' urged their hostess in a tone of apology. She seemed to be listening to the chimney growl under a cold sky, and listening with hard, placid eyes. 'But even the village gossips could tell that. When Mrs Randall came here to the house on that morning, both the front and the back doors were locked and securely bolted on the inside. All the windows were locked on the inside. If you will look at the fastenings in this dear place, you will know what that means.

'But, bless you, that was the least of it! I told you about the snow. The snowfall had stopped at 9 o'clock in the evening, hours and hours before Mrs Waycross was murdered. When the police came, there were only two separate sets of footprints in the great unmarked half-acre of snow round the house. One set belonged to Mr Wilkes, who had come up and looked in through the window the night before. The other belonged to Mrs Randall. The police could follow and explain both sets of tracks; but there were no other tracks at all, and no one was hiding in the house.

'Of course, it was absurd to suspect Mr Wilkes. It was not only that he told a perfectly straight story about the man in the tall hat; but both Dr Sutton and Mr Pawley, who drove back with him from Five Ashes, were there to swear he could not have done it. You understand, he came no closer to the house than the windows of this room. They could watch every step he made in the moonlight, and they did. Afterwards he drove home with Dr Sutton, and slept there; or, I should say, they continued their terrible drinking until daylight. It is true that they found in his possession a knife with blood on it, but he explained that he had used the knife to gut a rabbit.

'It was the same with poor Mrs Randall, who had been up all night about her midwife's duties, though naturally it was even more absurd to think of *her*. But there were no other footprints at all, either coming to or going from the house, in all that stretch of snow; and all the ways in or out were locked on the inside.'

It was Muriel who spoke then, in a voice that tried to be crisp, but wavered in spite of her. 'Are you telling us that all this is true?' she demanded.

'I am teasing you a little, my dear,' said the other. 'But, really and truly, it all did happen. Perhaps I will show you in a moment.'

'I suppose it was really the husband who did it?' asked Muriel in a bored tone.

'Poor Mr Waycross!' said their hostess tenderly. 'He spent that night in a temperance hotel near Charing Cross Station, as he always did, and, of course, he never left it. When he learned about his wife's duplicity' – again Hunter thought she was going to pull down a corner of her eyelid – 'it nearly drove him out of his mind, poor fellow. I think he gave up agricultural machinery and took to preaching, but I am not sure. I know he left the district soon afterwards, and before he left he insisted on burning the mattress of their bed. It was a dreadful scandal.'

'But in that case,' insisted Hunter, 'who did kill her? And, if there were no footprints and all the doors were locked, how did the murderer come or go? Finally, if all this happened in February, what does it have to do with people being out of the house on Christmas Eve?'

'Ah, that is the real story. That is what I meant to tell you.'

She grew very subdued.

'It must have been very interesting to watch the people alter and grow older, or find queer paths, in the years afterwards. For, of course, nothing did happen as yet. The police presently gave it all up; for decency's sake it was allowed to rest. There was a new pump built in the market square; and the news of the Prince of Wales's going to India in '75 to talk about; and presently a new family came to live at 'Clearlawns,' and began to raise their children. The trees and the rains in summer were just the same, you know. It must have been seven or eight years before anything happened, for Jane Waycross was very patient.

'Several of the people had died in the meantime. Mrs Randall had, in a fit of quinsy; and so had Dr Sutton, but that was a great mercy, because he fell by the way when he was going out to perform an amputation with too much of the drink in him. But Mr Pawley had prospered – and, above all, so had Mr Wilkes. He had become an even finer figure of a man, they tell me, as he drew near middle age. When he married he gave up all his loose habits. Yes, he married; it was the Tinsley heiress, Miss Linshaw, whom he had been courting at the time of the murder; and I have heard that poor Jane Waycross, even after *she* was married to Mr Waycross, used to bite her pillow at night because she was so horribly jealous of Miss Linshaw.

'Mr Wilkes had always been tall, and now he was finely stout. He always wore frock-coats. Though he had lost most of his hair, his beard was full and curly; he had twinkling black eyes, and twinkling ruddy cheeks, and a bluff voice. All the children ran to him. They say he broke as many feminine hearts as before. At any wholesome entertainment he was always the first to lead the cotillion or applaud the fiddler, and I do not know what hostesses would have done without him.

'On Christmas Eve, then – remember, I am not sure of the date – the Fentons gave a Christmas party. The Fentons were the very nice family who had taken this house afterwards, you know. There was to be no dancing, but all the old games. Naturally, Mr Wilkes was the first of all to be invited, and the first to accept; for everything was all smoothed away by time, like the wrinkles in last year's counterpane; and what past *is* past, or so they say. They had decorated the house with holly and mistletoe, and guests began to arrive as early as 2 in the afternoon.

'I had all this from Mrs Fenton's aunt (one of the Warwickshire Abbotts), who was actually staying here at the time. In spite of such a festal season, the preparations had not been going at all well that day, though such preparations usually did. Miss Abbott complained that there was a nasty earthy smell in the house. It was a dark and raw day, and the chimneys did not seem to draw as well as they should. What is more, Mrs Fenton cut her finger when she was carving the cold fowl, because she said one of the children had been hiding behind the window-curtains in here, and peeping out at her; she was very angry. But Mr Fenton, who was going about the house in his carpet slippers before the arrival of the guests, called her "Mother" and said that it was Christmas.

'It is certainly true that they forgot all about this when the fun of the games began. Such squealings you never heard! – or so I am told. Foremost of all at Bobbing for Apples or Nuts in May was Mr Jeremy Wilkes. He stood, gravely paternal, in the midst of everything, with his ugly wife beside him, and stroked his beard. He saluted each of the ladies on the cheek under the mistletoe; there was also some scampering to salute him; and, though he *did* remain for longer than was necessary behind the window-curtains with the younger Miss Twigelow, his wife only smiled. There was only one unpleasant incident, soon forgotten. Towards dusk a great gusty wind began to come up, with the chimneys smoking worse than usual. It being nearly dark, Mr Fenton said it was time to fetch in the Snapdragon Bowl, and watch it flame. You know the game? It is a great bowl of lighted spirit, and you must thrust in your hand and pluck out a raisin from the bottom without scorching your fingers. Mr Fenton carried it in on a tray in the half-darkness; it was flickering with that bluish flame you have seen on Christmas puddings. Miss Abbott said that once, in carrying it, he started and turned round. She said that for a second she thought there was a face looking over his shoulder, and it wasn't a nice face.

'Later in the evening, when the children were sleepy and there was tissue-paper scattered all over the house, the grown-ups began their games in earnest. Someone suggested Blind Man's Bluff. They were mostly using the hall and this room here, as having more space than the dining-room. Various members of the party were blindfolded with the men's handkerchiefs; but there was a dreadful amount of cheating. Mr Fenton grew quite annoyed about it, because the ladies almost always caught Mr Wilkes when they could; Mr Wilkes was laughing and perspiring heartily, and his great cravat with the silver pin had almost come loose.

'To make it certain nobody could cheat, Mr Fenton got a little white linen bag – like this one. It was the pillow-cover off the baby's cot, really; and he said nobody could look through that if it were tied over the head.

'I should explain that they had been having some trouble with the lamp in this room. Mr Fenton said: "Confound it, mother, what is wrong with that lamp? Turn up the wick, will you?" It was really quite a good lamp from Spence and Minstead's, and should not have burned so dull as it did. In the confusion, while Mrs Fenton was trying to make the light better, and he was looking over his shoulder at her, Mr Fenton had been rather absently fastening the bag on the head of the last person caught. He has said since that he did not notice who it was. No one else noticed, either, the light being so dim and there being such a large number of people. It seemed to be a girl in a broad bluish kind of dress, standing over near the door.

'Perhaps you know how people act when they have just been blindfolded in this game. First they usually stand very still, as though they were smelling or sensing in which direction to go. Sometimes they make a sudden jump, or sometimes they begin to shuffle gently forward. Everyone noticed what an air of *purpose* there seemed to be about this person whose face was covered; she went forward very slowly, and seemed to crouch down a bit.

'It began to move towards Mr Wilkes in very short but

quick little jerks, the white bag bobbing on its face. At this time Mr Wilkes was sitting at the end of the table, laughing, with his face pink above the beard, and a glass of our Kentish cider in his hand. I want you to imagine this room as being very dim, and much more cluttered, what with all the tassels they had on the furniture then; and the high-piled hair of the ladies, too. The hooded person got to the edge of the table. It began to edge along towards Mr Wilkes's chair; and then it jumped!

'Mr Wilkes got up and skipped (yes, skipped) out of its way, laughing. It waited quietly, after which it went, in the same slow way, towards him again. It nearly got him again, by the edge of the potted plant. All this time it did not say anything, you understand, although everyone was applauding it and crying encouraging advice. It kept its head down. Miss Abbott says she began to notice an unpleasant faint smell of burnt cloth or something worse, which turned her half-ill. By the time the hooded person came stooping clear across the room, as certainly as though it could see him, Mr Wilkes was not laughing any longer.

'In the corner by one bookcase, he said out loud: "I'm tired of this silly, rotten game; go away, do you hear?" Nobody there had ever heard him speak like that, in such a loud, wild way, but they laughed and thought it must be the Kentish cider. "Go away!" cried Mr Wilkes again, and began to strike at it with his fist. All this time, Miss Abbott says, she had observed his face gradually changing. He dodged again, very pleasant and nimble for such a big man, but with the perspiration running down his face. Back across the room he went again, with it following him; and he cried out something that most naturally shocked them all inexpressibly.

'He screamed out: "For God's sake, Fenton, take it off me!"

'And for the last time the thing jumped.

'They were over near the curtains of that bay window, which were drawn as they are now. Miss Twigelow, who was nearest, says that Mr Wilkes could not have seen anything, because the white bag was still drawn over the woman's head. The only thing she noticed was that at the lower part of the bag, where the face must have been, there was a curious kind of discoloration, a stain of some sort which had not been there before: something seemed to be seeping through. Mr Wilkes fell back between the curtains, with the hooded person after him, and screamed again. There was a kind of thrashing noise in or behind the curtains; then they fell straight again, and everything grew quiet.

'Now, our Kentish cider is very strong, and for a moment Mr Fenton did not know what to think. He tried to laugh at it, but the laugh did not sound well. Then he went over to the curtains, calling out gruffly to them to come out of there and not play the fool. But, after he had looked inside the curtains, he turned round very sharply and asked the rector to get the ladies out of the room. This was done, but Miss Abbott often said that she had one quick peep inside. Though the bay windows were locked on the inside, Mr Wilkes was now alone on the window seat. She could see his beard sticking up, and the blood. He was dead, of course. But, since he had murdered Jane Waycross, I sincerely think that he deserved to die.'

For several seconds the two listeners did not move. She had all too successfully conjured up this room in the late 'seventies, whose stuffiness still seemed to pervade it now.

'But look here!' protested Hunter, when he could fight down an inclination to get out of the room quickly. 'You say he killed her after all? And yet you told us he had an absolute, alibi. You said he never went closer to the house than the windows ...'

'No more he did, my dear,' said the other.

'He was courting the Linshaw heiress at the time,' she resumed; 'and Miss Linshaw was a very proper young lady who would have been horrified if she had heard about him and Jane Waycross. She would have broken off the match, naturally. But poor Jane Waycross meant her to hear. She was much in love with Mr Wilkes, and she was going to tell the whole matter publicly: Mr Wilkes had been trying to persuade her not to do so.'

'But –'

'Oh, don't you see what happened?' cried the other in a pettish tone. 'It is so dreadfully simple. I am not clever at these things, but I should have seen it in a moment: even if I did not already know. I told you everything so that you should be able to guess.

'When Mr Wilkes and Dr Sutton and Mr Pawley drove past

here in the gig that night, they saw a bright light burning in the windows of this room. I told you that. But the police never wondered, as anyone should, what caused that light. Jane Waycross never came into this room, as you know; she was out in the hall, carrying either a lamp or a candle. But that lamp in the thick blue-silk shade, held out there in the hall, would not have caused a bright light to shine through this room and illuminate it. Neither would a tiny candle; it is absurd. And I told you there were no other lamps in the house except some empty ones waiting to be filled in the back kitchen. There is only one thing they could have seen. They saw the great blaze of the paraffin oil round Jane Waycross's body.

'Didn't I tell you it was dreadfully simple? Poor Jane was upstairs waiting for her lover. From the upstairs window she saw Mr Wilkes's gig, with the fine yellow wheels, drive along the road in the moonlight, and she did not know there were other men in it; she thought he was alone. She came downstairs –

'It is an awful thing that the police did not think more about that broken medicine-bottle lying in the hall, the large bottle that was broken in just two pieces. She must have had a use for it; and, of course, she had. You knew that the oil in the lamp was almost exhausted, although there was a great blaze round the body. When poor Jane came downstairs, she was carrying the unlighted lamp in one hand; in the other hand she was carrying a lighted candle, and an old medicine-bottle containing paraffin oil. When she got downstairs, she meant to fill the lamp from the medicine-bottle, and then light it with the candle.

'But she was too eager to get downstairs, I am afraid. When she was more than half-way down, hurrying, that long nightgown tripped her. She pitched forward down the stairs on her face. The medicine-bottle broke on the tiles under her, and poured a lake of paraffin round her body. Of course, the lighted candle set the paraffin blazing when it fell; but that was not all. One intact side of that broken bottle, long and sharp and cleaner than any blade, cut into her throat when she fell on the smashed bottle. She was not quite stunned by the fall. When she felt herself burning, and the blood almost as hot, she tried to save herself. She tried to crawl forward on her hands, forward into the hall, away from the blood and oil and fire.

'That was what Mr Wilkes really saw when he looked in the window.

'You see, he had been unable to get rid of the two fuddled friends, who insisted on clinging to him and drinking with him. He had been obliged to drive them home. If he could not go to 'Clearlawns' now, he wondered how at least he could leave a message; and the light in the window gave him an excuse.

'He saw pretty Jane propped up on her hands in the hall, looking out at him beseechingly while the blue flame ran up and turned yellow. You might have thought he would have pitied, for she loved him very much. Her wound was not really a deep wound. If he had broken into the house at that moment, he might have saved her life. But he preferred to let her die: because now she would make no public scandal and spoil his chances with the rich Miss Linshaw. That was why he returned to his friends and told a lie about a murderer in a tall hat. It is why, in heaven's truth, he murdered her himself. But when he returned to his friends, I do not wonder that they saw him mopping his forehead. You know now how Jane Waycross came back for him, presently.'

There was another heavy silence.

The girl got to her feet, with a sort of bouncing motion which was as suggestive as was vaguely familiar. It was as though she were about to run. She stood there, a trifle crouched, in her prim brown dress, so oddly narrow at the waist after an old-fashioned pattern; and in the play of light on her face Rodney Hunter fancied that its prettiness was only a shell.

'The same thing happened afterwards, on some Christmas Eves,' she explained. 'They played Blind Man's Bluff over again. That is why people who live here do not care to risk it nowadays. It happens at a quarter-past 7 –'

Hunter stared at the curtains. 'But it was a quarter-past 7 when we got here!' he said. 'It must now be –'

'Oh, yes,' said the girl, and her eyes brimmed over. 'You see, I told you you had nothing to fear; it was all over then.

But that is not why I thank you. I begged you to stay, and you did. You have listened to me, as no one else would. And now I have told it at last, and now I think both of us can sleep.'

Not a fold stirred or altered in the dark curtains that closed the window bay; yet, as though a blurred lens had come into focus, they now seemed innocent and devoid of harm. You could have put a Christmas-tree there. Rodney Hunter, with Muriel following his gaze, walked across and threw back the curtains. He saw a quiet window-seat covered with chintz, and the rising moon beyond the window. When he turned round, the girl in the old-fashioned dress was not there. But the front doors were open again, for he could feel a current of air blowing through the house.

With his arm round Muriel, who was white-faced, he went out into the hall. They did not look long at the scorched and beaded stains at the foot of the panelling, for even the scars of fire seemed gentle now. Instead, they stood in the doorway looking out, while the house threw its great blaze of light across the frosty Weald. It was a welcoming light. Over the rise of a hill, black dots trudging in the frost showed that Jack Bannister's party was returning; and they could hear the sound of voices carrying far. They heard one of the party carelessly singing a Christmas carol for glory and joy, and the laughter of children coming home.